Method Acting

Franklin U 2
Book Seven

N.R. Walker

Copyright

Cover Artist: Tal Lewin (Caravaggia13)
Editor: Boho Editing
Publisher: BlueHeart Press
Method Acting © 2024 N.R. Walker
Illustrated Edition

All Rights Reserved:

This literary work may not be reproduced or transmitted in whole or in part in any form or by any means, including electronic or photographic reproduction, except in the case of brief quotations included in critical articles and reviews, without express written permission.

This literary work may not be reproduced or transmitted in whole or in part in any form or by any means, including information storage and retrieval systems, or for use in AI training software.

This is a work of fiction, and any resemblance to living or deceased persons, companies, events or places is purely coincidental. Licensed images are used for illustrative purposes only.

Warning

Intended for an 18+ audience only. This book is intended for an adult audience. It contains graphic language, explicit content, and adult situations.

Trademarks

All trademarks are the property of their respective owners.

Blurb

Chase Soria

Every budding actor knows acting is a difficult gig. There will be grueling auditions and punishing rejections. If you're lucky, there'll be roles that pay the bills and even roles that won't.

Roles we don't believe in.

But that's what acting is—acting as if we *do* believe in them.

So when the semester's production project is announced and I'm cast as one of the leads, I'm ecstatic. A lot of responsibility, a lot of work, but I'm up for it. Even when I find out what my role is and who my partner is. Amos, the brooding James Dean wannabe, is my on-screen boyfriend. Which is great, except for the fact he hates me.

I can do this. It's just acting.

Nothing more.

Amos Beddington

The 90s are back, apparently. *90210* and *Friends,* but with a reality TV spin, which means cameras following us around as if they're capturing the everyday lives of Franklin U students.

Me, but not me.

Me, with no more than a character description, no

script or screenplay. Method acting, being the character 24/7, not just when the cameras are rolling. With a campus boyfriend.

Method acting is immersive and intense, and it can be confusing if the lines begin to blur. I mean, I've dreamed of being with the irritatingly gorgeous and annoyingly popular Chase Soria, and now I have to be his on-screen boyfriend?

I'm a good actor, sure. But how can I be convincing when I'm not sure I can even convince myself?

Method Acting

FRANKLIN U 2

N.R. Walker

Chapter One
Chase Soria

"Morning, everyone!" Deirdre sang. "Welcome back for spring semester!"

Deirdre Wicks was a bright and bubbly person. She was loud and tended to overpronounce words as if her life was a permanent stage production of *The Sound of Music*.

Which, given her position as Performing Arts Director at Franklin U and her love of stage theater, wasn't surprising. I liked her, though. Everyone did. Her cheerfulness was contagious.

"We have a great production planned for you," she added. Everyone waited for her to continue, to hear what our semester project would be. Relishing in everyone's undivided attention, she raised a hand. "Before you get too excited, let me make this clear. It will be a full production. Not everyone will get the roles they so sorely desire, which is the first rule of acting. You know that, and if that is an obstacle you cannot overcome, I would suggest perhaps looking for another career."

We all knew this. It was drummed into us every chance they got.

Not everyone was going to make it. Not everyone was going to get the roles they loved, believed in. Few made it to the big time. One willingly went into acting for the passion, the love of it. Not the fame and fortune of Hollywood.

Blah blah blah.

Did I want to go to Hollywood? Did I want to be on the A list?

Hell yes, I did.

I could see my name up in lights, in tabloids, in reviews.

Chase Soria.

It was a name meant for big things.

I wasn't afraid of hard work, of busing tables until I got a big break. We'd all heard the stories of actors who'd lived in their cars before they made it. Not that I wanted to live in my car.

But I understood it took grit and determination to make dreams a reality.

And I understood it would involve roles I didn't believe in.

Roles that challenged me and tested my drive to pursue acting.

Roles that tested me personally, physically, and emotionally. That made me question what I thought I knew about the world around me and what I knew about myself.

"Are you ready?" Deirdre said with a sly smile. "I don't know if you're ready."

She paused for dramatic effect.

"This term's production will run for the first half of

this semester, starting today. That will include preproduction, filming, editing. It will count for sixty percent of your overall grade."

Sixty percent?

She definitely had our attention now.

"Method acting!" she announced.

Hmm, okay then . . .

"We're bringing the 90s back," she went on. "Think 90210, and Friends. Think Melrose Place, but with a twenty-first-century twist. We're doing reality TV!"

Wait, what?

Chatter erupted around the room. Excitement, disbelief, so many questions . . .

"Eight leads, eight friends—three couples, two best friends. Two weeks preproduction, two weeks of filming. Full production includes filming, postproduction, editing, color grading, sound, and . . ."

She paused again. Her smile made me nervous.

"We'll be live streaming!"

Wow.

Well, it was exciting and daunting, and then Deirdre started running through roles. Director of photography, assistant director, unit production managers, script continuity, camera operators and grips, picture and sound editors, and people around the room began to buzz as they got the roles they clearly wanted.

And then came the eight leads.

A quick glance around the room told me the eight remaining people were seniors, all of us theater majors, me included. Admittedly, we didn't have a huge class . . .

But damn.

I was one of the eight leads.

Everyone was split off into their preproduction groups, leaving Deirdre with the eight of us. She handed us each a manila folder. "Phoebe and Jess, you're the best friends."

Phoebe and Jess both squealed, excited.

And then I looked at the others and began to do the math.

"Max and Holly," Deirdre said. "You're couple number one."

And the math wasn't mathing . . .

"Tucker and Didi, you're couple number two."

Aaaaand there it was.

Deirdre smiled at me. "Chase and Amos, you're couple number three."

Amos and I . . .

I turned to Amos and he looked as stunned as me.

Could I be his on-screen boyfriend?

It was all acting, right? It was no different pretending to be the boyfriend of Amos or Didi or Holly. I didn't know them, or have any interest in any of them on any personal level, so gender made no difference. Right? Don't get me wrong, this was not a he's-a-guy thing.

I was bi. I'd been with guys before. I was not opposed to dick, mine or someone else's.

But Amos Beddington?

He was reclusive and broody. Tall, lean, longish dark hair and dark eyes. He idolized James Dean. He'd even done a re-enactment of *Rebel Without a Cause* for his final last year. I mean, he'd done it well, and he did have that natural X factor that most actors could only dream of . . .

"Is this going to be a problem?" Deirdre asked, looking between us.

Was it a problem?

"No," Amos answered simply.

He said it so nonchalantly, so blasé. Like he couldn't have cared less if he tried. With his Keanu Reeves hair and handsome face and a confidence I envied.

"Yeah, no," I added, trying to play it off as aloof as he had. "No problem. Not at all."

"Good," Deirdre said. She gave us that stage-worthy killer high-watt smile. "Because we've got a lot of work to do. Starting now."

Chapter Two
Amos Beddington

The eight of us sat at the round table reading the very brief script outline. The thing with reality TV was that, yes, while it was technically scripted, a lot of it wasn't. This was an exercise in method acting, after all. We were to become the character. We were to behave, to act, to be in our everyday lives as the character would be.

Which was ourselves, but not entirely.

We had character names, but these characters were to be us. They would go to our classes, hang out with our friends. For as long as there was a camera on me, I was Elijah. Elijah James, whose boyfriend of twelve months was Dominic Davis.

Dominic, played by none other than Chase Soria. Chase, who was super popular, hot as hell, loved by all. Insatiable flirt, serial dater, but never serious. Apparently. Not that I'd noticed.

Not that I cared.

Not that I'd known that he's dated both girls and guys,

a different person every other week, but was happy to keep his options open, impossible to nail down.

Not that I'd heard these things. Not that I'd cared.

Because I knew damn well he'd never looked at me.

That I knew of.

Because for all the times I'd looked at him, never once had I caught his eye.

I clearly wasn't his type.

Not that I cared.

Maybe he wasn't my type anyway.

Maybe I could lie to myself about that because, while I told myself the all-American guy next door was not my type, I kept finding myself drawn to him. Spotting him in a crowd, seeing him every time he crossed the quad, or finding myself wishing he'd look my way just once . . .

So yeah, this whole production was going to be a true test of my acting skills.

How to act the part of his boyfriend convincingly while acting like I didn't care.

"Elijah James," I read out loud when it was my turn. "Twenty-year-old fine arts student, gay. Boyfriend of Dominic Davis." I gave a quick glance up to Chase, though he was reading along, not looking at me. "We met in our second year of college. Elijah is brooding, serious. Aloof and mysterious and prickly to everyone but those who know him."

I glanced again at Chase, as I often did, to find him still reading along, still not looking at me, and wait . . . did he smile at that?

What did that mean? That I was prickly?

I went back to my outline. "Elijah is loyal and fiercely protective."

So, my character was basically me.

Had he been written with me in mind?

And after everyone had read their character traits out loud, I realized all these characters were similar to the actor portraying them. And then I realized it was for good reason.

So they'd be believable.

So we could spend this entire production being this character, method acting, without too much disruption to our normal lives.

"My character is basically me," Chase said. "Funny, well-liked, popular."

"Humble," Holly added.

Chase laughed. "No, that's not listed here."

"They're all like us," Max said.

"Because this is method acting," I said flatly. "It's so we can still be ourselves, basically. Just with different names and..." I made myself not look at Chase. "And partners."

Max made a face. "Yeah, my girl ain't gonna be too happy. Not gonna lie."

"It's just acting," Didi said.

"We know that," Tucker replied.

And that was the truth. Actors had to play the role of lover or partner to their costars all the time. The real-life partner or spouse had to deal with that. Was it easy? Probably not. But it *was* part of the deal.

It was acting.

"I'll talk to her," Holly offered.

Max gave her a smile. "Thanks."

"Anyone else here got a girlfriend or boyfriend they need to explain this to?"

Jess shook her head. "Phoebe and I are just friends in this, so it's not the same."

Tucker and Didi both shook their heads, then Holly did the same. "Single."

Chase grinned. "Very happily single."

Jess chuckled. "We know. You were crowned King Player at the end-of-semester party, remember?"

They all laughed. I had no clue what they were talking about. Very obviously wasn't at that party . . .

Then all eyes fell on me. I remembered they were waiting for my answer. "Single," I admitted.

Not happily, but whatever.

Chase turned the page. "My biggest obstacle will be convincing everyone I finally got nailed down by one person."

That earned a few laughs, but Phoebe's eyes landed on me. "You've got some expectations on your character already," she said. "Being the one that nailed him down."

"The whole enigmatic and mysterious thing will totally work in your favor," Holly added.

"Enigmatic and mysterious thing?" I asked.

I wasn't sure what that was supposed to mean.

"The whole James Dean thing you have going on," Chase explained. He spared me the briefest glance, then shrugged. "Dominic would totally fall for that whole vibe."

Right.

If they meant loner, on the outside, no friends, then sure. *The James Dean thing* was a nicer way to put it.

Our character arcs were laid out, although very thinly.

We had some milestones and some overall plot points to aim for. Fabricated dramas and some juicy elements to keep the viewers enthralled, but this was very much about the lives of students in college. A group of friends finding themselves in an ever-changing world of social media, studying, parties, and relationships.

The premise was great.

It was exciting, and it had the promise of some groundbreaking stuff. A modern-day *90210* with a reality-television twist, all livestreamed, no room for error.

Personally, I hated reality television. I thought it cheapened the art of acting and brought down the quality of decent television viewing.

But despite my best effort to sound like my grandfather, reality TV was an entertainment phenomenon of the twenty-first century, and that shouldn't be ignored. As an artist in the industry, I'd be foolish to turn my back on it.

It was an opportunity to push my limits and to explore acting as a craft.

This was what I told myself.

Was I convinced?

The jury was still out.

"So," Deirdre said as she waltzed back into the room. "How are we feeling? Excited?"

We all kind of said yes, but not with the enthusiasm she was after, clearly.

"Well, look alive," she said. "Preproduction is two weeks. That means you've got two weeks to get to know your on-screen partner. Get acquainted, become familiar. Partner off and pretend it's your first date—ask each other fifty questions."

Well, that I could do.

"Because," Deirdre added with her trademark grin, "tomorrow begins the workshops where we'll get a whole lot more familiar with each other, if you know what I mean. There will be intimacy exercises in touching, holding hands, cuddling, and kissing exercises. You know the drill. So go," she said, shooing us out. "Go on your first dates."

Chapter Three
Chase

Yikes.

Yikes with a capital *Y*.

Why indeed.

Why did this feel different?

Why did I ever agree to this? Why did I ever sign up for acting in the first place?

Why was I so damned nervous?

It was just acting. And if there was one thing I could do, it was act.

So, with a resolve I didn't quite rightly feel, I stood up. "Come on, boyfriend of one year," I said to Amos. "Let's go get acquainted."

Amos straightened his folder, picked it up, and stood. He never said anything—he rarely did—and he followed me to the far corner of the room.

I sat down with my back against the wall, legs outstretched, and he did the same beside me.

There was a good foot between us, and while it wasn't

awkward, it wasn't comfortable. He just wasn't an open person. He had a hard exterior that wasn't easy to break.

"You up for this?" I asked.

His eyes narrowed as he stared at his Chucks. "Sure. It's just acting, right?"

"Right."

"You work at the Bean Necessities, right? The coffee shop across the street? That's where I've seen you."

He nodded. "Yep."

And he offered nothing more, so I figured I'd just dive straight into the deep end. "So, have you ever kissed a guy before?"

He frowned, though his pale cheeks flushed a little pink. "I have, yes."

I nodded slowly. "You're gay, right? Is that what I heard?"

His dark eyes cut to mine. "You heard?"

"I'm bi," I replied. "And I've been to the LGBTQ center a few times." I didn't want to admit that I hadn't been there in a while, but still. "We talk."

"You gossip."

"No, we talk. We discuss things and we open up to each other. It's a safe place, and Ross might have mentioned you."

"Ross . . ." Amos sighed. "I dated Ross in my freshman year."

"He's a nice guy," I allowed. "And he never gossiped or spilled any deets. He mentioned you *in passing* two years ago; I think you must have been dating at the time. I don't even know why I remembered . . ."

Sure, Chase. Just give yourself away in the first two minutes.

You remembered because you noticed Amos, and you remembered that he was gay every single time you saw him.

Amos pulled at a thread near the hole in the knee of his jeans. "He is. We just . . . we're still friends, I guess. We weren't compatible for anything more."

"So have you dated anyone recently?"

He shot me a look that pretty much said *what business is that of yours.*

"You know, in case I gotta watch my back if the world thinks we're a thing."

Amos rolled his eyes and sighed. "No. No one recently. What about you? Still a serial non-dater to be forever playing the field?"

I wasn't sure what to make of that. Was that snarky sarcasm pure distaste? Or did I detect something else?

Keep dreaming.

He's the sarcasm king.

"Forever playing the field," I replied. Then I shrugged. "It's how I like it. I'm too young to be tied down. I want to be free to see as many people as I can, and as long as they know from the get-go that it's a one-time thing, then no one gets hurt."

He made a face. "No one's warranted a second look?"

"Look? Sure. I look all the time. But a second date?" I sighed. "Nah."

"That's kinda sad."

Sad?

I shot him a what-the-fuck look. "How is that sad?"

"You could've completely bypassed your one person, just disregarded them because of your own rules."

"My one person? Like a soulmate?" I tried not to laugh. "Do you honestly believe in that?"

Amos pressed his lips together and pulled at the loose thread in his jeans some more. "I don't know. Maybe I do." Then he shrugged. "The idea that there's one person we can connect with better than any other person, that we understand, that we gel with. I think that's true. Do I believe in the 'one person is half my soul' kind of soulmate, and I need to find them?" He made a face. "Statistically speaking, I think that's improbable. Some people are supposed to be in our lives short term; other people forever."

Okay, wow. I wasn't expecting things to get so deep right off the bat.

He exhaled loudly. "I think it's all kinda connected with past lives and who we were, and maybe your best friend in this life was your brother in your past life. Stuff like that. I think it's all connected somehow, like our souls recognize each other. Kinda weird, and I don't know why I just said all of that, sorry."

"Don't apologize. It's a nice idea."

We were quiet then for a few seconds.

"Anyway," he went on, then cleared his throat. "So we really do need to convince the entire campus that you, the serial non-dater who never does repeats, is suddenly interested in dating one person?"

"Well . . ." I grimaced. "Just how good are you at acting?"

"It's not me I'm worried about. How are you going to

stop flirting with everyone? You have a wandering eye and a smile that—"

He stopped mid-sentence.

"I have a smile that what?"

He rolled his eyes. "You know damn well," he mumbled. "You totally play it up. All-American boy next door, pretty blue eyes, Colgate smile, and a killer dimple. You know exactly what you're doing when you aim that at people."

I laughed because what the fuck?

I leaned in close and fluttered my eyelashes. "You think I have pretty eyes?"

He scoffed, seemingly unaffected. "It won't work on me. I'm immune."

My grin was for naught because he wasn't looking at me. "Immune to what?"

"To the bullshit."

"Ouch. My smile and pretty eyes aren't bullshit."

"You use them to get what you want."

"That's not fair. You use your spiky James Dean vibe to keep people away."

That made him look at me. "Spiky James Dean?"

I chuckled. "Yes. You use it so people avoid you. So you don't get asked to do group projects or go to parties."

He conceded a shrug. "Because it works."

"How is that any different from what I do?"

He stared at me, his dark eyes scrutinizing. Anyone else might have looked away and apologized, but I wasn't falling for it.

"Okay, that's fair," he mumbled.

I laughed, victorious. "We're not that dissimilar."

That made him scoff. "Pray tell, how the fuck did you come to that conclusion?"

I was still smiling. "You'll see."

He rolled his eyes and sighed. "We're supposed to be getting to know each other."

"We are."

"Like background information."

"Us or our characters?"

He opened his folder. "For the sake of simplification, it says we should just use our own family's background. Makes sense, I guess. What about you? How's your family stack up?"

"I have a younger sister. She's nine. Pretty sure she wasn't planned, but now she's the princess of the family. If you think I'm spoiled, you ain't seen nothing. My folks are still married, living their best lives in Palm Springs. What about you?"

"I'm from Phoenix. My parents split when I was five. It was amicable, I guess. They both remarried, both still kinda talk. I have two older brothers. One's an electrician, one's an accountant. And then there's me."

The way he said that last part didn't sound too happy. "Do your folks not agree with you majoring in acting in college?"

He shrugged one shoulder. "They don't mind, though I'm sure they think I'll end up doing something else and I just need to get this out of my system."

I made a face. "That sucks. I'm sorry."

"It's not so bad. My mom always wished she was a writer or a painter, and she's always doing some kind of craft. Loves books. So she can appreciate my creative side."

"And you've always loved acting?"

"Always. I'd put on little skits at dinner when I was three. And in kindergarten I got mad because my teacher would tell me to stop pretending, but I wasn't pretending to be Hiccup Haddock. I was acting. I *was* Hiccup Haddock."

"*How to Train Your Dragon?*"

"I loved those books."

"They were books?"

He gave me an annoyed side-glance and sighed. "What about you? Always wanted to be an actor?"

"Always. When I was younger, it was movies like *Spiderman* and *Star Wars*. The actors would get to live out those epic roles and get lightsabers for real. Then when I was a teenager, I'd see the cool actors with the great one-liners. From shows like *The OC* and *Pretty Little Liars*. Man, I loved those."

Amos squinted at me. "Those are your top two shows? Your preteen self was kinda predictable."

"Oh, okay, Mr Too Cool, what were your top two shows when you were preteen?"

"*Baskets, Mr. Robot, Pose. Boardwalk Empire, Westworld, Naruto.*"

"*Naruto?*"

"*Naruto: Shippuden* is intelligent writing."

"But it's not character acting. It's animation with voice acting."

"I'm still allowing it."

"Then I can allow *Rick and Morty*."

Amos cracked a smile. He actually smiled.

Kinda.

"I would also allow *Rick and Morty*."

"It's hilarious." I grinned and relaxed with a sigh. Still leaning against the wall, I nodded toward where Phoebe and Jess were chatting and giggling. "I don't think those two will need to be acting much. They're already good friends."

"I think that's why Deirdre chose them." He nodded to where Max and Holly were sitting and talking. "I think she paired us all pretty well."

Oh?

"Then why us?"

"Because I'm gay; you're bi. We'd have no real issue with showing affection to a guy. It's one less obstacle for someone like Tucker or Max. I guess Deirdre thought she was doing the others a favor."

"Gee, thanks."

"You know what I mean."

I did, but still.

"It's all acting. Kissing you or anyone else—it doesn't mean anything," I said, absolutely not trying to convince myself that he was no different. Then I realized something and began flicking through the folder. "Just how far do you think we're expected to go? We're a couple that's been together for a year, right?"

"What do you mean? Like full-on sex scenes?" He made a face, though his cheeks pooled the prettiest pink. "No. Surely nothing too explicit. Holding hands, kissing, that kind of stuff. It's PG-13, right?"

"Right."

"If you're not comfortable doing that, we just have to say. They can't make us—"

"No, it's fine," I said. "I don't have a problem with it. Do you?"

He shrugged. "Guess not. It's just acting, like you said. And anyway, if we're gonna take it to the next level, we need to get over it, right?" Then he winced. "I mean, take our acting to the next level, not the intimate scenes."

I snorted. "Yeah. We'll be fine."

He nodded, and I wondered if he had any better luck convincing himself than I did.

I didn't know why he rattled me so much.

Because you like him, idiot. Because he never fell for your charms like everyone else. He never fawned over you, never even looked your way.

And that gets under your skin more than any attempt at flirting.

"So," he hedged. "I guess we'll need to start convincing people."

I grinned at him. "Leave that to me."

He gave me one helluva mean side-eye. "Do I even want to know?"

I laughed, and when class was over and everyone filed out of the room, we were all feeling much better about the production. It was exciting, and I was looking forward to spending more time with Amos.

Real or not.

As me or as my character Dominic.

I met Tater and Jimmy at the edge of the courtyard, and seeing Amos already walking away with his head down, I seized my opportunity.

"Amos!" I yelled.

He stopped and turned, scowling.

I grinned at him. "Tomorrow."

He replied by extending his middle finger while still holding the strap of his backpack.

I laughed.

"What the hell is that?" Tater asked beside me.

That was the start of convincing the student body of Franklin U that I could be a one-man guy.

"Nothing," I said, slapping him on the back. "You know what? I'm famished, and I'm thinking we should eat at the coffee shop today."

Chapter Four
Amos

I hated that Chase was actually a nice guy.

I hated that he was ridiculously hot, with his perfect teeth and sparkly blue eyes and his perfect fucking dimple. I hated that he was actually serious about this production and making it the best he could.

He took his acting craft seriously.

His craft of sitcom acting, mind you—like that was barely one rung higher than reality TV on the ladder of credibility—but still . . . he was serious about it.

And he was good at it.

He'd make a perfect male lead in a sitcom like *Friends* or *90210*.

He was made for it.

Or blockbuster movie leading roles for the blue-eyed American dreamboat, like the next Brad Pitt or Austin Butler. That's the kind of actor he was.

I was more of a weird Finn Wolfhard or Keanu Reeves. I could fill the quirky roles like *Stranger Things* or *The Matrix*.

Or the serial killer roles like *Dexter*.

Or yes, James Dean. He was a remarkable actor who never got the chance to explore what he was capable of or show the world his true talent.

And because I'd done a showcase on him, I was labeled a James Dean wannabe. And that wasn't terrible.

Successful and hot weren't bad ways to start. Dead at twenty-four, not so much.

Was James Dean ever a barista? Did he need to bus tables at a college coffeehouse and make drinks with a fake customer-service smile?

I highly doubted it.

Though it was good practice for acting. I just had to *act* like a good barista who liked people.

That's how I thought of it anyway.

I tied my apron around my waist and ducked in behind the counter, slipping into work mode alongside Mason.

"Hey," he said. He was a senior like me and he'd worked here for as long as I had. Over two years now. He was the type to have his head down and work and not engage in small talk, which was why I liked him.

Working at the Bean Necessities really wasn't that bad. It was close to my dorm. I just had to walk across the road, basically. I was luckier than some. Given I didn't have to commute, I didn't need a car. There were no crazy late nights. Some early morning starts but they weren't the worst.

Plus, I got free coffee and sandwiches with a staff discount.

Not too bad at all.

"How was your day?" Mason asked.

"Pretty good so far. How about you?"

He checked his watch. "I finish in five, so it's getting better every minute."

I glanced around the kinda quiet shop. "You can clock out now if you want. I got this."

He brightened. "You sure?"

Just then, four people came in, loud and . . . familiar.

Because of course *he'd* come in here today.

"Damn," Mason mumbled. "Maybe next time." Then he smiled at the guys who'd just walked in. "Hey, what can I getcha?"

Jimmy was at the front. "I'll take an iced Americano."

"I'll have the same, with a turkey sub," the second guy replied. His name was Tate, I was pretty sure. They called him Tater Tot, which was awful.

"Chase." Jimmy gave him a nudge. "Whaddya want?"

Chase was too busy looking at me, apparently.

"Oh," he said, giving his head a bit of a shake, then looking at the menu as if he'd never seen it before. "Uhhh. Yeah, iced coffee, double shot, and a club on rye, thanks. Oh, and a bran square with raspberries and a bottle of water." He rubbed his belly and his eyes caught mine. "I'm hungry."

Christ.

They paid for their order and I started on their drinks while I pretended not to notice how Chase kept looking over at me.

Jimmy gave him a decent elbow. "Dude, the fuck?"

"I'm just looking at something," he replied. "Shut the fuck up."

Tate gave me a quizzical once-over before shooting

Chase a what-the-fuck look. I couldn't hear exactly what he said after that but it was clear they were talking about me.

Because Chase had called out to me across the courtyard just half an hour ago and now he was here, turning his head to look my way.

Well, he did say to leave "convincing people he could like me" up to him.

It must have been convincing because his friends were giving him shit.

Though it was more of a "why him?" kind of ribbing.

Like he could never be interested in someone like me.

I was soooo not his type.

But he was putting in some effort to make it look convincing, so maybe I could do the same.

I put their drinks on the end of the counter. "Jimmy."

Of course Chase stood up. "I'll get them," he said, quickly dashing over toward me.

"Which one's mine?" he asked.

"The one with your name on it," I replied.

He grinned. "This is fun, isn't it?"

I noticed over his shoulder that his whole table was watching us. So I gave Chase half a smile that was more glare than pleasant, and I leaned over the counter so it would look to our audience like we were having a private conversation.

"You might wanna take it down a notch," I murmured, "or they'll think you're having a medical episode."

Chase laughed and I rolled my eyes, turning back to my work while he took the drinks back to his table.

Mason clocked out and it was busy enough for me that

Chase didn't try to intervene, though I did catch him looking my way a few times.

Jeez. Dial it down.

A while later, I just happened to look up one time to see them leave. Jimmy gave Chase a shove out the door and they laughed as they headed across the street. And I managed to finish my shift and get back to my room and not give Chase Soria one more thought.

Not even when I had my nose in my psych textbook for most of the night. And not even at breakfast . . . because I definitely didn't look for him.

And I most certainly wasn't disappointed when he never showed.

I did have a sociology of theater class that was an actual distraction because, for one whole hour, I didn't give Chase Soria, or his character Dominic, one thought.

It was a blessed sixty minutes because as soon as I walked out of the lecture hall, I heard a very familiar voice yell out to me.

"Hey, Amos, wait up!"

I turned to see him give his buddy one of those cringey bro-handshakes, before he jogged over to me while his friend squinted in my direction, confused.

"I didn't know you'd be here," he said, far too cheerfully. "We got preproduction now, right?"

I gave his buddy a pointed look, where he'd now sprouted a few friends, and they were all looking at us, mystified. "They're about to stage an intervention."

Chase laughed and, completely ignoring them, began walking to the rehearsal hall. "They'll be fine. They'll get over it."

"Am I that big of a leap from your norm?" I asked, kinda joking, kinda not.

"Well, I've never dated an emo before."

I stopped walking. "An emo?"

He gestured to my clothes. "Rage Against the Machine tee-shirt, which I like, by the way. Black jeans and black Chucks. What would you call it?"

"This is my grab-what-the-fuck-ever look. Tomorrow will be whatever's-left-before-laundry-day look. I wasn't aware it was a whole identity."

"Is everything you own black?"

I didn't even have to think about that, so I sighed instead. "What's your point?"

"Nothing. It's just your vibe. I like it."

"And not everything I own is black. I do own some . . . gray."

Chase laughed. "Right. So do you like Rage Against the Machine, or you just into the merch?"

Into the merch. God help me.

"I do like them. Their political analogy of domestic and foreign policies of the government is insightful."

He made a face. "Isn't . . . isn't it just music? Like heavy metal kind of music?"

I stopped walking again and gave him a serious what-the-fuck look, then because I wasn't even going to begin that whole tirade, I settled for an eye roll and a sigh, then kept walking.

I got to the door and held it open for him, gesturing for him to enter before me. "People with zero concept of irony and appropriation first, please."

He laughed, and I had to wonder if there was anything I

could possibly say that would offend him. I'd always known he was a smiley kind of guy, that everyone loved him, that he was easygoing and friends with everyone.

Everyone except me, that is.

"So do your friends think you've lost your mind?" I asked, sliding my gear onto a table.

Chase grinned at me. "How good am I? How convincing was I in the coffee shop yesterday?"

I conceded a nod and I even almost smiled. "I was leaning toward overkill, but they certainly noticed."

He laughed. "They noticed, all right. And I got twenty questions about us."

"And?"

"And what?" He shrugged. "I'm playing it so cool. I just said we got talking in class and you were kinda cool."

"And they clearly don't believe you."

He smirked. "They will. I'm a good actor, remember?"

Hm. Yeah. The way he was checking me out and calling out to me across the courtyard . . . yeah, he was a good actor.

"Okay, teams," Deirdre said, walking in. She wore gray tights with a gray tunic, but her glasses, headband, and lipstick were all bright orange. Oh, and her shoes. Let's not forget those.

"Quick. Call Ronald McDonald," Chase mumbled beside me, as if he'd read my mind. "See if he's missing his shoes."

I choked down a laugh, which of course Deirdre saw. "Excellent, two volunteers," she said. "Amos and Chase, you're up."

Up for what?

"Come to the front," she said, waving us forward impatiently.

Chase and I both walked to the front of the room and stood beside her. "Preproduction workshops are important to foster a relationship between your characters to make it believable to the audience. Now your characters, Dominic and Elijah, have been together for a year. So you will be comfortable with each other, touching, holding hands, hugging. Being in each other's personal space, right?"

Chase nodded and I shrugged. "Right."

I guess.

"Soooo," she said, as if we were slow on the uptake. "Maybe stand a little closer."

With considerable effort, I resisted sighing.

But we shuffled a little closer to each other.

Deirdre looked at us as if we were props that didn't quite look right. Then she grabbed Chase's hand and put his arm around me, then made him half back-hug me, with his chin on my shoulder.

"Relax into it," she said. "Shake your shoulders, let go of the tension."

I tried, even though I wasn't relaxed because Chase's hands were on me and he smelled so good.

"Okay, within two weeks, you need to make it look like this is as natural as breathing," Deirdre said. "Try holding hands."

Well, holding hands was easy.

Still awkward but not as much.

"Now I want everyone to do this with your partner," Deirdre said. "Yes, you guys too," she said to Phoebe and Jess. "Best friends can hold hands."

The other couples stood up, all couples holding hands.

We tried a few exercises, walking holding hands, sitting holding hands, laughing at how ridiculous it was. Then facing each other holding hands, standing a foot apart, then standing closer, enough for our bodies to almost touch, now not really laughing at all. It was strangely intimate.

But after about twenty minutes, it almost felt natural. Except it was Chase Soria . . .

"Okay," Deirdre said. "Now face each other, holding both hands. And I want you to just look at the other person. I want eye contact. It might be awkward to begin with and that's fine. This production will require levels of trust between you. This will help foster that."

So I stood there, holding Chase's hands in mine, and stared at him.

At his perfect face and his pretty blue eyes. At his . . . not-so-straight nose, at his slightly uneven eyebrows.

"Your eyes are really dark," he said. "Like I can hardly tell where your iris and pupils start or end."

Oh.

I hoped I didn't blush.

"Your face isn't symmetrical," I said, trying to play it cool. "I always thought you had a perfect face but it's really not."

He snorted. "Gee, thanks."

"You have an old scar on your cheekbone. It's very faded." I'd never noticed it before.

He nodded. "You know how your parents used to say *don't run with scissors*?" He shrugged. "Well, don't run with scissors. Not even safety scissors in pre-K."

I smiled at that. "Do you always do what you're told not to do?"

He flashed me that Hollywood smirk. "Every chance I get."

I rolled my eyes, trying to remain immune to his charms.

"Why do you roll your eyes so much?"

"It's less rude than saying 'oh for fuck's sake' out loud."

Chase laughed. "Yet the emphasis is much the same."

"That's why I do it."

"So you always thought I had a perfect face?"

God, I was hoping he'd missed that.

"I used to, yes. Until I saw it close up."

"Ouch." He was hardly offended. In fact, by that damn smirk, I'd say he liked it. "So define perfect."

"Generic Hollywood."

Now he wasn't smirking. He made a sad face. Maybe even offended. "Ouch!"

I shrugged. "It's the whole boy-next-door thing you have going on."

"It's generic?"

I nodded. "Pretty much. In a Brad Pitt kind of way."

He turned his head, looking to the wall instead. "I'm trying to decide if I should be offended by that."

I squeezed his hand, kinda pulling on it so he'd look at me again. "If we were characters from *The Breakfast Club*, you'd be Emilio Estevez."

"And you'd be Judd Nelson," he shot back. "No, you'd be the goth chick."

"Her name is Ally Sheedy, and that is a compliment, so thank you."

Chase stared at me. Kinda glared. I liked that I got under his skin. Then he sighed, annoyed. "Her makeover in that movie was a travesty."

"Agreed."

"And I wouldn't be Emilio Estevez," he went on. "I'm not a jock."

"But you're not a geek or nerd either."

"So I'd be Molly Ringwald?"

"Well, princess, if the tiara fits."

He growled at me, rightfully annoyed now, but it faded into a smile. "I wasn't aware insults were part of this semester's production."

"I think your character Dominic personally loves it," I said. "Pretty sure he loves that Elijah takes none of his shit and doesn't care about the popularity game."

He snorted. "Is that right?"

"Yep. Lucky for Dominic, Elijah's love language is snark and sarcasm."

"You're just saying that because you want to be able to be an asshole to me."

I cracked a smile. "Correct."

"Ah, boys," Deirdre said.

Both me and Chase turned to find everyone staring at us, no longer holding hands.

Oh.

We'd missed something.

I dropped Chase's hands and took a step back, ignoring the smiles from the others.

"Okay, now we're going to move into group bonding exercises," Deirdre said. "I want everyone to form a circle."

Oh great.

I hated these things.

I would've preferred to be holding hands with Chase doing one-on-one stuff than group stuff. Group *bonding activities* felt a little too kumbaya for me.

But we did what Deirdre instructed. Holding hands as a group and doing breathing and yelling exercises. Basic acting stuff. But it was a good way to end the first session.

We took a break, grabbed a drink, not really getting any time to chat—thank god.

"Right, guys," Deirdre said. "No time to waste. Because now we're going to be doing some intimacy exercises."

Intimacy exercises. With Chase Soria.

Fuck.

My.

Life.

Chapter Five
Chase

Intimacy exercises.

Awesome.

For all his brusqueness and prickliness, Amos wasn't that bad. He wasn't the asshole he pretended to be.

My guess, without knowing him that well, was that he was an introvert who liked to appear unapproachable so people would leave him alone.

I could respect that.

Because the more I got to know him, the more I liked him. And I could see when he fought a smile or the way his cheeks grew slightly pink.

His tough-guy act was simply that. An act.

And he was a very good actor.

But even though he pretended not to like me, I knew he did.

As much as it annoyed him.

As much as I enjoyed annoying him.

I wanted to say these intimacy exercises would be weird

and uncomfortable, but the truth was, I enjoyed them a little too much.

"Amos stand here," Deirdre said. Then she put me in front of him. "Chase, you're here."

I was about to ask if this was more staring-at-each-other exercises when she said, "Chase, close your eyes."

Okay, then. Not staring.

"I want you to imagine you have no sight. Lift your hands and touch his face. Feel his jaw, his cheekbones, eyebrows."

Oh boy.

"Picture his face in your mind," Deirdre said.

And so I did.

I ran my hands up his neck to his jaw. I felt him swallow. I felt every breath, the rise and fall of his chest, his pulse under my palm.

His skin was warm and smooth, and I could smell him. His deodorant or cologne, maybe.

I liked it.

I ran my thumb over his chin, feeling the slightest stubble. Up to his lips, and I expected him to flinch or pull back, but he never moved. His lips were soft and warm.

His eyebrow, his cheekbone, down his jaw. And I could picture his face in my mind so clearly, now that I'd mapped it out. I liked what I saw, what I felt.

I really liked how he smelled.

"Okay, now swap," Deirdre said.

I'd been so lost in the exercise her voice startled me. I blinked my eyes open, and of course Amos was closer in real life than he'd been in my head.

"How was it?" Deirdre asked him. "How did it feel?"

"Private," Amos replied. "Intrusive. I'd normally not let anyone touch my face." Then he shrugged. "Or be in my space, at all, really."

She patted his shoulder. "It's not easy, I know. But you're pushing your comfort-zone boundaries, well done. Physicality is important for acting. Take a deep breath, okay."

"I'm more of a touchy-feely kinda guy," I volunteered. "You can touch me all over."

Deirdre snorted. "It's not that kind of exercise but I appreciate your enthusiasm." She left us for the next couple, giving me a parting glare. "Faces only, please."

Amos looked at me, disgusted. "That was gross. Makes me not want to touch you at all. You're like an old penny. I don't know where you've been."

"I am not an old penny, thank you very much."

"I'll need more hand sanitizer."

I smiled at him and mouthed, "Fuck you."

He made a sad face. "Excuse me, Miss. He said a bad word," he said, mimicking a little kid's voice.

I rolled my eyes. "I really want you to keep your eyes open just to make this so much more awkward for you, but this is an exercise in trust, apparently. Close your eyes and do your worst."

He was quiet for a second, as if he was sizing up the argument and if he could be bothered. I thought he might leave me standing there like an idiot, but he mumbled something under his breath before he closed his eyes. Then he put his hand on my chest.

He was feeling his way up to my throat, my neck, my jaw.

He kept one hand on my neck, holding my head still, and probably for spatial awareness, while his other thumb drew lines on my face.

He mapped me out like I did to him, and god, seeing him this close up without the dagger in his eyes . . . like I was seeing the real him.

He had his eyes closed, concentrating. His eyelids were pale, his lashes long.

"What do I look like in your mind?" I murmured. "And don't say generic Hollywood."

Fucker smirked.

He seemed to consider this question as he touched my hair, down the line of my nose.

"Hmm," he mused. "Prince Charming from *Shrek 2*."

I snorted, because what the fuck.

My eyes were well and truly open now. "Really?"

He opened his eyes and smiled at me. "I could have said you looked like Shrek when he was human, so be grateful." Then he shrugged. "Or when he's not human."

"Very funny. And anyway, Prince Charming is hot. I'll take that."

"He's a giant douche."

"Yes, but I said *looked* like, not *is* like."

He rolled his eyes but he *did* almost smile. I was also taking that as a win. "Anyway, your nose is slightly crooked and one eyebrow is a little higher than the other. And you need to shave."

"Wanna know what you look like?"

"No."

"A masterpiece."

He stared. "Don't be ridiculous," he mumbled.

"I mean it. An actual masterpiece. I mean, it's a Picasso, but they *do* consider that art."

He sighed. "I take it back. You're not Prince Charming or Shrek. You're Donkey. Insufferable and not funny."

"Are you kidding me? Donkey is freaking hilarious." Then I had to imitate him. "'I'm making waffles!'"

"Boys," Deirdre said, and yet again, everyone was watching us. They were smiling, but still . . . we'd missed whatever the class was doing.

"Sorry."

Amos fought a smile. An actual real smile.

Damn.

"Okay, that's class," Deirdre said. Then she put up her hand. "Before you go. Normally these on-screen relationships have many weeks or even months in preproduction to work on their chemistry, but we don't have that luxury. So you have homework."

Oh great. I was pretty sure I knew where this was going.

"Spend time with your partner. With your friends or not, I don't care. Do something together outside of this classroom. Because tomorrow?"

She paused . . . and we waited.

"Tomorrow we take a deeper look at character assessment and the relationships between all of you, couples included. The rest of you should be okay because your relationships are emerging as the production begins, but Chase and Amos," she said, looking right at us. "Your characters have been together for a year. I need you to be comfortable with each other. Close, touching, and it needs to look natural. Tomorrow there will be more intimacy exercises for you both."

"Yay," I deadpanned sarcastically. "Can't wait."

The class dissipated and I turned to find Amos already walking over to collect his bag.

"So," I hedged. "Homework..."

"If you think I'm hanging out with you and your friends, you're delusional."

"What's wrong with my friends?"

"Nothing. I'm sure they're great guys." His left eyebrow quirked up then flattened. It gave the impression that he did *not*, in fact, think my friends were great guys. "Just not my scene."

"And what is your scene?"

His gaze cut to mine, as if he actually considered telling me the truth about what he spent his time doing. But then he schooled that brief flicker of honesty away and slung his backpack over his shoulder.

"I gotta work tonight."

"Why didn't you say that?"

"I just did."

I groaned. God, he was so frustrating. "Well, we gotta spend time together whether we like it or not. What time do you finish?"

He pulled his phone out and thumbed through a few screens. "Eight."

"Then I shall see you at eight."

"I have two hours now if you..."

"I told the guys I'd hit the gym with them before I knew we'd have homework."

He made a face, as if even the thought of going to a gym smelled bad. "I thought you said you weren't a jock."

"I'm not." I pulled up my shirt and showed him my abs. "But I like to look good, and maintaining a six-pack is hard work."

He rolled his eyes. "You really are going for the Hollywood generic, aren't you?"

I dropped my shirt, a little pissed that he wasn't the slightest bit impressed. "Oh, come on, even you have to admit these are hot."

"Sure. If you want to look like a fossilized trilobite."

I deflated, because damn. Ouch. "Now I'm sad."

Of course *that* made him smile. "I'm sure your friends will give you the bro ego-boost circle jerk or bro-jobs, or whatever it is gym bros do."

"If you could please give me the name and address of any gym that you know of that does bro-jobs, please let me know."

He rolled his eyes and walked out.

"See you at eight!" I yelled after him.

"Only because I don't have a choice," he replied before he was out the door and gone.

I sighed to the now-empty room, collected my bag, and dragged my feet to the gym.

"Hey, man," Jimmy said. He gave me a second look. "What's up?"

I sighed and threw my bag into the locker. "Nothing. I just . . ." I spun around to face him. "I'm a likable guy, right? I mean, everyone likes me. I'm fun to be around. I'm nice to people. Well, I'm not a dick to anyone. But I'm kinda all right, aren't I?"

He stared at me, seeing I was serious, and closed his locker door. "What the hell brought this on? Of course you're likable. You're better than just kinda all right, Chase. Three-quarters of this campus wants you to dick them. Girls, guys. Why you askin'?"

"Why only three-quarters?"

He snorted. "Gee, I don't know. Because lesbians and asexual people exist, Chase. And straight guys." He put his hand to his chest. "Now I love you, but not *that* much. Dude, why are you . . . who's got you doubting yourself?" Then he pulled his head back and looked down his nose at me. "Is it that emo guy? What's his name?"

Jesus. He made that leap pretty fast. "What? Who?"

"The guy at the coffee shop, the guy you called out to across the quad, down the hall . . . What's his name . . . Armistice, Amish, Amy—"

"Amos."

He grinned. "Holy shit."

"He said I'm generic."

Jimmy laughed. "Holy shit."

"It's not funny. He called me generic. Actually, it was generic Hollywood. That's what I am. Generic Hollywood."

He stared at me, eyes wide, mouth open in some horrified smile. "Holy shit."

"I know!"

"No. Holy shit because he's got you."

I squinted at him. "Got me what?"

"Figured out. Bent outta shape." He put his hands up as if his words were up in lights. "Bamboozled."

"The fuck is bamboozled?"

"What he's got you."

"Oh, fuck off. He has not."

"You finally met someone who doesn't like you."

"I dunno. I'm starting to wonder about you and where this conversation is going. You seem a little enraptured in my misery."

He laughed and gave me a shove. "I just never thought I'd see the day."

"The day what?" Tater said, walking in and dumping his gym bag.

"The day Chase meets someone who doesn't fall at his feet."

"It's not about them falling at my feet," I said. "It's about them not even liking me. Without even getting to know me."

Tater's eyes went to me. "For real? Why don't they like you? Everyone likes you."

"Not everyone," Jimmy added, far too cheerfully. "Emo Amos."

"He said I'm generic Hollywood and that my abs looked like a fossilized trilobite." I snatched up my phone. "I don't even know what that is." I began to google it, and as soon as I saw the first pic, I groaned. "Look. He thinks I look like this."

I showed them the pic.

Tater pressed his lips together, but Jimmy burst out laughing.

"It's not funny," I said. I mean, it wasn't *that* funny.

"Tell me," Jimmy said. "Are you mad because he called you a generic Hollywood fossil? Or are you mad because he's not interested in you?"

I stared at him because obviously it was the first one . . . and maybe a little of the second. Okay, maybe more of the second one than I liked to admit.

Tater snorted. "Have you ever had anyone ever be *not* interested in you?"

"Fuck off, both of ya. I'm hitting the gym."

Jimmy patted his stomach. "Gotta keep the trilobite in shape." Tater laughed.

I hated them both.

And using that petulance and the irritation at Amos brushing me off, I shoved my headphones in, pumped up my gym playlist, and hit the treadmill first, then weights, then did laps in the pool.

By the time I was done, I was exhausted and starving, and my mind was clear.

More or less.

We came out of the aquatic hall, bag over my shoulder, towel around my neck with my hair still kinda wet, and we all but ran into Georgia and Taylah and their group.

"Hi there," Georgia said to me.

I tousled the towel through my wet hair. "Hey," I replied. I knew the look she was giving me. The smile, the eyes. I'd seen them before; I'd acted on them before. She was a great girl, smart and fun, and she lived by the no-dating rule, same as me. I mighta been interested in that look, for one night . . .

Except I was supposed to be acting interested in someone else.

A certain someone who thought I was generic.

Georgia certainly didn't think I was generic.

"We're heading down to Shenanigans," she said, still smiling at me. "You guys should come with us."

Man, I was so tempted...

Jimmy clapped me on the back. "Sounds good, right?"

I groaned. "I wish I could." I met Georgia's gaze so she'd know I wasn't flaking out because of her. "I really do, but I have a homework assignment for drama class. It's a group thing. I can't skip out." Then I looked at Jimmy. "But you guys should totally go."

I knew they'd really liked to have gone and they certainly didn't need me to. I wasn't the social glue here.

Jimmy gave Georgia a bit of a smile. "You girls don't mind if it's just me and Tater?"

"Not at all," she said, giving him a bit of a once-over.

Yep. He was totally going.

Bolstered by this confidence, Jimmy gave me a shit-eating grin. "A homework assignment with anyone from your drama class in particular?"

"Shut the fuck up," I said, giving him a shove. "And have some wings and beer for me." I rubbed my stomach. "Man, that sounds good." I took a step back. "Have fun, guys."

"Here," Jimmy said, taking his and Tater's gym bags and shoving them into my chest. "Take these for us? Thanks."

They laughed, and I carried everything back to our house. Mundell House, part of the Liberty Court, was just a short walk from campus. I loved the house we lived in. I loved living with my friends. I loved the parties, the weekends of watching football or hockey or playing volleyball on the beach.

I loved this campus. Especially this time of year when the days were barely warm and the evenings were getting cool, right on the beach. T-shirts during the day, hoodies at night. The breeze, the trees, the sunset.

It was freaking beautiful.

I didn't even mind carrying all their shit home. I dumped it in the laundry room—they could take care of it later. I made myself a quick sandwich, got changed into some sweatpants and a T-shirt, grabbed a hoodie, and headed back toward campus. To the coffee shop.

It was only seven thirty but an iced coffee sounded good, and I had some studying to do, so . . . And with a bit of luck, it would annoy Amos.

There were a few people at tables, most studying, some talking, their books closed on the table in front of them. Another guy was behind the counter, and I wondered if Amos was even here, if I'd gotten the time wrong, or if he'd bailed . . . or lied.

But then he came through the staff door with a tray and I got a sliver of satisfaction at seeing him do a split-second double take when he saw me.

It was infinitesimal. But it was there.

I ordered my iced coffee with the other guy. His name tag said Mason. Maybe I'd seen him around before . . .

Amos was restacking stuff, cleaning things down, and getting the store ready to close, I guessed.

He ignored me.

So I took my drink to the far booth, liking that I was kinda hidden—so I didn't keep turning and looking for Amos—took out my book, and began reading, taking notes.

I didn't notice people at the other tables clear out, but when a plate with a muffin on it appeared in front of me, I looked up to find everyone gone.

And Amos standing there.

He put a knife and fork by the plate. "If you're hungry," he mumbled, then turned and walked back to the counter.

It was a raspberry and white chocolate muffin and . . . had he warmed it up for me?

I looked back at the counter, but he must've been in the backroom. Mason was talking through the door to someone . . . The outside lights were off, the register was closed, the counter covered.

Shit.

I didn't mean to keep him. I began to pack up my book when Amos came out with a drink in one hand, a plate in the other. Without a word, he slid into the booth.

Then Mason called out. "Lock the doors on your way out, okay?"

"Yeah, no problem," Amos replied.

Then it was just Amos and me in a closed coffee shop with most of the lights off. "Uh, what's going on?"

"I'm starving," he said, picking up his panini and taking a bite.

"Do you always get left alone here?"

He shrugged. "Sometimes. Mason wanted to leave, some date thing with his girl. I dunno. I said I'd mop the floors so he could go."

I looked around at the very un-mopped floors. "Well, I hate to be the one to break it to you . . ."

"Food first." He took another bite, then nodded to the muffin, then to me.

"Yeah, I like these. I just wasn't sure it was meant for me."

He rolled his eyes and swallowed his mouthful. "I gave it to you, didn't I?"

"Well, you put it in front of me and said if I was hungry . . . And I just wasn't sure. Coming from anyone else, I'd think I could eat it. But coming from you, that could be 'if you're hungry, too bad because this isn't for you.'"

He snorted and finished chewing his food. "If you don't want it, I'll have it."

I took the knife and cut the muffin in half. "Here."

I was hungry and clearly, so was he. But I could eat something else when I got back to the house. He lived in the dorms, and I wasn't sure what he'd get to eat after the dining hall was closed.

"Thanks," he said, taking his half. He nodded to my textbook. "So, what's the book for?"

"Documentary Theater."

He screwed his nose up. "I hated that class."

I ate a few mouthfuls of the muffin. It was actually really good. "This is so good."

"How was your gym session?"

"Well, there was no circle jerk, if that's what you're asking."

He smiled. He actually smiled. It changed his whole face like the light replaced the dark.

Not that I'd tell him that.

"And I was kinda pissed," I admitted. "Though anger makes for good motivation in the gym. Drives me to focus. I killed some decent calories today."

"What were you pissed about?"

"The word *generic*." I nodded and took a small forkful of muffin. "And how much I hate that word."

His gaze met mine and his smile became a grin. "Oh, generic, as in generic Hollywood."

I pointed my fork at him. "That would be the one."

Amos chuckled. "Well, that's good to know. If I ever need to get under your skin, I'll know which weapon to choose."

I smirked at him because, goddammit. As much as he irritated me—and god knows he irritated me—this banter with him, the constant back and forth, was so much fun.

I liked that he challenged me.

To be fair, most people just went along with whatever I said. I could fabricate the biggest load of bullshit and all my friends would just nod and smile, go along with it, even beef up the story a little. They'd eat it up, knowing it was all a story, and smile at me.

But not Amos.

Amos didn't give an inch. He took none of my shit, and I kinda liked that.

"And which weapons would I need in battle against you?" I asked, stabbing some more muffin and shoving it in my mouth before I could tack anything on that might come across as flirting.

But when my eyes met his, I think he might have taken it as flirting anyway.

The way he chewed on the inside of his lip, trying not to smile, his eyes full of . . . something I couldn't quite read.

"Why would I give you ammunition to use against me

for free?" He sipped his drink. "I think you need to figure that out on your own."

"How is that fair? Nothing bothers you."

"Yes it does."

"What? Like this conversation?"

"Somewhat, yes."

Then I remembered something he'd said in class today.

"You don't like people in your personal space. Touching your face."

Amos's eyes met mine. "You were listening."

I pointed to my ears. "My mother would say they're not painted on."

He sipped his drink, looking around the darkened café. "Plenty of things bother me. Some more than others."

"So I won't touch your face," I said. "When we're acting like boyfriends and shit. You need to tell me where it's okay to touch, where it's not okay. If we need to be . . . affectionate in public. I don't want you to be uncomfortable."

"Well, you don't need to make it weird."

"I'm saying this shit so it doesn't get weird."

"I've had boyfriends and . . . whatever. I let them touch me. Personal touch is fine." He made a face. "God, you make me sound like a freak. I'm not a germaphobe or anything. Or a prude, or whatever. I just like my personal space, and I don't like crowded places. If there's too many people . . . it just gets overwhelming."

That sounded like an overreaction. Or a sore spot. An exposed nerve, perhaps.

"It's okay, Amos. Whatever you want to do. I'm down." He might not like talking about this, but we needed to figure out some details. "You know what you need to do?"

He rolled his eyes. "This'll be good," he mumbled.

"You need to act."

He looked at me then. "To act?"

I nodded and slid out of the booth. "Let's do something stupid, like *Hairspray*."

Amos scoffed. "*Hair*—where?"

I looked around. "Here."

"What the hell for?"

"To get used to each other."

"I don't need to act out a scene from the worst musical of all time to know you. The fact you suggested *Hairspray* tells me all I need to know. You could have at least suggested *West Side Story* or *Rent*. Or *Hamilton*, for god's sake." He slid out of the booth. "What you can do is put the chairs up on the tables for me so I can mop the floor."

Well, yes. That I could do.

I'd done a few tables when he came back out with the mop and bucket. He started behind the counter first, and as I lifted another chair up onto the table, I thought about what he'd said.

It says all I need to know about you.

What did he choose? *West Side Story* or *Rent*. What did they say about him?

Both great choices. They told me he was an outsider, someone who struggled but was a fighter. Someone who was brave. A classic. Cool, vintage.

While I was generic.

Maybe he was right.

I slid another chair onto a table, and another . . . and it

reminded me of something. Something I'd always loved, secretly, and watched a dozen times. And I wondered if I could show him a small piece of the real me.

If I could be brave like him.

Before I lost my nerve, I took out my phone, found the instrumental on YouTube, and pressed play.

As soon as the music started, Amos stopped mopping and watched me. But in that moment, I wasn't in the Bean Necessities after closing time.

I was transported to a stage, to Broadway, in front of a full audience, with a full orchestra.

Transported to the barricades in some French revolution.

I sang about a grief that can't be spoken, of a pain that goes on and on. Then I sang about empty chairs at empty tables.

The whole café was my stage as I lifted every chair, sliding it atop a table. Like I felt everything Marius felt as he sang that song for his fallen friends. Like I was singing for my life.

I sang about revolution, about a tomorrow that never came. I sang to the phantom faces in the window, to the shadows on the floor. I gestured to the table in the corner, where my friends would meet no more.

I belted out the crescendo, my voice straining as I held the note. Like I was ten years old at home alone, acting the whole scene in my parents' basement. Like no one was watching.

Except someone was.

When the song ended, Amos stood there with the mop handle in the crook of his arm so he could clap. He was grinning, a full-on grin. Something I'd never seen him do, ever.

And so help me god, it was breathtaking.

He nodded slowly, still smiling. I wasn't embarrassed. I was nervous, strangely enough. I wanted him to approve.

"There he is," he said.

Huh?

"There who is?"

His eyes locked with mine. "The *you* you don't show anyone else."

Chapter Six
Amos

So maybe Mr. Generic Hollywood wasn't so generic after all.

Well, okay, he still was . . .

But watching him sing "Empty Chairs at Empty Tables" as he lifted the chairs like props . . . Damn. He was something else.

Surprising, to say the very least.

I hadn't expected that out of him.

The emotion, the heart. The talent.

He was quiet afterwards and he helped me clean and lock up, and soon enough we were walking across campus to my dorm. I wasn't sure what to say, not wanting to make things awkward between us.

If we were supposed to act like boyfriends, the very least I could do was stop being sarcastic or rude. He'd shown a part of himself to me that I highly doubted he'd shown anyone else, ever.

Hell, in the last three years I'd been in his drama classes, been in stage productions, and done improvs with him, and I'd never seen that side of him.

"I used to act out *Les Mis* when I was younger," he said, clearly feeling the need to explain. Or maybe to open himself a little more. "Or any musical, really. My mom had DVDs of a whole bunch of them, so I'd go down in my parents' basement—it was a family room with old couches and a TV and DVD player. You know, like the kids' room with old bookcases, board games, that kind of thing."

I nodded. "Sounds fun."

"It was. Anyway, if I was ever home alone, I'd put on a musical, crank up the volume, and act them out. I'd use the furniture like I was on stage. *Les Mis* was always a favorite." He sighed. "I haven't done anything like it in years."

"You should," I said. "And I don't want to inflate your ego or anything, but you were good."

Chase smirked at me. "A compliment from you. Wow."

"Don't get used to it."

"How could I? When an insult follows swiftly behind."

"I haven't insulted you tonight."

"Yeah, I'm still kinda stuck on the generic thing."

I chuckled and stopped walking. When he looked at me, wondering why, I nodded to the dorm. "This is me."

He seemed surprised. "Oh. Okay. I didn't know . . . I'm down at the Mundell House."

I nodded, because of course he was. "What's your plan for tonight? A few beers? Studying?"

He glanced in the direction of his place, into the dark. "Uh, nothing, actually. The guys were going down to Shenanigans, but I'm not feeling it, ya know."

Goddammit.

Was I really about to do this?

I took a deep breath and resigned my fate. "Well, we are supposed to do some homework," I said. "Did you want to come up to my room?" I cringed. "There was no way to say that without it sounding like an invite for something else," I added. "Which it isn't. Just so you know."

Chase's eyes met mine and he smiled. "Oh, believe me, I know."

I sighed and trudged up the steps and held the door for him. "Yes or no, make it quick or the invite is rescinded, in three . . . two . . ."

"All right, jeez," he said, brushing past me. "I'm still not sure if that was a threat. Is that what that was?"

I started up the stairs, not stopping to see if he was following. "My threats have less subtlety. Believe me, you'd know."

He said nothing until the third flight. "Christ. You have to walk up these every day?"

"Several times."

"Isn't there an elevator?"

"Do you whine this bad all the time? Or am I just lucky?" I got to the landing and turned to watch him trudge up the last few steps. "There is an elevator, but this way I don't have to go to the gym."

"Maybe I overdid it at the gym today."

"Maybe you shouldn't let the opinions of others get to you so much," I said, leading the way down the hall to my room. "Why do you care so much about what I think anyway?"

"Isn't it good to care how other people think and feel?"

I unlocked my door and pushed it open. "No. It's the

opposite of good." I hit the lights and tossed my bag onto my desk chair. I waited until he was inside before I closed the door behind him. "Concerning yourself with what other people think of you is the biggest waste of mental headspace."

"You don't care what other people think of you?"

I wasn't sure why he seemed so surprised by this.

"Not at all. My parents, perhaps. I want them to be proud of me, sure. But I don't seek approval or validation from anyone. I know who I am. I'm a good person, and I'm nice to others. I mind my own business. If they don't like me, that's their problem."

He studied me for a bit, then conceded a sad smile. "I wish I could do that."

"Why can't you? Just start telling yourself it doesn't matter what people think of you. Do what makes you happy and stop giving a shit what other people think. You'll be so much happier."

He let out a laugh. "Is it that easy?"

"It's exactly that easy." I sat on my bed, opened my laptop, and waited for Netflix to load. "How are you going to own Hollywood if you wear the expectations of everyone?"

He sat down on the end of my bed with a sigh. "I dunno . . . I just . . . feedback is good though, right?"

"That depends. Is it feedback on your craft, on the art of your acting, of the character you play? Or is it someone's opinion and preconceived expectations? Because those are two very different things. If it's the former, then sure. If you can take it constructively and if you can learn from it, then yes. If it's the latter and if it's gonna eat you up inside, then hell no."

He smiled at me then. "You really have it all figured out, dontcha?"

"Not at all. I just don't care what people think, as a general rule." I shrugged. "I know people don't like me; they also don't know me. I know they think I'm weird, or emo, or eccentric or whatever. I don't give a fuck what they think. Their opinions mean nothing to me. They can bend themselves all out of shape, use up all that mental energy." I hit Play on my laptop. "I'll just be over here watching *Rick and Morty*, living my best life."

His smile was more genuine now. "I love *Rick and Morty*."

"Same."

"I'm gonna try thinking more like you. Letting shit go and not caring what they think."

"Would you do musical theater if you didn't care what people thought?"

His eyes narrowed at the computer screen as he considered this. "Mm, I dunno." Then he scooted back on the bed to rest against the wall, his feet dangling over the edge. "I mean, do I want Hollywood? Or do I want Broadway?" He sighed then. "I don't know. Hollywood, I think."

I wasn't convinced.

"The Chase I saw singing his heart out in the café earlier was a very different actor than the Chase I see in the classroom."

"That was just for fun. It wasn't serious."

I didn't need to point out the obvious. That he should

do what was fun, what made him happy, because from the look on his face, I was almost certain he knew.

"You could be the next Hugh Jackman," I said instead. "Blockbuster movies and theater on the side. Win an Oscar *and* a Tony."

He grinned at me. "Yeah, maybe."

We watched *Rick and Morty* for a bit, laughing at the ridiculousness and crudeness, and it wasn't weird. There was no awkwardness, no need to fill the silence.

Not on my part, anyway.

"What do you think we'll be doing tomorrow?" Chase asked.

"Tomorrow? In what?"

"Deirdre said we'd be working on more intimacy exercises."

Oh.

I sighed. "Not sure. Physical closeness probably."

He nodded slowly. "Yeah."

And then it was kind of awkward.

"Are you okay with that?" he asked. "I mean, I know we talked about it on day one, but are you really? Okay with it, I mean?"

I shrugged. "Sure. Are you?"

"Yeah, I'm down. It's fine." He frowned as Rick did something hilarious, which kinda told me he wasn't watching the show. "Are you okay with kissing? I mean, it's gonna be weird, of course. But we're both professionals, right?"

"Sure. Haven't you had to kiss people in a play before? Or embrace or whatever?"

"Yeah, sure. But this is different. It's . . . it's a reality TV show. It's supposed to be like our normal, everyday lives." He looked at me then. "And like I said, I'm a touchy-feely kind of person. If I'm with them, I like to show affection. And I know you're not like that—you don't like physical touch—so maybe we should work on that."

"Work on what, exactly? Because that sounds like you want me to adapt to you, and not you adapt to me."

"See? This is what I mean," he said quickly. "We need to work out a middle ground that looks believable and something you're comfortable with."

"I don't *not* like physical touch," I said. "I told you that. I just have . . . boundaries. And limits."

He seemed genuinely happy to hear this. He shot forward, sitting now with his feet on the floor. "Okay. So what are your limits?"

"People. In general."

He snorted. "Like a social battery?"

"Exactly. You get buzzed hanging out in crowded places. I get drained by it."

"Okay, fair enough. That's easy. When you've had enough, we leave."

"*We* leave? Are you expecting me to go places with you?"

"Well, yeah. As part of the show. There's gonna be social settings."

I groaned, because I hadn't really thought of that. "Yeah, okay. Fair enough."

"And the touching," he hedged. "Is holding hands okay? Hugging?"

I grimaced. "God. If you have to, I suppose."

"Kissing?"

"In public?" I wasn't one bit sorry for the face I made. "I can't think of one reason where it's necessary to suck face in public."

He snorted. "Because the love you feel for someone is greater than your opinions of others . . . Hey, I thought you didn't care what other people thought?"

"I don't."

"But you do, clearly."

"Some things are supposed to be private."

"Well, I think we're expected to kiss at some point." He shrugged. "And who knows, maybe we can ask if our kissing scenes are done in private. I'm sure if we tell Deirdre it's a hard limit, she'll be okay with it. They're still working on script adaptations anyway, so we can tell her tomorrow."

Goddammit.

"I don't have a problem with it," I said, feeling the need to explain myself. I wasn't sure why. "It's just acting, I get that. And the real script adaptations won't start until filming does. It's a reality show. The script writers and scene guides need to adapt and change shit on a daily basis because there will be factors out of our control. We're working with the general public, with the students and faculty. And they're not in on it. They don't have scene guides or anything. This is pure method acting, ad-libbing, and rolling with it." I shrugged again. "So, if there's kissing . . . if the scene calls for it, and if it feels right, then we can do that."

"So tomorrow if we have to practice kissing, you'll be okay with it? I don't want you to do anything you won't be comfortable with."

"I'll be fine," I replied, aiming for a nonchalance I didn't feel. "As long as you brush your teeth beforehand."

He laughed. "Same. Oh, you're not allergic to peanuts or anything, right?"

"No."

"Good. Because I love me a good PB&J sandwich."

I rolled my eyes but did concede a smile.

"Okay, let's start with this," he said, scooting back on the bed, sitting against the wall with his legs outstretched, feet over the edge. He patted the bed next to him and held out his hand.

"You want to hold my hand?" I asked, sidling up next to him.

"Might as well start now."

I resisted sighing but I did whack my hand into his. He chuckled, then maneuvered our palms and threaded our fingers until he was comfortable.

"See, this isn't so bad," he said, keeping his eyes on the computer screen.

Yeah, this isn't so bad at all . . .

His hand was big and strong, calloused from the gym. Warm and, man, the human touch felt nice.

We watched the whole next episode with our hands joined, resting a bit on his thigh and mine. It wasn't weird . . .

Well, the only weirdness was that it wasn't weird. That it felt completely natural. Nice, even.

He left after the next episode ended, and I showered and got into bed, thinking about how he'd sung that *Les Mis* song, thinking about how his hand felt so good in mine, and wondering if I'd have to kiss him tomorrow.

If I was dreading it. Or if that tightness in my belly was something else.

2

So, as it turns out, the intimacy exercises Deirdre had in mind were exactly what I feared they'd be.

"Chase and Amos," she said. "Stand together as if you're waiting for someone to get out of class. You've got time, you're relaxed, and no one else's around."

Chase parked his ass against a desk and pulled me between his legs, one hand on my hip, his other hand holding mine, our fingers lazily interlocked. It was casual, relaxed.

"Perfect," Deirdre said. "Now face each other."

"Oh good," I mumbled. "More staring exercises."

"Yes, more staring exercises," Deirdre said. "Get used to it. Look into each other's eyes as if you love him."

I would . . . I just had to roll my eyes first.

Chase chuckled and tugged on my hand, making me focus. And we did the staring thing.

I understood it built trust and it helped build a bond, but staring into his blue eyes, seeing every fleck of gold and black, it felt . . . personal.

Then Deirdre was beside us and she put a notebook to my lips. "Hold this and lean in the way you'd kiss him. Keep the notebook in place, so there's no lip-touching. Hold eye contact. There are varying stage kisses," she said. "There is an art to the choreography of a stage kiss. How to position faces, how to create the illusion of a kiss, but sometimes it calls for actual lip contact."

I knew intimacy exercises were a real thing, actors did them all the time. There were even professional intimacy coaches and scene coordinators on most sets. But god, this was crazy.

I took the notebook, keeping it pressed to my lips, and pretended to kiss him.

The jerk smiled.

I wanted to hit him with the notebook.

But as weird as it was, it did help with getting used to having our faces close together, having him in my personal space, and mimicking the action of a quick kiss.

It was about becoming familiar. For this to become a habit so it looked natural.

Then we had to switch positions. Me leaning against the table, Chase had to hold the notebook. It was all pretty much the same, and after five minutes, it did kinda feel like it was no big deal.

Boring, even.

Then it was a piece of paper. No notebook, just a single sheet of paper.

More intimate, yet still a barrier between us. I could feel his lips through the paper, but there was no direct lip contact. A little unnerving at first, but after a few minutes, it felt fine.

He kept making funny faces with his eyes. Every time we leaned in to fake a kiss, he'd go cross-eyed or wink or raise one eyebrow. I don't know if he was just trying to lighten the mood, or make it less serious to make me more comfortable, but it worked.

It made me kind of mad that it worked.

It made me kind of mad that I liked it.

"Okay, guys, we're going to try this," Deirdre said. She handed us a pack of pretzel sticks. The crunchy kind that was about six inches long, lightly salted.

"Ooh, I like these," Chase said, opening the packet.

"Good," Deirdre said. "Put the end in your mouth. Amos, start at the other end, and you're both going to bite the ends until your lips touch."

Oh.

Lip contact.

Okay then.

Chase put one end of a pretzel stick in between his teeth, and I put the other end in between mine. "Like this?" I asked Deirdre.

"Yep. Now eat."

Chase snorted and began to bite his way up the pretzel, getting closer and closer. I only got a few bites in before his lips met mine.

Warm and all too brief.

He pulled back with a laugh, chewing his mouthful of pretzel. Then he put another one in between his teeth. "Your turn."

So I did the biting this time, crunching my way up the pretzel until our lips touched.

It was silly and fun, and I could see why this was a technique used to acclimate to intimacy between actors. It made a game of it.

Well, Chase did.

"My turn," he said, putting a pretzel stick between my

lips. He didn't even give me a chance to bite it. He just munched his way up the stick until his lips met mine.

"Now you."

I met his gaze and began to slowly bite up the pretzel, and he smiled around it as I got closer. "I can't kiss you when you smile," I mumbled around the half-eaten pretzel in my mouth.

He laughed but pursed his lips, so I finished it, pecking his lips.

We did it a few more times, each time becoming more familiar, more fun. Until he put the packet down. "I need a drink," he said. "Too many pretzels."

He walked over to our bags, grabbed my water bottle too, and brought it over to me. "Thanks."

We sipped our drinks as Deirdre came back over to us. "How'd you find it?"

"Fine," I answered. "It's a good way to practice."

She gave me a nod, then turned to Chase. "And?"

He shrugged. "It's fine, but I don't think we need it. I could kiss Amos right now and it'd be fine." He looked at me, his raised eyebrow asking if I agreed.

I half shrugged, embarrassed and nervous, and . . . I wasn't sure. "I guess."

"And we discussed boundaries and consent. We'll be fine."

"Did we discuss consent?" I asked.

"Well, yeah. I asked if you'd be okay with general affection or kissing. You said yes."

"Actually, I said I can think of no good reason why kissing in public should be a thing. For anyone, not just us."

Chase snorted. "But you said if it was required for a scene, then yes."

I sighed. "True."

"So I have your consent?"

"Yes."

He grinned and waited.

And waited . . .

"What?"

"Aren't you gonna ask me?"

"I did. You said yes."

"Consent is ongoing. Ask me again. In front of Deirdre."

I sighed. "Do I have your consent to hold your hand? Or to kiss you if there is no other reasonable course of action applicable and under duress we *have* to kiss?"

Chase laughed. "Such a romantic."

"Yes or no?"

"Yes."

Deirdre was looking between us like a tennis match, her smile slow spreading. "Okay, then let's try it."

"Kissing now?" Chase asked.

He suddenly didn't look so confident.

"Yes," Deirdre replied. "Would acting out a scene help? We can pick a classic scene, any scene you like."

"No," he said, shaking his head. "It'll be fine. Won't it?" He looked at me. "I mean . . ."

Yep. Confident Chase was gone.

"For god's sake." I sighed, walked up to him, slid my hand around the back of his neck, and kissed him.

He froze, in shock for half a second before he caught up and he reciprocated the kiss.

Warm lips, soft mouth. His hair felt good in my hands.

Instinct told me to fist his hair and open his mouth with my own, but that's not what this was. This was acting, and this was practice for filming, nothing more.

I pulled back, his lips parted, his eyes half-closed.

"Done," I said. "First one is out of the way."

Deirdre was staring at us, shocked. "Well, that's one way to do it, I guess."

Chase was staring at me, his cheeks pink. "Well, that was . . ."

"What?" I asked.

"Unexpected."

I pointed to my lips. "Your turn. Get it over and done with. It's easier that way."

Taking the clinical approach was better than the alternative.

So he did exactly what I did. Put his hand around the back of my neck and planted his lips on mine. More of an over-pronounced smooch than a kiss.

"What the hell kind of kiss was that?" I asked. "Like a joke kiss?"

"Boyfriends are gonna joke around," he said. His cheeks were still pink. "They're gonna be familiar enough with each other to joke around, right?"

Hmm. "I guess."

"You want a real kiss?"

"Just more convincing, and not like you'd kiss your favorite aunt."

"Who the hell kisses their aunt like that? Just how close is your family?"

I rolled my eyes. "Shut up. You know what I mean."

"Fine," he said. Then he did the opposite of before. He stepped in close, his eyes on mine, and he put his hand to my face, his thumb tracing my bottom lip. "You want a real boyfriend kiss?" he murmured, his voice a rough whisper. His gaze drew down to my mouth, then back up to my eyes. Then he pressed down on my lip, pulling my mouth open and sliding his thumb away, he covered my lips with his.

Open mouth, soft lips. He tilted his head and raked his hands through the hair at the back of my head, pulling on the strands.

It made my knees weak, and I was just about to give him my tongue when he pulled back.

He smirked. "Was that a joke kiss?" he murmured, his eyes looking at my lips as if he wanted more.

Someone cleared their throat, and we both turned to find Deirdre and the rest of the actors watching us.

"Practicing," I said. "Practicing kissing."

"Looks like you got the hang of it," Holly said, fanning her face.

Max laughed. "Don't let us interrupt."

I took a step back, trying to clear my head, to calm my racing heart.

Because that didn't feel like practice to me. And if that's how Chase kissed, then I was in for one helluva few weeks.

How am I gonna get through this?

Chapter Seven
Chase

I wasn't gonna let Amos win.

Admittedly, when he'd kissed me first, I hadn't been expecting it. No, I hadn't expected him to be so brazen. I hadn't expected him to take charge. It knocked me off my guard a little, not gonna lie.

I'd tried to mimic his professionalism. His separation from craft. If he could kiss me like it meant nothing, then I could do the same. Admittedly, the big old smooch I'd given him wasn't my finest work and then he called it a joke kiss.

A joke kiss.

And I wasn't having that. So I kissed him like I would kiss anyone, anyone that I was interested in, anyone that I wanted to take to bed, and he was into it. When I'd fisted his hair, I felt the rumble in his throat. The moan damn near made me almost shove my tongue in his mouth, and I had to stop myself before I did. I wanted to push him against the table and kiss him for real—all hands, teeth, mouth, tongue. Bodies.

I'd almost done exactly that.

So close.

He tasted like pretzels and toothpaste. He smelled of deodorant or cologne. I wasn't sure what it was—timber and honey, or maybe it was just him.

I liked it.

I was beginning to like him.

When I'd left his room last night—after we'd sat on his bed, holding hands and watching *Rick and Morty*—I walked home, telling myself it wasn't real.

Because it *wasn't* real. It was acting. It was all preparation for this semester's production in our final year.

Just like the kiss.

It wasn't real.

It wasn't me, and it wasn't Amos. It was our characters. It was Dominic and Elijah. They kissed, not us, and that's what I told myself for the rest of the day and well into the night.

I told myself it was no big deal. I told myself not to read into it.

So I'd been a little competitive. That was nothing new. He'd been brazen enough to kiss me first when I had been suddenly overcome with nerves and apprehension, so if he could be aloof and removed, then so could I.

Except now, I couldn't stop thinking about him, about that damn kiss. About how he'd felt against me, about how he'd reacted. How he'd tasted.

How he'd blushed and been all shy afterwards.

It'd pleased me to know that it had affected him as much as it had affected me. And the great part was—or maybe it was the torturous part—now we had to keep doing it until we made it look natural.

"Why are you so quiet?" Tater asked. "Everything okay?"

"Yeah, everything is great. Why do you ask?"

"Because you've been quiet. And you've got your thinking face on."

"That's not his thinking face," Jimmy said. "That's his caught-feelings face."

I gave him the stink eye. "Oh, fuck off."

He just laughed. "A bit like that time when you thought you caught feelings for Georgia before you talked yourself out of it. But this is worse. You've caught bigger feelings this time."

I leveled him a not-impressed glare.

Tater blinked in surprise. "Holy shit. For real?"

Jimmy's grin widened. "And if I were a betting man—which I totally am, by the way—so five bucks says it's a certain someone who doesn't like you . . . What did he call you? Generic?"

I sighed so loud it was a borderline groan.

"Oh my god. Like, for real?" Tater was grinning now too.

"No, not for real. And he apologized for the generic comment." Kind of. Not really, but whatever. "And he *does* like me."

"You're not denying it," Jimmy said, putting his hand out. "You owe me five bucks."

"You can suck my dick," I said, batting his hand away.

"No thanks." Jimmy sized me up, serious now. "Honestly though? Are you good? Ain't like you to get bent outta shape over someone."

So typical of Jimmy. Joked until he could see it was time to be serious. Like now. And it wasn't like the whole drama production was some big secret. We were allowed to tell people. Maybe telling them would help.

I began with another sigh. "So this production for drama is a thing for a few weeks. It's a focus on method acting."

"Okay," Jimmy hedged.

"What's method acting?" Tater asked.

"It's a style of acting," I explained, "where the actor stays in character. Not just when the camera rolls but always. At home, twenty-four seven. You become the character."

"Marlon Brando was famous for it, right?" Jimmy asked.

I nodded. "It can be intense."

"Like an undercover cop," Tater added. "Like if he infiltrates a gang, he has to be that character all the time."

God bless him. I adored the guy. He really wasn't the brightest, but that was actually a pretty good comparison. "Right."

"And?" Jimmy asked.

"And this is like a *90210* reality TV twist. They're gonna film us in our everyday lives."

"As another character?"

I shrugged. "Yes, but each character is very similar to our own person, so we can play the part for the whole project."

Tater blinked. "For how long?"

"We have another week or so of preproduction and then filming for two weeks. Which doesn't sound long, but it's twenty-four seven for two weeks."

"Wow," Tater said.

I nodded and sighed again. "And my character has a boyfriend." I winced. "A long-term boyfriend. Been together a year."

Jimmy's smile was slow spreading. "Lemme guess. The generic guy."

I really hate that word.

"His name is Amos. And *he's* not generic. He thinks *I'm* generic. Well, he did. I don't know. He told me he doesn't think of me as generic anymore." Which made me so stupidly happy. "He does like me. I know he does."

Jimmy smiled at me. "So he's finally on the same page. Thank god, because I was beginning to think you were going to pine forever."

"I'm not pining. And it's not . . . it's not like romance or anything. He doesn't like me like that."

"But you like him like that."

I scoffed because that was ridiculous. "Look, this project is a pretty big deal. I'm gonna have to spend time with him, and he'll be spending time with me, here and around you guys. I need you to not make it weird." I ran my hand over my face. "And there'll be cameras around, so you might not wanna walk around naked . . ." Then I shrugged. "Or do. I don't care. The editing team is gonna need to learn how to pixelate and blur, so whatever. Although it's being live streamed, so I don't know . . ."

Tate looked around the house. "There's gonna be film crews? Here?"

Jimmy blinked. "Live streamed?"

I nodded. "Yep. Though I think they wanna try and keep it at Amos's room, mostly. Less distraction for you guys, and he's in the dorms and so are three of the others, so it'll be like *Melrose Place* or some shit. God, I don't even know. There's minimal outline, minimal script. They just gave us some quick character profiles and some plot lines to make it interesting."

Tater blinked. "What's Melrose Place?"

I resisted sighing.

"And your character and Amos's character are banging?" Jimmy asked. "So you gotta act all lovey-dovey with him all the time, day and night?"

"As long as there's cameras around, I guess. We just need to stay in character. It's about method acting. Capturing the psyche of our characters, their mental headspace."

"And bed space."

I rolled my eyes and sighed, then I groaned. "Pretty sure it won't go that far."

"But you gotta act like you've been together a year. Pretty sure couples who've been together for a year are fucking on the regular," Jimmy said.

I ignored that.

Tater looked confused. "I dunno if I could ever be an actor. Having to kiss your costar. I mean, what if you hated them? What if they ate tuna and pickled onions for lunch?" He made a face. "Or what if they had poor dental hygiene? Or if they were just a terrible person? I could never pretend to like someone who made fun of other people."

He was such a sweet guy.

"That's why it's called acting." But then I conceded. "And there are general rules and etiquette for brushing teeth etcetera before you suck face."

Jimmy's eyes cut to mine. "Have you kissed Amos yet?"

I didn't even have to answer out loud. Apparently just looking at him was enough.

"Oh, this is perfect," he said, clapping his hands. "So did you kiss him? Or did he kiss you?"

That time I sighed. "We practiced," I replied. "They're called intimacy exercises. It sounds dirty, but it's just stuff like touching, holding hands, and just being comfortable in their personal space."

"So there was no tongue?" Jimmy pressed.

"No, there was no tongue. You perv."

There was no way I was telling them how I'd almost given him tongue. How I'd had to stop myself from slipping my tongue into his mouth.

"It's not like that," I added. "We're professionals. Well, we're not paid for this, but we take it seriously. It's worth a good chunk of our semester grade. We have to nail this."

I knew I'd said the wrong thing as soon as I'd said it.

"Shut up, Jimmy," I said before he could open his mouth. He snorted instead.

"So when do we meet him?" Tater asked. "Officially, I mean. Are you bringing him here? And the film crew? Will I be in anything? I'll have to let my mom know to watch."

"I don't know how much you guys'll be in it," I answered. "Probably not much. Maybe just background stuff, like extras. But if we go to the bar or the coffee shop . . . It's more about us. There are four couples. Three romantic couples, one set of best friends."

"So, tell me," Jimmy said. "How did you and emo-boy's characters meet? You're not exactly running in the same circles."

"It's in our character briefs," I replied. "We met in drama class."

He grinned at me. "So, do your character briefs say which one of you tops or bottoms?"

"Hey, Jimmy," I deadpanned. "Fuck all the way off."

2

"I told my friends," I said.

Amos and I were sitting on the floor in the drama room. We were supposed to be acting as if we were home alone watching TV. He had his legs outstretched, crossed at the ankles. I tapped his knee. "Open your legs."

He did a double take. "I beg your pardon?"

"Move your leg," I said, physically moving his legs apart so I could lay down between his legs, my back to his chest. I snuggled in a little, using his upper pec as a pillow. "That's better."

"Are you comfortable?" he deadpanned.

"I am now. And shush, we're supposed to be watching TV." I pointed to the non-existent television. "I love this episode."

He leaned back on his hands, and I did my very best to feel any particular hard bits that might have jabbed me in the lower back, but I was disappointed . . .

"So you told your friends about what?"

"About us."

"What exactly about us did you tell them?"

"That we're on-screen boyfriends, and if you come around to the house, they have to be nice to you."

"Oh." He paused. "Would they have not been if you didn't ask?"

"Yeah, of course they would. They're nice guys. Well, they can be dicks to me, but they'd never be dicks to you."

"Dicks to you? You call Tate Tater Tot. I'd consider that you being a dick to him."

"Everyone calls him that." I shrugged. "Because he has the brain function of a potato."

"You're a bully to him. And he puts up with you, why?"

"No, I'm not a bully . . ." I sighed. "Maybe . . ." Christ. "I didn't make the name up. I didn't start it."

"Well, maybe you can stop calling him that."

I felt duly admonished. Probably rightfully so, but I was nothing if not petulant. "You can't talk. You called me generic."

He sounded amused. "Did I touch a nerve?"

Yes.

"No."

I hated that we were having this conversation while I was lying on him with his knee raised. "You know, if I was ever going to be lying all over someone like this, I would've thought they'd be saying nice things to me." I pulled at a thread in the hole in his jeans. "Say something nice to me."

He sighed. "You're not generic. Feel better now?"

"Yes."

I did. Immediately.

"So about my friends," I began. "I know you're not a

fan of anyone who doesn't meet your cool-recluse vibes, but they're good guys."

"Hm."

"Well, you're gonna have to spend time with them at some point, so maybe work on acting like you can tolerate them," I said flatly. "What about your friends? You tell them yet?"

"You might find this hard to believe, but I don't have a lot of friends. I try not to socialize. It's exhausting. There are people that I work with, people that I have classes with."

Figuring we were doing the whole get-used-to-touching thing, I took his hand and brought it around to rest on my belly, threading our fingers. "You don't hang out with anyone?"

"Not really. I do sessions with the study club. Sometimes we go to Bean Necessities afterwards."

I played with his fingers. It all sounded so sad to me, even though I understood his social battery depleted easily.

"So does hanging out with me like this tire you out?"

He didn't answer, and when I tried to turn around to see his face, he held me in place. "Shush," he said. "I'm trying to watch TV. This is my favorite episode."

I chuckled and settled back against him, surprised by how comfortable this was. Me sitting between his legs, resting my back to his chest, his arm draped across my stomach.

I thought maybe I could begin to feel the press of something against my lower back . . . maybe it was his jeans. But then he brought his right leg up.

"You're not very comfortable," he said.

"You're very comfortable," I replied.

"You're too heavy. And bulked up. Are those muscles from hard work or genetics?"

I wasn't even offended by that. "Both. My dad's a big guy. And my mom's brothers are all over six feet. But I do work out and swim. You should come along one time."

"And swim? Are you insane?"

He sounded like I'd asked him to give me one of his kidneys. "Swimming's good for you." I took his hand and brought it up to my pec, giving myself a squeeze. "See?"

He pulled his hand away and gave me a shove. "Ew. You have moobs."

"I do fucking not." I half turned around, leaning against his bent knee, and pulled up my shirt to show him my pec. I poked it. "This is a pectoral muscle. It's not soft. It is not a moob, thank you very much."

"Christ, put it away," he mumbled, but not before he'd copped a good eyeful, his cheeks pink. "Do you have to get naked every chance you get?"

"I'm not naked." I pulled my shirt back down, then eyed his chest and stomach. "You're so skinny, I bet you got abs under there."

Then I made the mistake of trying to lift his shirt, and he did some lightning-fast maneuver with his legs that half turned me inside out, and before I knew it, I was on my stomach, one leg bent up in some kung fu lock-hold and my hand pinned to the floor above my head.

He pinned me to the floor, his lips at my ear. "You do not have permission to do that."

Then a bunch of feet came through the door and stopped. Well, I could assume there were bodies attached to the feet, but from how I was being pinned down, I couldn't really see . . .

"Well, I see you two are getting along just fine," Deirdre's voice said.

"Need some more private time?" Max asked.

"We were just discussing consent," Amos said.

"I can see it's going well," Deirdre said. "Chase, are you okay?"

"Oh, I'm great," I squeaked out. "This is kinda hot, actually. Not gonna lie."

Amos gave me a shove before he got off me, but when I got up and caught a glance at him, he was smiling.

I sat up and swung my leg around him, grabbing him and giving him a back-hug with my chin on his shoulder. "That was fun. You've got some kung fu moves."

He sighed. "You're lucky I'm allowing this."

I chuckled. "I *am* lucky you're allowing this." Then I sighed. "But this is nice." I gave him a bit of a shake. "Relax. I'm not going to do anything to you."

He exhaled and some of the tension left his shoulders. "Only because you know you'd lose."

"Letting you win isn't technically losing."

"You didn't let me win."

"No. But I will from now on. I had no idea how much fun wrestling was. I'm forlorn to think about all the hot body rubbing I've missed all these years by not being on the wrestling team."

He snorted. "Forlorn."

"It means pitiful and forsaken."

He growled. "I know what it means."

"Ooh, do that again. That was hot."

"Deirdre? I'd like to request a partner change."

I laughed and tried to do the leg maneuver he did to me, but it failed spectacularly and he ended up pinning me to the floor again, this time on my back with my hands on either side of my head. Our faces just two inches apart. He was actually smiling. "You lose again."

"I'm letting you win on purpose."

He gnashed his teeth at me, then jumped up to his feet. He offered me his hand, which I stupidly took—thinking he was helping me to my feet—only for him to let go of me so I fell on my ass.

"Deirdre?" I said from the floor. "I'd like to request a partner change."

I don't know why no one took me seriously. Even Amos laughed.

2

THE NEXT DAY we spent the day with the camera crews. It was one thing getting familiar with Amos and being partnered with him, but it was another thing getting used to having cameras on us in a reality TV sense.

Being aware of angles and the camera without any stage direction wasn't as easy as I thought it would be. The reality-television aspect of this meant candid filming, and not looking down the barrel of the lens was difficult given there was no fixed camera angle.

We acted out scenes from *Friends*, just small skits, as a group of eight. Our designated camera crew was Daniel and Bridgette. Daniel held the camera with a stabilizer and Bridgette was his assistant. He did all the filming, she walked behind him, guiding him so he didn't bump into poles or people.

We'd need to get very comfortable with them being our shadows and in our faces, while pretending they weren't there at all.

Amos seemed to be able to do it a lot easier than me.

"I'm surprised you struggle with it," Amos said with a frown. He packed up his bag and slung it over his shoulder, ready to leave now that class was done.

"Why?"

"Because you always have eyes on you," he said. "Wherever you go, people watch you."

"No they don't."

They did, but I wasn't admitting to knowing that.

He rolled his eyes. "For an actor, you can't lie for shit."

"You know, contrary to popular belief, I don't actually ask people to look at me."

"I never said you did. And I get it. You look like a young Brad Pitt. People are gonna look."

"Are my genetics a crime now?"

"Sure. Looking like generic Hollywood is a federal offense."

I glowered at him. "I hate that word. And you took it back. No returns."

"Should I just call you Hollywood?"

"I'd rather you didn't. And anyway, you look like Keanu Reeves from *My Own Private Idaho*."

He considered that and smirked. "Thanks. He was hot in that."

I sighed. "My point is, people look at you too."

He held the door for me as we walked out. "And *my* point is," he said, "just pretend the cameras are people. The people who watch you. You know they're there but don't act like you know. They're the extras on your stage, not the other way around."

I thought about that. "That actually makes sense. I dunno why it's so different for me," I admitted. "I'm used to having a stage or a set, an audience or the camera that has a fixed location, ya know? This is random."

"Like freeform," he said. "You've done that before."

True. "Jeez. Are you right about everything?"

"Mostly."

I stopped walking when I realized where we were—at the door to his dorm. "Oh. What are we doing here?"

He nodded to the building. "Well, *I'm* going to get changed for work. I have a shift in twenty minutes. I don't know what you're doing."

I checked the time on my phone. "I can hang out at the coffee shop while you work," I said. "I need to study anyway."

"Well, it's a public space. I can't technically stop you."

"Gee, thanks."

"Are you aware that Daniel has been filming us since we left the rehearsal hall? Don't turn around. Keep it natural."

Shit.

"Uh, no, I wasn't aware."

"See? You can do it. Like the dozen or so people who watched us walking to my dorm together."

"I wasn't aware of them either." Goddammit. "You distracted me with arguing."

He damn near smiled. "Well, if we're gonna give them

something to talk about, you should maybe come up to my room."

I wasn't sure why that gave my heart a little kick. "I do like being propositioned."

He sighed, turned, and walked inside. I had to rush to catch up before the door closed. "You know," I said, taking the stairs behind him. "If we're gonna convince people that we like each other, it might help if you actually like me."

"I'm an excellent actor."

"You also have a great ass," I said.

He stopped walking and I gestured to his said great ass. "What? If you waited for me to walk with you, your ass wouldn't be in my face." I shrugged with zero shame. "I'm not complaining."

He pursed his lips and gestured ahead of him. "Be my guest."

I grinned at him as I went in front of him. "If you want to look at my ass, you just gotta ask. Because I am not opposed to being checked out."

"Have you considered not being a douche?"

I groaned. "Have you considered using the elevator?"

"Stop your whining."

"Stop looking at my ass."

By the time we got to his floor, I stood at his door as he unlocked it and pushed it open, and I was pretty sure he either wanted to kill me or kiss me.

It was hard to tell.

He dumped his bag and took his work uniform into his bathroom to get changed, so I sprawled out on his bed and checked my phone.

Sure enough, the first thing to pop up on my socials was

a photo of me. And Amos, walking across the courtyard, not even five minutes ago.

The caption read *Soooo is this new?*

Damn, people were fast.

The first comment was, *Saw them together the other day,* and the next comment was, *Chase just went into the dorms with him.*

Oh great.

"Uh, Amos?" I said, loud enough for him to hear. "They're talking about us."

A second later his door opened. "Who is?"

I showed him my screen. "People. There's a pic of you and me taken just now, walking across the courtyard, and into your dorm."

He ran his hand through his hair. "Really?"

"Fast, huh?"

He didn't seem too surprised. "I guess it was bound to happen."

Another comment appeared. *Hope Amos knows Chase doesn't date.*

Next comment. *He only ever nails and bails.*

"Oh, that's not very nice," I said. "I do not nail and bail."

Amos raised an eyebrow. "Sorry?"

I held up my phone like the incriminating evidence it was. "User Aprilshower05 would like to protect your honor, advising you to please be aware that I don't date anyone, to which LochVanessMonster said no, I only nail and bail." I held up my pointer finger. "In my defense, I do not nail and bail. Expectations are outlined prior to any nailing and therefore the bailing is more of an anticipated departure."

Amos snorted. "Right. That's a nicer way to put it."

"I thought people liked me," I said, pouting, genuinely kinda hurt over the nail-and-bail comment. "I've never been dishonest to anyone about anything like that. Everyone knew what they were getting into, and they agreed before anything began."

"Why are you telling me this?"

"Because it matters," I said. Because it did matter. It mattered to me. "Nice that they wanted to warn you though," I said, still pouting. "But they make me out to be a bad person just because I don't want a long-term relationship with every person I meet, and like I'm some kind of manwhore. Which I'm not. It's not like that." I finished with a shrug. "I don't want you to think bad of me."

"I don't think bad of you," he said quietly. "And I don't care what they think. But for the sake of the performance, now you're supposed to be serious about being with me."

"Which is fine. We can make it believable, right?"

He pulled his other shoe on and laughed as he nodded to my phone. "Apparently I'm not the one who needs to be convincing."

"I'll be the best boyfriend ever, you'll see." I glanced at my phone again, and seeing more comments, I groaned and turned it off. "I don't want to see what else they say."

He went to his door so I followed him. "I don't know what you're worried about," he said. "If anyone around here does the nailing, it will be me."

I was so stunned, I couldn't speak. So he opened the door and shoved me out of it, laughing.

And there in the hall was Daniel, camera rolling.

Chapter Eight
Amos

I don't know what made me say it. Maybe so he would stop thinking about what people were saying, and maybe so he would realize that it's not all about him.

Though, to be fair, they were bad-mouthing him, not me. But maybe it would do the ego of the great Chase Soria some good to know that he is not the perfect pretty boy he thought he was. I mean, he was still a pretty boy.

Though, also to be fair, he was much softer than I'd thought he was. He genuinely cared what people thought of him. He wanted people to like him, and it bothered him when they didn't.

I, on the other hand, didn't care what people thought of me.

For the next two hours, Chase sat in the end booth at the coffee shop. He ignored the crowd for the most part, and although he had his textbooks in front of him, I was pretty sure he ignored those too.

I saw him a time or two checking his phone, scowling at whatever he read until he tossed it onto the seat beside him and ignored that as well. He tapped his pen, pouting out the window. So when I had a ten-minute break, I put two iced coffees on the table and sat across from him. "Hey," I said softly.

"Oh, hey." He seemed genuinely surprised to see me as though he'd been lost in thought. "What time is it? Are you finished?"

"Nah, just a break. Still got two hours to go."

He winced. "I kinda lost track of time."

"You've been staring out the window a lot," I said, then sipped my drink. "You okay?"

"Yeah, sure."

"Don't let the comments bother you. People are gonna talk."

His eyes cut to mine. "They think I'm a bad person."

"Who gives a fuck what they think? Chase, as an actor, you're gonna get a lot of critique and feedback and horrible reviews and scathing social media attacks. You need to learn to ignore it."

"I know, I just . . ."

"You just what?"

He huffed out a sigh. "You're right. But by then I'll be a millionaire and I can be sad about it in my mansion in Beverly Hills, dabbing artfully at my tears with hundred-dollar bills."

I snorted. "It's good to have goals."

He managed a smile. "I'm sorry. I don't know why I let it bother me so much. I know I'm not a bad person. I just also don't want you to think that I'm a bad person."

"I don't. I mean, when I first met you, I might have thought—"

"If you say the word generic one more time, I will tell everyone that I fell madly in love with you, wanted to be in a committed relationship—like actual boyfriends—for the first time in my life, and you broke my heart. Then you will be the bad guy and people will feel sorry for me, and I'll get pity-attention and free drinks at the bar."

"I was going to say, when I first met you, I might have thought you were conceited and full of yourself."

"Oh yay, that's so much better than generic."

"But you're not. You're actually not that bad a guy. Despite the repeated attempts to show me your moobs."

He gasped so loud, people at the next table looked over. He put his hands over his boobs. "Take that back." Then he gave his pec a squeeze. "Hm. That reminds me. Today was supposed to be chest day at the gym."

I sighed. How he could go from melancholy to funny in the blink of an eye . . . I got the feeling the funny side of Chase was his public persona. The quieter, more vulnerable side was the private side not many people ever saw.

"So you don't think I'm conceited or full of myself anymore?"

"Well, you aren't full of yourself, but maybe a little conceited."

"That's not even remotely true."

I rolled my eyes. "It might even be permissible given how good-looking you are." I wasn't even embarrassed saying that because everyone with functioning eyeballs could see he was gorgeous. "There's nothing wrong with knowing you're hot."

His grin was slow spreading. "You think I'm hot?"

"Everyone on this campus thinks you're hot."

"I don't care about everyone on this campus. You," he grinned at me. "You think I'm hot."

I let out a long-suffering sigh. "You're precariously close to entering full-of-yourself territory."

He laughed, keeping his gaze on mine as he leaned forward to take a sip from his straw. "Thanks for the drink, by the way."

"It was one of those pity drinks you mentioned earlier."

He snorted. "See? I told you it totally works."

I had to remind myself not to smile. "How long do you plan on sitting here?"

"How long is your shift?"

"I finish in two hours."

He made a face. "Well, maybe not that long. I was supposed to be writing this stupid essay. It's due for Professor Michaels."

"You can finish that in two hours."

"Can I?"

"Sure. If you stop staring out the window and ignore all the campus rumor bullshit." I pushed his open textbook closer to him. "Get writing. And if you get it finished by the time I'm done, I'll buy you a slice of pizza from next door when we leave."

He grinned at me in a way that made my heart take notice.

But then he went and opened his mouth.

"So before, when you said you'd be the one doing the nailing, what did you mean exactly?"

I slid out of the booth and stood up, getting back to work. "Write your paper, Hollywood."

2

I WAS surprised by how easy it was to be around him. Sure, we joked and there was a lot of snarky comments, but for the most part, being with Chase Soria was so easy.

I'd always assumed he would be the typical handsome and popular douche bag. Like so many of them were. But he wasn't like that at all, and I was pleasantly surprised by how compatible we were.

I also had to wonder how compatible we were in other ways.

I knew he was bisexual, and I had also assumed that he would top when he was with guys. But the more I got to know him, the more I realized I didn't know him at all.

Because I got the feeling he wasn't a top. And that made us a whole lot more compatible.

And that was something I tried not to think about.

Especially in class the next day, when we were back to sitting on the floor with him in between my legs and my arms around him. Not that we *had* to sit like that—no one else was sitting like that—but Chase had maneuvered us and made himself comfortable as the little spoon, taking my hand and holding it against his belly.

It was his new favorite way to sit, apparently.

I tried especially hard to not think about him being a bottom when he kept taking my hand and making me squeeze his pecs.

"Stop it," I hissed.

"You're the one that's obsessed with them."

I dug him in the ribs because I was absolutely not obsessed. He was. He squirmed, laughing, and grabbing my calf, he brought my leg around his waist.

"Jesus, are you all right there?"

He held me in place. "You're such a koala bear. And you said you weren't the cuddling type."

"You're wrapping me around you. This is all you. Because believe me, this is not my choice."

"But you could totally throw me down and pin me to the floor if you wanted."

"Is that . . . is that why you're doing this?"

He chuckled, holding my right leg and my left arm around him. "Of course it's not."

"Are you two okay there?" Deirdre asked.

The way everyone was now staring at us, I was pretty sure our talking had interrupted her lesson. Not that I'd heard any of it. I gave Chase another dig in the ribs for good measure. "Sorry."

He laughed but never let go of my arm. Or my leg.

I stopped fighting it and just resigned myself to cuddling him, which of course, made him happy.

He was like a golden retriever puppy. Cute and adorable, but also a big clumsy oaf.

And one hundred percent used to getting what he wanted.

Insufferable.

"What was that?" he murmured.

"I said you're insufferable."

"Okay, you two," Deirdre said, waving us forward. "Up here. Because you can't seem to stop talking or touching each other, you're going to do this exercise in front of the rest of us."

Chase threw off my arm and leg, then jumped up to his feet. "Oh, thank god, he finally let me go."

I growled, but it wasn't worth the reply. I stood up and went to the front, opting to stand on the other side of Deirdre, away from Chase.

Surely whatever exercise this was couldn't be worse than being wrapped around him . . .

"So," Deirdre said. "You're going to venture out into the public as a couple."

Oh god.

It was so, so much worse.

"Like a trial run. Let's see how the camera angles work, the sound quality, etcetera." She held up her iPad. "We'll be watching you here, live streaming it, okay?"

"Okay, the love of my life," Chase said, using his theater voice. He held out his hands toward me.

"If you keep that up, this will be a reality TV *Dexter* episode," I said. "Where I kill you on live stream."

Chase just laughed. I was beginning to think him antagonizing me was his new favorite sport. And maybe, just maybe, I didn't half mind it either.

But as soon as the camera team was ready, Chase took my hand and pulled me out the door. "So, Elijah," he said, using my character name. "What did you want to do after dinner tonight?"

We headed out across the courtyard, holding hands. In public. The two-person camera crew a few feet directly behind us, but still. It was weird.

"I don't know, Dominic," I replied. "Study, most likely."

"There's a twilight beach volleyball game. I'm playing, so you should definitely come watch."

"Why would I do that?"

"Because, boyfriend," he said, giving my hand a squeeze. "It's what a good boyfriend would do."

"If you were a good boyfriend, you wouldn't make me go out where there are people."

He laughed as we got to the street, and I realized we were heading for the taco truck.

"But you don't work tonight, so . . ."

"No, but I do have to study."

"I'll help you study after."

"Your idea of helping is very different from mine. Don't you have an essay due?"

"I finished it the other day," he said. "Remember? You made me do it and bribed me with pizza. Which totally worked, by the way."

"Are you bribing me with pizza?"

"Nope. You get to watch me shirtless on the beach playing volleyball. That's your prize."

I sighed, turned to Daniel, and stared right at the camera. "Deirdre, I know you can hear this. It's not too late to swap partners. Someone who doesn't threaten me with having to see him naked."

"Semi-naked," Chase said. "Do you wanna see me fully naked? Because that's a whole other rating level. Pretty sure we don't have clearance for an R rating."

I sighed and gave him a shove toward the truck. "Shut up and order your tacos."

Chase laughed again, then ordered a bunch of tacos and two sodas. He handed one to me. "Oh," I said, surprised. "Thanks."

Then he held up the tray of tacos to share. "See? I'm a good boyfriend."

"Pretty sure the word I used before was insufferable."

He gestured to a bench seat in the shade. He sat first, and I sat down next to him, but not close enough, apparently because he shuffled over so our thighs were pressed together.

He offered the tray. "Taco?"

Bridgette pressed her earpiece. "Deirdre said we have some wind interference."

So while they dealt with that, Chase and I ate the tacos and sipped our sodas.

"I wasn't joking about volleyball," Chase said quietly. "I am playing. You should totally come and watch."

I made a face.

"You don't have to sit with the crowd if you're sick of people. You can just sit on the side, away from everyone."

I grimaced at the thought. "I'll think about it."

"Then I will totally help you study. I mean it," he added when I shot him a disbelieving look. "You totally helped me smash that essay out. If you hadn't made me do those two hours the other night, I'd never have done it. And I do have a test next week, which I should totally study for." Then he nudged my shoulder with his. "You're actually good for my grades."

"Gee, thanks." I sighed, looking out over the ocean. It really was beautiful here. "Don't your friends miss you? You've been hanging out with me a lot."

"They know about the filming production. I told them I'd be scarce." He shoved in the rest of his taco and chewed it before washing it down with his drink. "You should totally meet them. At my place or something. I know you're not a fan of crowds, so I'm guessing the bar is out."

I sighed. "Will they be at the volleyball game tonight?"

He gave me a half-smirk as he bumped his shoulder to mine again. "So does that mean you're coming to watch?"

"My character, Elijah, is coming to watch Dominic play," I allowed. "Just so we're clear. Because Amos"—I put my hand to my chest—"would absolutely not."

He laughed, mimicking me with his hand to his chest. "Dominic loves Elijah so much."

Daniel held up his camera stabilizer. "That's much better," he said. "We're good to keep moving."

Bridgette nodded, holding her earpiece again. "Deirdre says to come back."

For a second, I forgot they were even there.

We stood up, dumped our trash into the garbage, and before we got to the street, Chase slipped his hand into mine again. "Dominic loves to hold hands."

"It's funny because Elijah isn't a fan," I replied.

"Hmm," he hummed. "Speaking of fans . . ."

There were people watching us. Other students smiling as they watched on. We were very clearly filming—Daniel was ahead of us, walking backward with his camera on us while Bridgette guided him.

It was clearly a shoot.

But the people coming out of class were stopping and watching us, smiling when they saw Chase and me holding hands.

At least they had the smarts not to interrupt.

But then Daniel backed away to the side, letting us pass him, so he could follow us instead. It felt weirder then, to be in the front, holding hands with Chase as we walked back to class.

I was more aware of the background noise then, of chatter and people talking, and how the sound techs would work around that. "Should we keep talking so the sound guys can differentiate between dialogue and background noise?"

"Probably," Chase said. "It might help. Let's run lines."

"Lines from what?"

"I don't know. It doesn't matter."

"If you say *Hairspray*, I'm dumping you."

"You mean Elijah is dumping Dominic."

"No, I mean Amos is dumping Chase."

"I think we need to have a *Hairspray* appreciation date."

"I think you need to stop talking."

He chuckled. "I can sing it if you'd prefer."

"I would not prefer that, no."

"What about *Rocky Horror Picture Show*?"

"Will you be Frank-N-Furter?"

"One hundred percent yes."

I laughed just as we got back to the rehearsal hall. I held the door for Chase and he walked through. When we were inside, he took my hand again and he did a theatrical bow, as if he was getting a standing ovation. "Thank you, thank you so much."

A few people did clap, though attention soon turned to the iPad. We watched it for perspective, to learn which angles were best and how dialogue worked with the sound quality. All the technical stuff . . .

But I also couldn't help but think how good we looked together. How the camera made Chase look even more handsome.

I also couldn't help but notice how much I'd smiled.

"Aww," Chase said. "Dominic and Elijah make such a cute couple."

Right, yes.

Dominic and Elijah.

Not Chase and Amos.

Keep remembering that, Amos.

Then Chase had his phone out already, scrolling his socials. "Oh, yep, we're topic number one on campus. We need to start advertising this show," he said, looking at Deirdre. "People are already invested."

Hm.

They sure are.

Chapter Nine
Chase

A trending topic in college news, sure. And that was exciting and so much fun.

But the comments still stung.

Told you they were acting. Chase doesn't date anyone.

As if Amos would be his type anyway.

Wonder what they're filming?

A "She's All That" remake with the Preppy Jock and the Emo?

"Ouch," I mumbled. "Now I'm a preppy jock?"

Amos didn't even look up. He didn't seem interested in any of it. "I told you not to read the comments. Why do you like to torture yourself?"

He'd been quiet since we got back. While the others did their thing and the tech crews set up sound, cameras, and production, he just kinda slunk off to the corner and sat with his back to the wall, knees raised. Not looking at his phone, not reading a book. Just picking at a thread in the hole on his knee and staring at nothing.

Was this him needing to timeout from people?

Probably.

But that didn't include me, right?

Of course not.

I went over and tapped his knee, then sat down right in between his legs leaning back against him. I was beginning to think this could be my new favorite spot.

"Are you okay there?"

"I am now." I sighed as I made myself comfortable, which included taking his hand and draping his arm over my chest. "I'm just going to assume that if you need less people time that does not include me. I'll be quiet, I just don't want you to be alone."

"I like being alone."

"And I like hanging with you, so can you see my conundrum?"

He sighed, long and loud. "And it's all about you, right?"

"See, you're getting the hang of this relationship with me. You'll be a pro in no time."

He sighed again, and I made good on my promise to be quiet.

If he needed silence, I could at least give him that.

And anyway, I wasn't lying. I liked hanging out with him. That silence that most people thought was him being shy or emo or reclusive, I actually found kind of comforting.

It was peaceful.

The hard exterior was now almost like a reassurance. The stoicism and reluctance he had around other people felt like a safety bubble, and I found myself enjoying that. I didn't have to put on an act, I didn't have to try and be funny, there was no audience. I could just be . . . me.

I liked it a lot.

After almost everyone was gone, Deirdre came over to us. "How are we feeling? Everything okay?"

I waited for Amos to answer first. He didn't.

"Yeah, I'm fine," I said. "Not sure about this guy, though." I tapped his leg. "If he's just processing or just needs some non-people time."

"I'm fine," he replied quietly.

Deirdre gave him a pointed nod. "If you need to talk about anything, you come find me. Any time, day or night, okay?"

He nodded.

"Are you comfortable with the displays of public affection?" she asked him. "I know you said you were in the beginning, but how are you feeling about it now?"

He took a second to answer. "Yeah, I'm fine with it."

She looked at me, sprawled out using Amos as a recliner. "I can see *you're* fine."

I shrugged. "Yep." Amos said nothing else, and I got the feeling her being here, although well-intentioned, wasn't helping. "Amos and I need a minute. We're just gonna chill for a bit, if that's okay," I said. "If you need us to leave . . . ?"

"No, you're fine," she said, taking the hint and backing off. "You know where to message me."

She left us alone and soon enough it was just him and me. "Thanks," Amos mumbled.

"That's okay," I replied. "Kinda got the feeling you needed some alone time."

He snorted quietly. "And yet, here you remain."

"Because you being alone includes me."

"I think you need to google the definition of alone."

"I did. It says to be by oneself with Chase."

He chuckled, and I made no attempt to get up, get off him, or to move his arm from where it was still draped around me.

It was really freaking nice.

"Is this what couples do?" I asked. "Because this feels good. It's relaxing and comfortable."

"Glad *you're* comfortable."

I laughed, but yeah, still not moving.

"And yes, I believe this is what couples do."

"Is this cuddling or snuggling? You know, if I wanted to give it a name."

"Cuddling. I guess. Not sure the definition is so specific. Snuggling, I'd assume, is more intimate."

"More intimate than this?" Because to me, this was pretty damn intimate.

"Like on a couch or bed, more body contact."

"Naked body contact?"

He laughed. "Not sure. Probably, yes. Naked cuddling? Though not all snuggling requires nakedness."

"It should. I love being naked."

He sighed again, but I was sure he was smiling. Without looking up, I could just tell.

"Did you want to talk about anything we did today?" I asked. "Was how I acted as Dominic okay with you? You need to tell me if I cross a line or anything."

He was quiet again for another second, like a pause, while he decided how honestly he was going to answer. "It was fine. I just . . . your character is very you. Dominic is very Chase-coded. And while Elijah is still introverted like me, my character is expected to conform to yours." He sighed with a shrug. "I know it's for ratings and whatever. Introverts and quiet book-types don't make very interesting reality TV stars."

I sat up and stared at him. "Are you kidding? Introverts make the best characters. All mysterious and shit. And you guys always get to be the serial killers and psychos. You know, it's the quiet ones you gotta watch."

It was an attempt to get him to smile, and it kinda worked. "Gee, thanks."

"I get it," I said, putting my hand on his knee. "And people are gonna be watching us. Watching you. That's a lot, I get it. So if you need to decompress alone, then I get that too."

"Like you're leaving me alone right now?" He gestured to the empty room, then to him and me. "Alone, but with you."

I grinned at him. "Exactly!"

"So, everything is about you."

I gave his knee a shove. "See? You know exactly what it's like to be in a relationship with me."

His lips twisted into something that was almost a pouty smirk. "God. Even being in a fake relationship with you is a lot."

I laughed and jumped up to my feet. I held out my hand and pulled him up. "Come on, I need food."

"You always need food."

"Oh my god, you are so good at this."

He was smiling when we picked up our bags, just as some girls—freshmen—came barreling in. They stopped when they saw us, giggled, and got all shy, so I grabbed Amos's hand and pulled him out of the room.

I dropped his hand as we got outside and we headed toward the dining hall. "I get the feeling we need to get used to that," I said.

"Would you ever get used to it?"

I held the door open for him to go inside. "Hell yes. Fame and fortune all the way."

"So you need security to get groceries?"

"Dude. Fame and fortune. I'm talking enough fortune so I can pay someone else to shop for me."

He rolled his eyes and took a tray. I was surprised he was going to eat but never made a point to mention it. I was just glad. I took a plate of pasta and salad, some fruit and a juice, then threw on some bread as well.

He chose pretty much the same, just not as much, which was fair.

We sat down at the back of the dining hall. He faced the wall; I faced the room. I was kinda glad he couldn't see the people watching us.

"I think it'll settle down once filming starts," I said after we'd eaten a bit. "People will be used to seeing the cameras around. Pretty sure Deirdre said there were announcements going out about the filming and to remind people to please not interrupt or act like idiots in the background."

He nodded slowly. "Yeah, given it's basically an insight into life at FU, I'm guessing they don't want any bad raps. I mean, they're calling it some fictional college, but everyone will know it's here."

"True." I stabbed some pasta with my fork, wondering how I should say this . . . "And once the bulletin goes out, people will know I'm Dominic and you're Elijah, so when they see us with the cameras around, they'll know we're in character." I made a face at my lunch. "I mean, just in case you . . . if you don't want people to think you and me are . . . dating for real."

He looked at me then. "I don't care what people think. I've told you that. But you do, clearly."

"No, not like that," I said quickly. "I don't care if people think I'm dating you. I don't care if they see us together. It's their idea of who I should date that makes them write stupid comments on social media. But at least writing our character names next to our real names will remind them that we're just acting."

He did a weird thing with his eyebrows that kinda came off as sarcastic without him having to say a word. He was so good at silent acting. "Sure."

God.

Now I'd made it weird, and I wasn't even sure how.

"So are you still coming to watch me play volleyball tonight?"

He pushed his food around with his fork, frowning at it. "I thought that was Dominic talking."

"Sure it was. He asked Elijah to come watch." I tapped his foot with mine under the table so he'd look at me. "Kinda hard for Elijah to come watch if you don't bring him."

He rolled his eyes again, but the corner of his mouth curled up a little. "This method acting really is something, huh?" He ran his hand through his hair, and so god help me, it looked good. "Being in character full time is harder than I thought it would be."

"And we haven't started filming yet."

He chewed on the inside of his lip for a bit. "Hm."

Why did he somehow look ten times hotter to me than he ever had in that moment? The angle of his jaw, the line of his neck, his dark hair where his fingers had left track marks . . .

"What time is volleyball?"

I grinned at him. "You're such a good boyfriend."

Volleyball started at six.

It was just a pickup game, a bit of fun with the guys. I'd felt as if I'd been neglecting my friendships so it was good to spend some time with them.

Especially on the beach at twilight. The sand was cool underfoot, the sun was getting low, the fading light made everything look like they'd used a photo filter. The day was winding down, class was finished, dinner had been had. It was playtime.

People were coming across the campus to watch, which was normal. It was a great night to sit on the pier or the steps to the beach, grab some snacks from the food trucks, and chill with friends.

But I hadn't seen Amos yet.

"Christ, Chase," Jimmy said, throwing my water bottle to me. "It's been two hours since you saw him last and you're already looking for him."

Fuck.

"I just don't want him to be by himself," I said. Which

was redundant because I knew he would be by himself. "He's not big on crowds or people in general. This is out of his comfort zone."

More crowds came down as we were warming up, and by the time the first match started, we had a decent audience.

Still no Amos.

I tried to tell myself not to be disappointed, but that was a fat waste of time. I tried to not be distracted, tried not scanning the crowd, or looking for a familiar face with dark hair and a sly smirk. But that wasn't going too well either, apparently, because I missed a few easy shots and I wasn't really paying much attention to the game. We lost the first set.

"Oh, for fuck's sake," Jimmy said, sending the ball none too gently at my head. I caught it before it hit me—barely—and before I could spit out *what the fuck*, he pointed to the pier. "He's over there. He's been there for fifteen minutes. Now quit looking and pay some goddamn attention. I got two beers on this match."

I looked over toward the pier to where Jimmy had gestured, and sure enough, there he was.

Amos, in his black jeans with the knees out of them, black hoodie, and his Chucks. Without even realizing it, I was grinning at him . . . until Jimmy came over, took the ball from me, and shoved me into place.

When I took notice, people were smiling at me on the volleyball court—waiting for me so they could play?—and in the crowd too, but before I could even be embarrassed, the whistle blew and play began.

I was more focused for the second set. I managed some

points and a few kickass saves. And it helped that I had a reason to try and look cool now.

It was a tough game but a lot of fun, and we'd managed to win the second set. I was hot and sweaty and covered in sand, and knowing that people would be watching—hell, maybe that's why I did it—I grabbed my water bottle and jogged over to Amos.

"Hey."

He made a face, clearly horrified that I'd make a bigger point of drawing attention to him. "What are you doing?"

"I didn't think you'd come," I said, ignoring his question. I pulled up the hem of my shirt to wipe my forehead and then I had an even better idea.

I pulled my shirt off right in front of him.

I heard some laughter behind me, but I wasn't turning around.

"Very *Top Gun*," Amos said. "Iceman."

I wiped my abs over with my shirt and chugged some water. "You calling me Iceman is better than generic, so I'm taking that as a win."

"Iceman from *Top Gun* 1986 is the definition of generic Hollywood, but okay."

I threw my shirt at him. "Don't tell me you didn't like watching me play just now. I caught you smiling a time or two."

He held up my sweaty shirt. "Ew. What the hell am I supposed to do with this?"

"Hold it for me," I said, giving him the smile that usually got me whatever I wanted. "And you can't toss it because people are watching and you have to think, what would Elijah do with Dominic's shirt?"

Amos gave me an unimpressed glare. "He'd send it to the CDC and then have an acid bath, that's what Elijah would do."

I laughed and stepped in even closer. "He absolutely would not. He'd love it. Method acting, remember?"

I was probably pushing my luck with him, but to be honest, I really gave my shirt to him so there'd be more of a chance he'd stick around until the match ended. We were heading down to Shenanigans after the game and I wanted him to come with me.

So, he'd either hold it till the end or my shirt would be a lump of fabric on the sand, and he'd be nowhere to be found.

I had a feeling it'd be the latter.

But to my surprise, he stuck around.

Also to my surprise, we won the match. I played awesome in the final set; it helped that I played harder than I'd ever played in that final set. I told myself it was not because Amos was watching me.

But it absolutely was.

I wanted to impress him.

Even if he didn't care.

But did sticking around mean he cared? Or was he just acting the part of his character, Elijah?

Because sure, being in character one hundred percent of the time was very much an Amos thing to do. This was an exercise in method acting, after all.

But I wasn't entirely sure I was . . .

When the match ended, we walked off to our drink bottles and most of the crowd dispersed. Amos headed over and threw my shirt to me. "Good game," he said.

"Thanks."

Tater smiled at him, and I knew he was about to say something . . . *I mean Tate.* I really had to stop calling him Tater. "Hey," he said to Amos. "We're heading down to Shenanigans. Wanna come with us?"

Amos was clearly surprised and he shot me a wild look. "Uh . . ."

"Just for one drink," I said, striking while the iron was hot. "And food. It'll be fun." But remembering how peopling wasn't his favorite thing to do, I added, "We don't have to stay long."

Amos shoved his hands into his back pockets. "Uh, okay. Sure."

I grinned at him, and yeah, it wasn't my character Dominic that was happy. It was me. "Awesome."

He looked me up and down. "But only if you put your shirt on."

Jimmy grabbed my pec and tweaked my nipple. "These are his emotional support tiddies. Brings 'em out whenever he can."

I batted his hand away and rubbed my nipple. "Ow."

Amos almost smiled. "Emotional support tiddies. Makes sense."

I used my balled-up shirt to wipe off as much sweat and sand off my chest and arms as I could. "Leave my tiddies alone."

I was just glad he didn't call them moobs in front of Jimmy.

"It sounds better than emotional support moobs."

Aaaaand there it was.

I looked at Amos and sighed while Jimmy roared laughing.

"Thanks a lot," I mumbled. "Never gonna hear the end of that."

Tate gave me a sympathetic nudge. "Guess it's better than generic Hollywood."

Tate meant no harm, but Jimmy laughed again, and even Amos cracked a smile. I looked at all of them. "Is it National Pick on Chase Day today? Did I miss the memo?" I gave Amos a pointed stare. "You are supposed to be on my side."

Jimmy and the others picked up all their stuff and began heading toward the bar, and Amos and I fell into step behind them. There were some girls still on the steps watching us, so I slung my arm around Amos's shoulder, pulling him into my side.

"What are you doing?" he asked.

"It's payback for the moobs comment. Now Jimmy is gonna be a pain in my ass for weeks."

I'd pulled him so close he kinda had to put his arm around my waist. "You're all sweaty and gross," he said.

But he never dropped his arm, so I kept mine where it was. "Volleyball was fun. I'm glad you came to watch."

He made a scowly face. "I'm not staying here long, just so you know. Just enough to show face, play our part, then I'm bailing."

"Fair enough."

I was surprised he'd said yes to the bar at all, so even five minutes was a win.

Especially when he saw how crowded it was. A lot of

people meant close contact, and I was grateful for all the practice we'd done because it didn't feel weird at all.

It felt natural.

We managed to score a tall table by the wall, so I put Amos on a stool in the corner so he was kinda hidden and might feel more comfortable. It also meant I could maybe press him against the wall if it got extra crowded.

Not my original plan, but I didn't object when it happened.

Neither did he.

I found myself somehow between his legs, my arm around his shoulder, a drink in my other hand.

Yep, all that close-contact practice had been a great idea.

"So," Jimmy said, looking at Amos. "You drew the short straw and won the consolation prize, huh?"

"I'm not a consolation prize," I said, sipping my drink. "So that's a real quick fuck you. I'm first prize all the way."

Amos smirked as he sipped his bourbon. "Your friends are great for your self-esteem."

"I know! I don't know why I keep them."

"Because shit-talking is our love language," Jimmy said, raising his glass.

We clinked our drinks together and Amos shook his head.

Amos's phone beeped with a message and I saw Deirdre's name on the screen. He tapped on it.

Casting just went out. Enjoy!

There was a link, which he clicked on, and there on the screen was the list of the cast.

Our names alongside our character names.

Chase Soria as Dominic Davis
Amos Beddington as Elijah James

I looked at Amos. "Well, Elijah. It's out there now."

"So it is," he replied, meeting my eyes. "Dominic."

I didn't even mind him calling me that, because our faces were just a few inches apart, and while Amos would never look at me like that, Elijah would.

Method acting sure was a mindfuck.

Taylah and Georgia were suddenly at the table. "Hey, Dominic," Taylah said with a drunk grin. She held up her phone. "And Elijah. Looking forward to the show."

"I knew there had to be a reason," Georgia said, looking at me.

A reason why I'd declined her offer the other night.

"Something like that," I said before sipping my drink. Because man, in that moment, I'd pick Amos a hundred times before I'd pick her.

Why?

I wasn't sure.

Because maybe you like the whole fake-relationship thing more than a meaningless fuck.

Fake relationship? Or the idea of a real one?

I downed my drink trying to shut that voice up.

"I think that's my cue," Amos said. He slid his empty glass into the middle of the table and stood up.

"Yeah, okay," I said, knowing he was never staying long. I gave Jimmy and Tate a nod. "Catch you guys later. Bye, girls." I gave them a parting nod, took Amos's hand, and pulled him through the crowd.

I didn't let go of his hand, not even when we were outside, the cool air a welcome reprieve.

"You can stay," he said, facing me.

"Nah, I can't." I tried to roll some tension out of my shoulders, giving his arm a bit of a shake because I was still holding his hand.

I didn't want to let go of it. No clue why. I just needed the contact. The connection.

"I wasn't feeling that tonight." I nodded toward the way back home and we began walking. "Kinda glad to leave if I'm being honest."

"So are we holding hands the whole way back?"

I gave his hand a squeeze. "The whole way."

He was trying not to smile, and it plucked at something inside me.

"Those girls," Amos said after a bit. "Was that Georgia?"

I groaned. "Yeah. Nice girl. We had a thing once. We're still friends, but I don't want a repeat."

"Oh, that's right. You don't do repeats. I forgot."

I shot him a sideways glance. "It's not that I don't . . . Well, okay, I didn't used to. I just never . . ."

I stopped talking, not even sure what I was trying to say. But now holding his hand felt weird. I let it go, missing the warmth of it, and the ache in my chest grew a little deeper.

And I *was* hurt.

Why? Because I never did used to want repeats, and that was a well-known fact. So why did him saying that hurt so much? Because him thinking less of me, thinking I wasn't capable of dating anyone . . .

Fuck.

"I dunno," I mumbled.

"You just never what?" he asked. "You dunno what? You're not normally at a loss for words, Hollywood."

I rolled my eyes at his stupid name for me, but it also kinda made me smile. He made me feel a bit better without even trying. "I dunno about a lot of things," I said. "Like what we're gonna watch when we get back to your place. Or what kind of pizza we're gonna order."

He snorted as he took the steps up to the entry hall of his dorm. "You assume a lot," he said, leaning his back against the door. But then, with that disarming smirk, he pushed the door open, waiting for me to brush past him.

Which I did, of course. A little closer than was completely necessary, but that was totally his own fault. I went up the stairs without waiting. "You're welcome, by the way."

"For what?"

"For the view of my ass when I'm walking up these freaking stairs again." I lifted the back of my shirt and tucked it into the back of my shorts. "There you go. Unimpeded view. Now you're welcome."

"Tell me, do people find your douchery charming?"

I stopped, mid-step, turned, and smiled at him. "Believe me, those who I've douched for, appreciated it very much."

He stared, cheeks turning pink, before he trudged past me. "I walked right into that one, didn't I?"

"You did, yeah." I followed him up the stairs. "Now it's me who should say thank you."

"Stop looking at my ass," he grumbled.

"It's a great ass," I replied, just as two girls came down

the stairs. They giggled, and I gave them a nod. "It's true. He has a great ass."

He stopped on the landing so he could glare at me, which, of course, made me grin at him. He also glared at me when he opened his door for me, and I grinned at him as I walked in.

This game was so much more fun than my uncertain, overthinking shitshow game from earlier. It was so much more fun to pretend not to have feelings.

I threw myself on his bed, head on his pillow. "So," I said, "pizza?"

"You know," he said, toeing out of his Chucks. "When we agreed to the whole method-acting thing, I was pretty sure it did not include you lying on my bed demanding pizza."

"Okay, one. I didn't demand it. I suggested it. Offered to order it, even. There was definitely a question mark implied, so that rules out any demands. And two, this is method acting. Me lying on your bed is exactly what a boyfriend would do. And we are acting boyfriends, amiright?"

He sighed. "You're impossible to argue with."

"Only when I'm right. Which is most of the time." I took out my phone. "So, meat lovers okay?"

"Get the spicy one. The Godfather, I think it's called."

So of course I had to do my best Godfather impersonation. He'd basically asked for it.

"'I'm gonna make him an offer he can't refuse.'"

I thought he might roll his eyes at me, but no. He replied with his own. "'It's a Sicilian message. It means Luca Brasi sleeps with the fishes.'"

I laughed, impressed. "Great quote."

He lifted my legs and sat on the bed with his back against the wall. He put my legs back across his knees, his hand resting on my thigh. "It's an underrated quote."

"And that's an underrated move," I said, gesturing to my legs. "Impress all the boys with that?"

He replied with a glare. "Don't get comfortable. You're going down to get the pizza."

"That's fine. I'll be taking the elevator. No point in taking the stairs if you're not there to ogle my ass."

He sighed. "*Rick and Morty* okay?"

"Perfect."

And I couldn't lie, this was perfect. Just chilling, easy company, stupid, funny shit to watch and pizza on the way.

"Tell me, is all dating like this?" I asked. "I mean, boyfriends. Is this what they do every night?"

"Why? Are you bored?"

"Are you kidding? This is like my ideal night right here."

He kept his eyes on the screen but his smile turned a little wry. "Yeah, I guess this is what boyfriends do."

"Man, I've been missing out. Add in some making out, maybe an orgasm or two, and it's a perfect night."

He turned slowly to face me. "Pardon?"

Oh shit. I just realized how that sounded.

"I didn't mean with you. Tonight. I just meant in general. If this is what boyfriends do. This, right here." I gestured to us. "Hanging out, chilling out watching shit on Netflix, and eating pizza. I mean, that's perfect. And I'm assuming most boyfriends make out because that's what couples do, right? And sex? That's all I meant. I didn't mean you. I mean, not that I'd be opposed to that. With you, because you're hot and everything." *Christ, Chase, stop talking.* "But that's not . . . I didn't mean . . . Fuck."

He was still staring, but the corner of his mouth did that thing . . . that almost curling thing that I was beginning to think was his trademark smirk. "Are you done?"

"Embarrassing myself? Not sure. The night is young. Anything's possible."

He pressed his lips together and watched the screen for a bit. "So you think I'm hot?"

I pulled his pillow over my head and groaned. "Is it possible to snuff yourself with a pillow?"

"Dunno. You try it, then we'll know."

I took the pillow and tried to whack him with it, but he deflected it easily. He gestured to his screen. "You're missing one of my favorite episodes."

I shoved his pillow back under my head and pouted for a bit, trying really hard not to think about how his hand was now resting a little further up my thigh.

"You're totally hot," I said, aiming for nonchalance, watching Rick and Morty do stupid shit. "Don't pretend you don't know that."

He shot me another glare, mouth open, just about to kill me with sarcasm and wit, no doubt, when my phone beeped.

"Ooh, pizza," I said. "Saved by the bell."

I pulled one leg back, sat up, and straddled him before climbing off the bed. The move stunned him, but I got in a quick grind before he could shove me.

"Do you need another lesson in consent?"

I stopped at the door. "Would that involve you pinning

me down with your body weight again? Because if so, then yes, I need another lesson in consent."

He lobbed the pillow at me but I was already out the door.

I jogged happily down the stairs and was at the bottom before I remembered the elevator existed. I grabbed the pizza and took the elevator back up to his floor. His door was unlocked so I just walked straight back in and joined him on the bed with my back to the wall, my thigh touching his.

I had no intention of moving. Lying all over him was my newest favorite thing to do.

I put the pizza on our laps. "The elevator is the way to go," I said, shoving the first slice into my mouth. "We should take that from now on. I'll forgo the ogling of your ass just not to walk up those stairs."

"Nice."

I wasn't sure if he was referring to my comment about his ass or me speaking with half a mouthful of food. I wasn't bothered either way. "I'll just have to cop an eyeful every other chance I get."

He bit into his pizza. "Shut up and watch the show."

So I did. And we ate the whole pizza, laughed our way through two more episodes, and by the end of the night, I was certain—without any doubt—that if we were dating for real, I would've spent the night. In his bed, in his arms.

I wanted to. Hell, if he'd offered, I would've been naked and face down on his bed in a heartbeat.

I even considered offering it.

But instead, knowing he'd have told me off and sent me

packing and knowing we were about to start filming in the next day or so, I couldn't risk ruining such a good thing.

The next morning, I found Jimmy and Tate eating breakfast before class. I came down, my mood bright and cheerful. "Morning."

Jimmy stared at me. "You were home late. Guess your smile says why. You finally got some."

I poured myself some juice. "Nope. Not like that. But I did have a revelation."

Tate looked very confused. "About what?"

"About me."

Jimmy smirked. "And?"

"About this whole dating thing. Being a boyfriend or whatever." I took a mouthful of juice while they waited. I swallowed, still smiling, too happy to care. "It's like the best thing ever."

Chapter Ten
Amos

Being boyfriends with Chase was terrible.

Even fake boyfriends, whatever. He was irritating, had far too much energy, and most of all, he was clingy.

Clingy.

So touchy-feely all the time.

He had to be touching me. Holding my hand, his arm around my shoulder, his leg over mine.

He was like a koala bear with separation anxiety.

He'd said he was a touchy-feely person right from the very beginning. So this shouldn't have been a surprise to me. I thought I was prepared.

I wasn't prepared for him.

For the warmth of his body. For the way he'd laugh. For how easily he draped himself over me.

Admittedly, I did put his legs over mine on the bed. But that was only because he chose to lie down and I had to sit where I could see the screen.

And we were used to touching, somewhat.

Like we'd touched at the bar. He'd planted me on a

stool in the corner, which was kinda sweet of him, not gonna lie. But then he'd stood beside me, between my legs even. He had his arm around me, so casually, so effortlessly.

So perfectly.

Then he'd held my hand.

Until he got all moody and sullen, then he'd dropped my hand and pouted like a baby. It was annoyingly cute. And I could see he was torn about staying, about what Georgia had said.

So a quick distracting compliment and subject change were in order, and he was back to his usual annoying self.

His funny, charming, sweet, clingy self.

Totally annoying.

And with filming about to start, I could only imagine it was going to get a whole lot worse.

I walked into the rehearsal hall to find everyone either crowded around the iPad or looking on their own phones. Chase was in the middle of it all, of course, holding the iPad.

He was grinning, and when he looked up and saw me, he groaned. "Babe. Where've you been? I messaged you."

Babe.

"Babe?"

He held the iPad up. "Yes. It's what boyfriends do. If you'd read my messages, you'd know what I'm talking about."

Phoebe took some pity on me and filled me in. "You and Chase are the stars of the show already. All the photos from last night are online."

"Photos from last night?" I mumbled. "What photos . . ."

I went to look on the iPad and Chase pulled me in between his legs and turned me around so I could lean against him and hold the iPad for myself.

It also meant he could sling one arm around my waist and rest his chin on my shoulder and watch the screen with me as I scrolled...

Through post after post, photo after photo. Of me and Chase.

On the beach, me holding his shirt. Him shirtless, again, his bare muscular torso looking golden in the fading sunlight.

Us walking to the bar, his arm around my shoulder.

Us in the bar, at the table, crowded in. Him leaning against me. He was laughing at something and... god, was I smiling?

I hadn't meant to look happy.

"I like that photo," he said, pointing to me. "You look so cute."

I ignored that and kept scrolling. The next photo was of me holding the door to my dormitory open for him, again smiling...

I had to stop doing that.

Why did I look so damned happy?

"I didn't see anyone take any of these photos," I mumbled.

"Me either," Chase mumbled.

The comments were much the same.

Chase and Amos, or is it Dominic and Elijah? Acting or real?

Chase doesn't date. It's all part of the act.
There's no camera crew.

They look too cozy to be acting.

Someone at Shenanigans said they were all over each other.

No cameras rolling, who do you think they're acting for?

Never noticed Amos before. He's hot.

Well, that's not humiliating. "Goddammit."

There were some photos of Tucker and Didi too, though they weren't even holding hands. Max and Holly too, though the comments were more about Max being cast with Holly when he already had a girlfriend and how hard it must be for her.

"Oooh," Deirdre said, sliding into the room with a clap of her hands. "Publicity is hot today."

Great. Awesome.

Publicity.

Not sure any of us were so enthusiastic about it.

"Filming starts tomorrow," Deirdre said. "We're gonna go through some final production stuff today and do some practice runs with the whole cast in the courtyard."

I handed Chase the iPad, not wanting to see any more.

"Someone said you're hot," he noted. "I mean, they're not wrong."

I sighed. "Did you write that? Was it you?"

He laughed. "Nope. But I do concur." He slid the iPad onto the next desk, then wrapped both arms around me, his chin still on my shoulder.

He was far too comfortable with this.

Deirdre came over for the iPad. "Well, you two look very relaxed."

I made a point of trying to remove Chase's arm from my waist and failing. "He's like those dryer sheets," I said.

"You know the staticky ones that stick to everything. He's like that."

"He's called me worse," Chase mumbled, seemingly undeterred. "Staticky dryer sheet is a compliment coming from him."

I sighed. "It's not too late for a partner change, right?"

Chase held onto me harder and Deirdre waved me off. "You two are the leading couple right now. The public's already invested. There's no way you're changing now."

Chase laughed like he'd won, and I sighed. Deirdre went off to do whatever she needed to do. "You're stuck with me," Chase said. His lips were precariously close to my neck and I tried to shuck him off, but it just made him worse. "Plus, I like this whole boyfriend thing. It's fun."

"I could be a prime case study for Stockholm Syndrome," I muttered. "Coerced into staying, now unable to leave. My tormentor believes I'll love him if he annoys me enough."

Chase just laughed and gave me a squeeze, and I resigned to him being stuck to me like glue for the rest of the class.

The fact I was beginning not to mind it was something I'd never tell him.

That it felt nice. That it was nice to rest my cheek against the top of his head when he had his head on my shoulder. That his knee on my thigh felt nice when we were reading scene outlines. That by mid-afternoon when he was tired, the way he weaseled himself in between my legs and leaned against me and closed his eyes felt especially good.

So I'd missed the contact, the closeness. The physical touch. It'd been too long since I'd been with anyone, and my body certainly liked the attention. Especially given the fact that Chase was bigger than me—more muscular, broader, and taller. He was Mr. Perfect Popularity.

And he was a bottom.

The guys I've douched for certainly appreciated it.

That was what he'd said. He'd all but admitted it to my face. So yeah, my body liked the idea of that too.

I'd had to jerk off when he'd left my room last night. To the fresh memories of his body close to mine, to his touch, to the smell of him on my pillow.

To imagine *the* Chase Soria naked in my bed. Underneath me, gripping the sheets as I sank into him. I imagined the sounds he'd make, the look on his face as he came . . .

It was the quickest jerk-off session ever.

It also made seeing him later kinda awkward, even though he had no idea of the fantasies I'd played out. The fantasies that still echoed in my mind. And it certainly didn't help that he kept touching me, kept his body as close to mine as he could without being indecent.

I *wanted* him to be indecent.

So yeah, if he wanted to keep lying all over me, keep me close with his arm around me, his hands on me, I wasn't saying no.

I pretended to be annoyed, but honestly it was all going into the memory bank for later.

The eight of us—the four main couples—spent the afternoon in the courtyard, walking the halls, sitting in the dining hall, going to the beach. Well, Chase, Max, and Tucker played frisbee and the rest of us sat in the shade. And of course, Chase had his shirt off . . .

Did it bother me that I was the only guy not playing?

Absolutely fucking not.

They should be grateful I was even outside.

But the camera crews worked angles and the sound techs did their thing. The editors and production team were already talking about cuts and lead-ins . . .

It was really happening.

Official filming started tomorrow, so yes, it was really happening.

Holly was kinda bummed though, and honestly, I didn't blame her at all. She was playing Max's girlfriend, and Max's real-life girlfriend, Jenna, was not too happy.

"She has to deal with it," Jess tried. "If she's going to date an actor, this is part of the process. If he's going to play lead roles, he's going to be partnered at some point. Don't feel bad."

Didi nodded. "I've spoken to Jenna, and she does understand . . . She's trying to be supportive but she just says it kinda sucks."

Holly sighed for about the tenth time. "Yeah, and I get where she's coming from. At least we're not as hands-on as you two," she said, looking at me.

"That's all Chase," I said. "He's like one of those magnetic monkeys we had as kids. You know with the long arms that hook on and don't let go. It's like that."

They laughed. "Oh, I had a purple one of those," Phoebe said. "I loved it."

Jess nudged her knee to mine. "Lucky you're both single, huh? You and Chase? No one getting mad that you're all over each other."

"You two are the most touchy-feely out of all of us," Holly said. "Thank god."

"Yep," Jess added. "People love the idea of you guys already. You have a ship name already. Domeli or Domijah, I think."

I resisted groaning. Because yeah, while dealing with shit like that was better than dealing with upset girlfriends or worse, bigotry. People had been accepting . . . from what I'd seen.

"I ignore all the online stuff," I said, shrugging it off. "I don't care what they say. I mean, I hope they'll like the show when it begins streaming but I don't play into any of that shipping crap. And why is his character's name first anyway?"

"It's a top/bottom thing, I think," Phoebe answered. "Sorry."

I rolled my eyes. "Jesus Christ."

I wasn't about to tell them they had that wrong. I wasn't even entertaining any idea of it.

Chase ran over and crashed onto the ground beside me, taking my drink and draining it, slurping the ice in the bottom. "Thanks. I'm parched."

"Are you allergic to shirts?"

He laughed and lay on his back, swatting me with the offending shirt. Then he ran his hand over his pec. "You love it."

"Oh yes, your emotional support tiddies. How could I forget?"

The others laughed, and he swatted me again with his shirt, only to then shuffle over enough to use my hip as a pillow. He covered his face with his shirt. "Wake me up when it's time to leave. Or whenever you've all had enough of checking me out. Whichever comes first."

The fact that he was ripped and tanned only served to annoy me. The fact he'd starred in my fantasies last night annoyed me too. And the fact that the waistband of his shorts outlined the planes and valleys of his V muscles and the bulge in his crotch . . .

It annoyed me that I noticed these things.

That I wanted them.

"We should do dinner tonight," Tucker suggested. He gave Max a nod. "Bring Jenna."

"Good idea," Holly agreed. "So she can see us as a work team."

Everyone kinda nodded, but it wasn't something I could do. "Gotta work tonight, sorry."

Chase put his hand up, his shirt still over his face. "I'm with him. If he's a no-go, then I'm out too."

He totally could still go . . .

"We could meet at the coffee shop?" Jess suggested. "It's probably gonna feature a bit anyway, in the filming and whatever, so it might be a good test run. Amos will already be there and that way Chase could come too."

Chase pulled his shirt from his face, his big blue eyes looking up at me. "Will there be iced coffee?"

I sighed and put his shirt back over his face.

Chase held my hand when we walked back to the rehearsal hall. He kept his arm around my shoulder while we did some filming at the lockers. He kept his chin on my shoulder, his hand slung on my waist as we filmed in the dining hall.

I knew people around campus were watching us and watching Chase and me especially.

And as an actor, for all the plays and stage productions I'd done, I was used to having an audience.

But this one felt different.

Personal, somehow. As if Chase and I were having our privacy invaded, even though we weren't.

But if we were going for the *Friends/90210* reality feel, we needed to be in familiar sets around campus, so filming at the Bean Necessities made sense. And Jerry, the owner, was fine with it. It was all publicity, he'd said, as long as his logo was showing, his customers weren't inconvenienced, and the business was perceived in a positive light.

Which I'm sure it would be.

But it was also my work. No one else had film crews at their work, and I tried not to let it bother me.

And, admittedly, as the other cast members all crammed into one booth, including Max's girlfriend, it was fun to watch.

It did have a *Friends/90210* vibe, and the cameras took some footage and some photos, and it was great for the production . . . but I wasn't sure how it would work if the café was super busy.

Not well, probably.

"Hey," Chase said, leaning against the end of the service counter.

I slid the tray of cookies into the fridge and closed the door, standing up. "Hey. Whassup?"

"You okay?"

I walked over to him, close enough so our conversation would be private. "Yeah, why wouldn't I be?"

"It's just that you haven't come over . . ."

I gestured to the counter. "Uh, yeah, I'm at work."

"Can you take a break?"

I checked the time. "Soon, I guess. Why?"

"'Cause it's not the same without you. They're all couple-y and I'm sitting there third wheeling it." He shoved his hands into his pockets. "And I don't know what to do with my hands when you're not there."

I snorted. "You mean, you have no one to accost."

"I don't accost you. I . . . touch you. Why would you say it like that? Now it's weird."

I snorted at that. "Yeah, *I'm* the one who makes it weird."

He made a face. Slipping his fingers under the waistband seam of my apron, he tugged me closer. "Take your break. Come and sit with me."

Jesus. Now we were not even an inch apart. His face was far too close to mine, his eyes playful and imploring.

"Has anyone ever told you you're annoying?"

"Yes. You tell me all the time."

"And needy."

"Well, I think that's a first, but I don't even mind."

My god, he was pitiful. I sighed. "Mason," I called out. "Gonna take my ten."

Chase grinned, and when we turned around, the whole cast in the booth was watching us, cameras too. Aaaand the table by the door.

Just great.

Chase took my hand and dragged me over. "Look who I found."

I was greeted with smiles and *heyyyy*s around the table, and before I could pull a seat over, Chase sat and pulled me onto his knee. He pressed his face into the back of my arm, kept one hand on my thigh, the other on my waist.

Okay then.

It was a very boyfriend thing to do, so I went along with it.

Then he took his half-finished iced coffee and held it up to my mouth so I could sip from his straw. I figured it was a boyfriend thing to do as well, so I went along with that too.

We got a few funny looks but mostly everyone at the table wasn't surprised. Were we taking the method acting thing too seriously? Or were they not taking it seriously enough?

Maybe because their character's couples weren't as established as ours. Elijah and Dominic have been together for a year. We had to establish a level of comfort around each other, and we'd done that.

I was comfortable with Chase. Despite my best efforts to not like the guy, I kinda did. He was easy to hang out with. Easy to joke with. Easy to antagonize and rankle.

Easy to sit on and cuddle with.

"Ready for your morning shoot?" Max asked, looking at me and Chase.

We were up first thing. The basic script was that Chase would leave from his place at Mundell House, then cross the campus to my dorm. It was intended to give the audience a view of the college campus, and it would set the scene. There'd be location shots of the beach, the courtyard, the campus itself.

In the opening of the series, the viewer would get acquainted with the college campus, following the cute guy up to the dorms where he would meet his boyfriend.

That was the opening scene.

No pressure.

From there, Dominic and Elijah would then stroll across to the dining hall, and the rest of the cast would come in for breakfast before heading to class.

Sounded easy.

"Ready as we'll ever be," Chase said. "Once shooting starts and we get used to the cameras being one step behind us, we'll be fine." He looked up at me, his lips pressed to my shoulder blade. "Won't we, babe?"

Babe.

"Sure thing," I replied. "Babe."

He chuckled. "See? We'll be fiiiiiine."

I rolled my eyes but took his drink and finished it.

Max's girlfriend gave me a timid smile, she still seemed uncomfortable and Max and Holly weren't even touching each other. It made me realize just how different Chase and I were.

We were so comfortable with each other.

Too comfortable, maybe?

When the camera crews asked Jenna to squeeze out of the booth so they could take some more shots of just the eight of us, it got really awkward and quiet.

I began to stand up. "Want me to—"

"No, stay there," they said. Chase pulled me back onto

his lap and smiled at the camera from behind my shoulder. "That's perfect."

I went back to work, and not long after the cast made their leave, they all yelled out goodbyes and waved, except Chase. He cleared the table for me, bringing empty cups to the trash, and he waited while Mason and I quickly closed up.

He even helped a bit, lifting chairs onto tables—without the *Les Mis* encore tonight—and soon enough, we were locked up and leaving. Mason waved us off, and Chase nodded toward my dorm. "I'll walk you back."

"You don't need to," I said, even though I liked that he did.

But he didn't hold my hand or put his arm around me, and I was surprised by how disappointed it made me.

"So," he began. "Do you think Jenna and Max will last?"

"She didn't look too happy tonight."

"I know, right?" he said, animatedly. Probably happy that I noticed like he did. "She has to understand it's just acting. I feel sorry for Max."

Just acting. It's just acting . . .

"Yeah, same," I said, though I wasn't sure . . . "And Holly. I feel bad for her too. It's not her fault."

He let out a groan. "It was awkward tonight. Did you see how she was looking at us?"

"I did, yeah."

"Man, I'm so glad we're not awkward like that." He shot me a questioning look as if he was seeing if I agreed with him?

"Yeah," I said. "We're not awkward. If anything, we're too comfortable."

"Too comfortable? What's that supposed to mean?"

"You pulled me onto your lap tonight."

"Hey, that wasn't me. That was Dominic pulling Elijah onto his lap."

"Right."

"That's the Dominic privilege. Elijah allows Dominic to do that. Amos, on the other hand, would not allow Chase to do that."

I laughed. "The Dominic privilege. I have a feeling Dominic is going to try and get away with all kinds of shit."

Chase laughed. "I think he might."

"Elijah might be a willing participant, but he will still put Dominic on his ass if he goes too far."

Chase laughed. "See, Dominic thinks that's foreplay, so he's totally on board with that."

I gave him a shove. "No, Chase thinks that's foreplay."

Chase laughed. "Dominic and I are very similar."

"I know," I said. "Much to mine and Elijah's disdain."

He laughed as we reached the steps to my dorm. "Well, here you are. Home, safe and sound."

"Dominic is a gentleman."

"And Chase," he added. "It was his idea."

I snorted. "Right."

"I'll see you back here bright and early," he said, rocking back on his heels. He looked around as if he were nervous. Chase Soria, nervous? Or was he being Dominic right now?

"Okay," I said. "Thanks for walking me back."

He gave a nod but said nothing else, so I turned for the door.

"Oh hey," he said. "Just before you go."

I stopped and he ran his hand through his hair. "Were you comfortable with me pulling you onto my lap? I know we discussed boundaries before, but filming starts tomorrow, so I just wanted to double-check that you're still okay with that kind of physical touch. I mean, you didn't object tonight, but the camera was rolling so I just thought I should ask to be sure."

Oh my god, he was actually nervous.

Chase Soria was nervous and double-checking consent.

There in the dark with only the building lights illuminating half his face, I could still see the uncertainty in the shadows.

I could also see the sweetness.

"It was fine," I said. "I was okay with that."

I was more than okay with it.

A grin broke out on his face. "Good. Same. It felt natural, so I went with it. Dominic would absolutely do that."

Right. Dominic.

"And Elijah would allow that."

His eyes met mine and he held my gaze for a beat. Then he turned and nodded to the dark. "Awesome. Okay, see you here, bright and early tomorrow. I'll text you before I leave so you know I'm on my way."

"Thanks."

He disappeared into the dark, no doubt heading back to his place.

I went upstairs, showered and changed, got ready for bed. I lay there, staring at the ceiling for what felt like hours. Remembering how it felt to sit on his lap with his arm around me. Remembering his face pressed into my shoulder. Remembering his hand on my thigh.

And remembering his face in the dark. How he'd asked me for consent again. How he'd smiled.

How he'd said it was his character that was so touchy-feely. How I'd said my character was okay with it.

When really it was me.

I didn't sleep for ages, my mind reliving every angle, every moment. And I slept through my first alarm and only realized he'd texted me when I was getting out of the shower.

Shit.

I threw on my jeans and a hoodie, had my socks on and one shoe in my hand when there was a knock on my door.

Who the hell was it? I didn't have time for talking, I had to get downstairs . . .

Still holding the shoe, I opened the door.

To find Chase standing there, grinning, Daniel and Bridgette behind him, camera on.

"Morning, babe," he said. Then he stepped in close, put his hand on my cheek, and kissed me.

Chapter Eleven
Chase

I kissed him.

I gripped his face and planted a soft kiss on his lips. He was surprised, but to his credit, with the camera rolling behind us, he was quick to adapt.

"Morning," he replied. "Running a bit late, sorry. I slept through my alarm."

"Because you work late," I said, going to his desk and grabbing his backpack, shoving his laptop inside while he pulled on his Chucks. His hair was still a bit wet, but damn, he looked good in all black: jeans, hoodie, hair.

Especially against his pale skin and the pink blush on his cheeks.

Damn.

Why did I kiss him?

Because I'd wanted to last night. Because it was all I'd thought about, and seeing him when he opened the door . . . it felt right.

It's what Dominic would do.

I mean, it was also what I'd do, but I was in character. I

was my character, and Dominic would definitely kiss his hot-as-fuck boyfriend every chance he got.

"I can think of better reasons to miss sleep," I added.

He looked up at me, tying his laces. There was definitely a for-the-love-of-god, don't-do-this-on camera look in his eyes. But instead, he stood up and took his bag. "I'm sure you could."

"Hurry up, I'm starving," I said, changing the subject and ushering him to the door. Daniel and Bridgette had to back out of the room with his camera, two steps ahead of us, and I needed to be more aware of shit like that.

"You're always starving," he said as we bounded down the stairs.

"Did you get your report done on time?" I asked, trying to keep the conversation rolling.

"Yep. Did you?"

"Yeah, but it wasn't my best work." I got to the bottom and held the door for him. "You *know* where I do my best work."

He walked past me, giving me a what-the-fuck glare that the camera couldn't see. "If that's your best then—"

"Then we need more practice," I finished for him, not letting him finish that sentence on camera. Okay, so maybe hinting at sex wasn't a good idea. I should have known he'd cut me off at the knees.

Lesson learned, Chase.

I fell into step beside him and took his hand, threading our fingers. "What time's your last class this afternoon?" he asked.

"Three. Then I was gonna hit the pool. Wanna come

watch me do laps? You've got tonight off work, so we can grab a pizza after. Let's see what the others are doing."

He gave me a side-eye before he smiled. "Okay. Sounds good."

Amos held the door for me this time, and Daniel followed us into the dining hall but stopped filming. The other camera crews were already there, the other guys seated at a table in the corner.

Deirdre and some of the production team were standing with placards that read *quiet please, filming*, and although the dining hall wasn't too full yet, there were enough people sitting around, breakfast forgotten as they used their phones to film the filming.

Amos and I quickly grabbed some trays of food and slid into the two spare seats at the table.

We were greeted with the usual "hey" and "morning" and we ran through small talk like we'd practiced. Talk about the food, about the hockey game, and our classes of the day.

"So," I began, "you guys wanna grab a pizza tonight? There's an outdoor movie at the beach tonight. I think they're showing *Jaws*. Elijah and I are going if you wanna hang out."

"Sounds good," Tucker said.

Max looked at Holly. "Wanna go?"

She smiled and tucked her hair behind her ear before she nodded. Acting the shy, smitten love interest to perfection. "Sure."

There was a beat of silence, and Jess was quick to fill it. "Hey, so did you hear about the two sophomores that got caught doing the walk of shame?"

Everyone laughed along, shocked but amused. Shocked that she would say that. There was no walk of shame. There was no scandal. The *real* scandal was the baseball sex scandal and subsequent fallout, but it wasn't like we could say *that* on camera.

Or the stats professor who slept with the student, only it wasn't a student per se but the student's twin brother that no one knew he had. Professor Brooks accused him of lying and cheating *in public*, outing himself in the process. It was big news around campus but honestly, how that wasn't caught on camera was the real scandal.

But Jess couldn't say that either. This *fake* scandal Jess mentioned was just a conversation starter, and it worked. Chatter around the table began, funny and smooth.

Until Didi checked her phone. "Shoot. Look at the time. We've got class in ten."

Phoebe jumped up. "And I'm on the other side of campus." She and Jess said they'd see us tonight and left with their camera team behind them.

Max asked Holly where she was heading next and they left; then Tucker and Didi did the same. "See you guys tonight," Didi said.

"Okay," I replied, watching them as they walked out.

Then it was just Amos and me.

Or Elijah and Dominic, I should say. Daniel was filming again.

"What've you got first?" he asked, stabbing some sliced apple with his fork.

"Documentary Theater."

He scrunched his nose up and it was the cutest thing ever. "I better go," I murmured. Then I pulled the cords on his hoodie, bringing him closer, and I pecked his lips. "See you at lunch."

Ignoring the color on his cheeks—because I'd just kissed him in front of the now-full dining hall—I got up, took my bag, and walked off.

"Okay, cut," Deirdre said, and the dining hall erupted in applause.

I went back to Amos and he stood up and gave me a gentle shove, but I wrapped my arms around him, and sitting my ass on the table, I pulled him in close.

He didn't fight it.

"That was great, guys," Deirdre said. "How'd it feel?"

"Yeah, it was fine," I said.

"We need to work on the small-talk dialogue," Amos said. "Even points of interest for us to talk about."

"Jess did great," I added.

Amos nodded. "She did." Then he gave me another shove, this time with his elbow. "And you kept talking about sex. Jesus Christ." He pointed to Daniel who was now looking at a replay of something. "If you keep throwing me under the bus with all the sexual innuendo, I'll look right down that camera and tell the world that Dominic cries after sex and calls me mommy."

I burst out laughing, and this time he pulled out of my arms. "I do have to go though."

I stood up. "Yeah. I'm headed that way. I'll walk with you."

We walked out, ignoring the eyes and smiles of everyone watching us, even though it gave me a thrill. As soon as we were outside, I slung my arm around Amos's neck as we walked. "Oh, that was such a rush. Doing improv like that. Don't you think?"

He laughed. "It was fun."

"The way everyone was watching. This is gonna be a fucking ride. I love it."

The thrill of the audience, the thrill of the cameras, the improvisation. I loved it.

"And," he added, "now everyone gets to see you swim laps because you went ahead and mentioned it, so now you gotta do it."

I was still too buzzed to care. "Me, shirtless and wet. The ratings will be huge."

He snorted. "Please tell me you wear Speedos."

"If you wanna see my junk, you just gotta ask. I have no objections."

He dug me in the ribs, making me drop my arm, and it was then I realized that Daniel was behind us with the camera.

Great.

Amos laughed and cut across the corridor to head to his class. Still smiling, he blew me a kiss. "Have a good day."

I had to admit, the kiss-blowing took me by surprise, and honestly, it wasn't Dominic who stood there smiling like a fool.

It was one hundred percent me.

"So how's it going?" Tate asked. We were at the gym, weight training. It was leg day, but I wanted to work my chest too. If I was gonna be shirtless on camera in an hour, I wanted to look good.

"Yeah, good so far," I replied, letting go of the barbell. "Though filming just started today. We'll iron out some kinks and things will be smoother as we go, I'm sure."

"And how's Amos? Or Elijah. I dunno which name to use."

I didn't correct him, because honestly, I wasn't sure. "He's . . . he's good, actually. Takes my bullshit and rolls with it."

Tate laughed. "Perfect."

"You know, Tate—" I said, stopping myself from using the not-funny nickname. "This whole boyfriend thing ain't so bad. Did you know the other night we ordered pizza and watched funny shit on TV. Like I would with you guys, but with him. We got to cuddle and stuff, and I realized that maybe dating someone wasn't so bad. If that's what dating people do."

Jimmy was staring at me. "You were . . . cuddling? Like in his room, by yourselves?"

"Well, yeah. Where else we gonna do that?"

"But . . . were there cameras? I mean, aren't you just supposed to do that in front of cameras?"

I shrugged. "Well, yeah. But it's all practice. We need to look comfortable with each other."

Jimmy wore a smirk. "Sounds like more than practice to me. Hey, Tater? I think Chase—"

"Don't call him that," I said gently. "It's not nice."

Jimmy blinked. "Oh, sorry, I . . ." He shrugged at Tate. "Sorry, dude."

Tate made a face. "'S okay." But then he looked at me. "Thanks."

Amos was right. I shouldn't have been surprised.

"And anyway, you're missing the point," I said, changing the subject. "What I wanna know, is that what dating people do? Because it was kinda awesome. And if we can watch *Rick and Morty*, eat pizza, and have sex, then I think I've been going about this no-dating thing all wrong."

"What did you think dating was?" Tate asked.

I shrugged. "I dunno. Boring monogamy and missing out on fun stuff."

Jimmy snorted. "Holy shit, you had a revelation."

"All I'm saying is it was fun. And maybe I wouldn't mind doing it again."

"Did you two . . . ?" Jimmy waggled his eyebrows at me.

"No. We just . . ."

"Cuddled?"

"Yeah, and we hold hands and put our legs over each other, and we kiss occasionally, but that's only acting. No tongue. And to be fair, I've kissed him. He's never kissed me."

They both stared, and Jimmy's smile became a grin. "So the fake boyfriend thing is kinda sounding real boyfriend-like to me."

Tate nodded. "It kinda does, yeah."

"I don't even do half of that with the girls I date," Jimmy added.

"You should do it," I told him. "It's awesome! That's what I'm saying. I had no idea it could be . . . so nice. I really should try this whole dating thing for real."

"Uh, Chase," Tate said gently. "It sounds like you already are."

"But we *are* acting," I explained. "It's method acting. It's supposed to be immersive. It's not real."

"But you want it to be," Tate said.

Well, shit.

"I dunno. Maybe."

"With him? Or just in general?" Jimmy pressed. "Did you have this epiphany because of him, to be with him? Or just dating in general?"

I tried to think about that. Imagining being like that with someone else . . . "I dunno. I . . ."

Goddammit.

Jimmy laughed and clapped my shoulder. "That's what I thought. You got it bad for the emo guy."

"He's not the emo guy," I said, probably way too short.

He raised both hands in surrender, and I let out a sigh. "Sorry. It's just . . . confusing. Is it our characters? Is it Dominic and Elijah? Or is it me and him?"

"I thought your characters were kinda based on you. Aren't you basically playing yourselves anyway?" Tate asked. And he mighta asked innocently, but the point he made needed no answer.

Because he was right.

God fucking dammit.

Laps of the pool, like always, helped clear my mind. Following that black center line in the lane, regulating my breathing, pushing my body, and using every muscle never failed to help.

I lost count of how many laps I'd done. I lost track of time, and I forgot that Amos was coming to watch.

That I'd asked him to come.

When I stood up at the shallow end, leaned against the wall of the pool, and tried to catch my breath, I saw him. Sitting there in the bleachers . . . with Jimmy and Tate.

Oh no . . .

And there, at the top of the stands, were Daniel and Bridgette, filming.

Double oh no.

Not that Amos couldn't hold his own, but Jimmy . . . Jimmy couldn't keep his damn mouth shut.

I pulled myself up the ladder, my legs tired and heavy, and made my way over to them. I wore the swim shorts most athletic swimmers wore. Not Speedos exactly, but a whole lot tighter than swimming trunks.

And from the way Amos's gaze drank me in, I wasn't about to cover up. Camera or not.

He totally fucking checked me out.

All of me.

It gave me a thrill I wasn't expecting, and all those silly fears and doubts about whether we were acting or if we were taking the role of boyfriends too far all just fell away.

Because he checked me out, and he liked what he saw.

If he was Amos or Elijah in that moment, it didn't matter. Because I didn't care either way. Me or Dominic, both knew appreciation when we saw it.

I took my towel and dried my hair, leaving the rest of my body dripping wet. And when I wiped the towel slowly over my pecs and down to my junk, I kept my eyes on Amos.

He scoffed and shook his head, finally looking away. "You have no shame."

"None," Jimmy said. "He has none."

I held my hands out, holding the towel away from my body. "What's not to be proud of?"

"Your ego," Amos replied.

Jimmy laughed and Tate smiled at me. "I love how he takes no shit from you. It's good for you."

"I need new friends and a new boyfriend," I said, loud enough for the camera to hear.

Amos stood up, smiling, and stepped down the bleachers and came to a stop right in front of me. Too close. Not close enough. "Swim practice is about to start, so we need to not be here when this pool is full of people."

Right. Whereas I loved crowds of people, he did not.

"I need to shower," I said. "Unless you wanna come back to mine? Then we can go to the movie on the beach from there. What's the time?"

Amos pulled out his phone. "Twenty minutes past four."

Damn.

I really had lost track of time.

He hadn't answered about the shower, so I tried the oldest trick in the book: I batted my eyelashes and pouted. "You haven't been to my place before," I whispered, certain the camera couldn't hear.

He rolled his eyes in defeat. "Fine."

I beamed at him and barely resisted saying *yay!*

Barely.

God, what had I become?

I wrapped my towel around my waist, tying it off, and still shirtless and a little wet, I threw my arm around his shoulder.

I knew the camera was on us, and I knew the viewers would love it.

And me. I did it for me too.

"Ugh, you're wet," Amos griped, but his arm came around my back and we walked to the door.

As soon as we were outside where the camera couldn't see us, he shoved me. "You're wet. And half naked."

I laughed. "I'm resisting so hard right now on saying any sexual joke, just so you can appreciate my restraint. I think you should appreciate that."

Jimmy and Tate laughed, but seeing Daniel follow us out the door, I took Amos's hand and headed toward my place. "Cameras are still on," I said quietly.

"Gotta ask," Jimmy said. "Are the cameras allowed in your bedroom? How far you gotta go?"

"It's a reality show," I answered. "You're thinking of Only Fans, you perv."

"Why?" Amos asked. "Would you watch?"

Tate and I cracked up laughing, and I was loving that he took no shit from my friends either. I dropped his hand, opting to put my arm around his shoulder again.

I liked touching him. I liked feeling his body close to mine.

He didn't object, and maybe that was because the camera was behind us. I liked to think it wasn't.

And maybe when this was all over, I could examine my need for physical closeness with him. I could pull it apart and dissect what was different about him—because I'd certainly never craved contact with anyone else like I did with him.

But first, I needed a shower, and to jerk off because, yeah, I liked the close contact a little too much.

His phone beeped and he took it out. "It's a message from Bridgette. They're gonna leave us here and pick up again at the outdoor theater tonight."

"Okay, cool," I said.

"Uh, that means you can drop your arm now," he said.

I kept my arm very much where it was. "I mean, I could. But would Dominic do that? I'm thinking Dominic wouldn't do that."

He sighed and shoved me off him. "Elijah would do that."

Jimmy and Tate both laughed.

When we got to my place, I showed him into my room and pulled my towel off. I was dry now, but I needed a freshwater shower to get rid of the pool smell. And to give him a full view of my body because I remembered how he'd checked me out earlier.

He walked into my room, looking around. Not that there was much to see. I was just grateful I'd made my bed this morning, not something I always did. I threw my towel over the back of my desk chair. "Make yourself comfortable. Help yourself to anything out of the fridge, and don't listen to anything Jimmy tells you. I'm gonna grab a quick shower."

I left him to it, taking the quickest shower of my life. I opted not to jerk off—probably something I'd regret later—and realized upon getting out that I probably should have taken some clothes with me to get changed back into . . .

So now he was gonna get a full show.

Maybe not taking a change of clothes was the best idea ever.

I went back into my room with a bath towel wrapped around me, wet hair brushed back, and not completely dry. He liked me wet before, so it was the least I could do.

He was lying on my bed, propped up against the headboard, scrolling through his phone. Looking all kinds of comfortable, looking all kinds of hot.

I grabbed some boxer briefs and pulled them on under my towel. I caught the way he glanced from his phone to me and back again. "You just love being naked, don't you?"

I pulled the towel away with a flourish. "Damn straight."

I had no qualms standing there in nothing but underwear, but Jimmy chose that exact moment to knock and open the door. "Oh," he said, stopping and giving me a double take. "Didn't mean to interrupt."

"You're not interrupting," Amos said, not looking up from his phone.

"Whassup?" I asked Jimmy.

Looking right at me, he lifted his phone and took a photo. "Snapchat."

I snatched up my towel and tried to flick him with it. "Oh, fuck off."

He just laughed. "Is that movie thing tonight for everyone?" he asked. "Or just the drama peeps?"

"Everyone," Amos answered.

"Cool." He pulled the door shut and disappeared.

Amos was still looking at his phone so I threw on some shorts and then I climbed onto my bed, over Amos, and planted myself in the crook of his arm, my head on his chest. "Whatcha lookin' at?"

He froze for a second. "Are you all right there?"

"Yep, much better now. Thanks for asking."

He dropped his hand to my shoulder. "Are you allergic to shirts?"

I slung my leg over his thigh. "Not allergic. It's just an intolerance."

His only resistance was a sigh, but then he kept scrolling on his phone. "To answer your question," he said, "I'm looking at what people are saying."

"About us? I didn't think you wanted to look." I squinted at the screen. "Oh my god, are we a hashtag?"

We were. We were totally a hashtag.

"That's hilarious."

He didn't seem impressed. "Hmm."

But there were pics of us in the dining hall, pics of him on my lap in the coffee shop the other night, pics of us walking down the hall. Videos of us walking hand in hand. There was even a video of us just twenty minutes ago, walking toward my place. It was when he'd asked Jimmy if he'd watch our Only Fans and I'd laughed and slung my arm around him. And he'd put his arm around my bare shoulder.

Much like he was doing right now.

Another pic of us at breakfast, everyone else sitting normally, but Amos and me... I mean, Elijah and Dominic were sitting far too close, leaning into each other.

And we had no idea people were taking photos. Sure,

the cameras were on us, but these were candid photos by other students. No wonder people were asking questions about whether we were together or not.

I was beginning to ask myself the same thing.

I couldn't take my eyes off us.

"We make a fucking hot couple," I said.

He snorted as he scrolled to the next pic. It was us in the coffee shop with all the cast, Amos on my lap, my arms around him, my face pressed into the back of his shoulder.

Jesus.

"Did you know people were taking photos of us?" he asked.

"Nope. Did you?"

"No."

"I mean, I know the cameras are on us. Daniel's never far away. But other students? Not a clue."

He kept his thumb on the photo of us at breakfast, studying some detail, before he scrolled onto the next one.

Which Jimmy had taken five minutes ago.

Me in my goddamn underwear, Amos lying on my bed.

"I'm gonna kill him," I said. "I didn't think he'd actually post it."

Like he was listening, my door opened and Jimmy stood there, camera ready again.

"Hey, asshole," I said, trying to get up.

"Two hundred and eighty-four likes in five minutes," he said, grinning like the shithead he was. "For what it's worth, I'm on the they're-not-acting side of the fan war."

Amos surprised me by hooking the pillow from behind his back at Jimmy's head so fast, he had to duck and pull the door shut. "Fuck off."

Jimmy laughed from behind the door and I grumbled. "I'll kill him later. I'm too tired to get up."

Amos settled against the headboard, and I put my head back on his chest. I wasn't lying. I was tired after overdoing it again at the gym and in the pool. And he was much too warm and comfortable.

He zoomed in on the pic of us, zooming in on me in particular.

"Looking for something?" I joked.

"Just checking it was decent, nothing showing, if you know what I mean."

"My junk? I'm in my underwear. It doesn't hide much."

"They're black, at least—helps hide outlines."

"Jesus Christ." I took his phone and zoomed in to see if the outline of my junk was at all visible. Thankfully, it wasn't.

I relaxed and he took his phone back. "Your swimming trunks are more revealing than your underwear."

"Oh, yes. And don't think I didn't *not* notice how you appreciated those swimming trunks."

He stilled, frozen. "I did not."

"You absolutely did. And you just gave yourself away because you should have said it was Elijah checking out Dominic."

He gave me a shove. "Oh, shut up."

I laughed. "It's okay with me. I have zero objections. In fact, I like you checking me out. Amos or Elijah, or both. I work hard for this body. I'm glad someone appreciates it."

"Half the campus appreciates it," he mumbled.

"Only half? That's disappointing."

He chuckled. "You just love the attention."

"And you hate it," I replied. "That's why we make a perfect couple."

He was quiet for a bit, and I couldn't be bothered correcting the *couple* thing.

He knew what I meant.

I ignored the pictures on his phone and closed my eyes. I couldn't ever remember feeling so relaxed. So peaceful.

So happy.

"Uh, he posted the video," Amos murmured. "Though it's more of a gif."

I cracked an eye open to watch. Sure enough, there were Amos and me, lying on my bed, exactly as we were right then. The door swung in, a shirtless me draped over Amos, me trying to get up, Amos throwing the pillow at the door.

That was the entire clip.

The caption read *Still not acting*.

"It has three hundred likes," Amos added.

I groaned. "I'll kill him later. I'm too tired. Do we have to go to the outdoor theater?"

"It was your idea."

"Past-me was a dick. Now-me is a much more reasonable person."

He chuckled, turned his phone off, and put it on my bedside. His arm fell back to my shoulder, so I hitched my leg a little higher on his thigh and closed my eyes.

"This is nice," I mumbled. "We should do this more often."

"Hm" was all he replied.

I told my dick to behave itself and snuggled in, ready for the best nap ever.

2

I WOKE up fully embracing Amos. He was on his side, holding me, his leg between mine, sound asleep. His dark lashes fanned his cheeks, his pink lips were wet and parted, and so help me god, I had to make myself not kiss him.

Don't do it. Don't kiss him. Don't pull him on top of you. Don't open your legs so he'd fit between them, so you could feel his dick against yours. Don't do it.

I wanted to kiss him so bad.

And not just a small peck like I'd done before. I mean, a deep kiss. I wanted to thread my fingers in his hair, tangle my tongue with his, and grind on his dick. I wanted his hands all over me.

And my dick was most definitely not behaving itself.

Christ.

But he was so attractive, especially in sleep. The frown was gone, the scowl. He looked peaceful and happy and so goddamn beautiful.

My door creaked open, and a hand appeared holding a phone, aiming the camera right at us.

"Post that photo and you die," I said. "I fucking mean it, Jimmy."

Amos stirred, pulling away from me, confused. He looked at the now-closed door. "What?"

I pulled him back close. "Nothing, don't worry about it."

He held his breath, then he let it out with a sigh. "I fell

asleep," he mumbled, clearly still trying to come to grips with the world.

"Best nap ever," I replied. "We should do this more often. Like all night. Except at your place because my friends are assholes."

He pulled away for real this time and sat up, scrubbing his hand over his face and through his hair. "What time is it?" he murmured, grabbing his phone. "Ugh."

He held it so I could see the screen. It was 5:42.

"Shit." I sat up, bending my legs to hide my semi. "We should get ready to go."

"I was just gonna wear this," he mumbled, pulling at his T-shirt.

"Yeah, same."

"Do you plan on wearing a shirt? Or is everyone getting to appreciate your emotional support tiddies?"

I snorted out a laugh, then took his hand and placed it over my pec, giving myself a bit of a squeeze. "These are Elijah's emotional support tiddies now."

I dropped my hand from his but he kept his hand right there, cupping my pec. "Are these like an A cup?"

I batted his hand away. "Fuck you."

He smirked. "Get up and put a shirt on." He stood up and stretched his hands over his head, giving me a peek of pale skin above the waistband of his jeans and . . . and a decent bulge at his crotch.

"Damn, Amos," I murmured. "Do you have a concealed weapon permit for that?"

He pulled his shirt down and gave me an annoyed glare. "Shut the fuck up and stop staring at my . . . me."

I gave my semi a squeeze. "Or we could skip the movie and stay in."

He stared.

Holy hell. Was that . . . was that *interest* in those dark eyes?

I stood up, adjusting my junk, not even attempting to hide my semi now. "For real, though," I said. "We could act out some roleplaying. I could be a really annoying jerk and you could give me another lesson in consent. But we'd be naked and you'd have to remind me over and over with your dick in my ass."

His mouth fell open.

"It's been a while since I've done that, and I—"

He threw my shirt at me. "Get dressed."

"Or? Was that a threat? Get dressed or what? You'll make me suck your dick? Because it's been far too long since—"

"Or I'll go home."

Oh.

I pouted. "That's no fun. The fucking and the dick sucking is so much more fun than that."

He glared, all serious business. "Chase."

"Fine." I sighed and pouted some more, but he was clearly not playing. I pulled my shirt over my head. "Did you wanna eat something here or should we grab something at the pier?"

He was still obviously a little mad at me for all the sexual innuendos and offers I could throw at him. "Tacos."

"Hell yes, tacos now and blow jobs later. Perfect night."

He glared and I held his gaze because this kind of foreplay was my favorite. He quickly realized I was still playing, so he looked away and rolled his eyes. "Shut the fuck up." He snatched up his phone and pretended I didn't exist while I found my slides.

"Christ," he mumbled.

I shot him a look. "If Jimmy posted that picture of us in bed, I *will* kill him. For real this time."

Amos looked at me then. "Which one? The one he posted before?" He held up his phone and it was the first pic.

"No, he tried to take another one. You were asleep." His eyes narrowed at me, and I held up both hands. "I threatened to kill him if he posted it."

"Let's go find him."

Jimmy was in the living room, on the couch with his leg over the side armrest, scrolling on his phone. "Hey, dickbag," I said, walking in.

"Oh look, it's the Sleeping Beauties."

"Stop posting shit," I said. "You got no right to do that."

He held his phone up. "Did you see how many likes you got? And about a thousand comments about how excited people are to watch the show when it airs."

Amos stood beside me. "Post anything else without our consent and I'll report you for stalking and invasion of privacy and have you expelled."

Jimmy stared at him, and Amos held his gaze, unflinching.

I slid my arm around Amos while grinning at Jimmy, giving him the bird. "What he just said." Then I looked at Amos. "Your lessons in consent are awesome. Though your lesson with me was much more fun."

He rolled his eyes, though I caught the hint of a smile.

"I didn't mean anything by it," Jimmy said. "I'm sorry. I didn't post the other one, and I can delete the first two."

"It's too late now. They're out there and probably reposted a hundred times," I replied. "Just don't do it again."

He stood up, his eyes wide. "I'm sorry. I am. I thought it'd be funny. I didn't mean anything. I swear."

I believed him. His apology was sincere.

"Funny?" Amos asked.

"Well, yeah. Because it's Chase. He's never done the boyfriend thing. He has an aversion to public displays of affection but now he's all clingy and pathetic. It's funny to see, that's all."

"Pathetic?" I stared at him. "Pathetic. I am not pathetic, fuck you very much."

Jimmy just shrugged and half-smiled, and Amos didn't argue. "Do you think I'm pathetic too?" I asked him.

"No," he lied.

"Great. Generic and pathetic. That's awesome. I love my life, love my friends."

"Just keeping it real," Amos replied.

"Well, if you could keep it real with less teeth when you're sucking my dick later, that'd be great."

Amos rolled his eyes at that, but he didn't deny it.

"Wait," Jimmy said. "What?"

"Nothing," Amos said. He gave me a flat stare. "Are we going?"

"We sure are. Tacos, *Jaws* on the big screen, and BJs later. Let's go!"

Amos shoved me into the doorframe as we walked out, and Jimmy laughed behind us.

Chapter Twelve
Amos

The outdoor theater was awesome. It was set up on the beach with a huge projector screen hanging on the side of the pier. People brought blankets and coolers, and I felt foolish for not thinking of that, but Jess and Phoebe had brought enough for everyone.

We set up toward the back to stay out of the way. We would have film crews moving about, so it was only fair.

We split the cost of a tray of mini tacos for all of us to share and enough drinks for everyone. We got comfy as the sun began to set, and Chase planted himself on me, like he always did—between my legs, his back to my chest.

Only this time, I had to keep thinking of terrible things so my dick wouldn't poke him in the back.

God, sleeping next to him, wrapped around each other, had been incredible. I wasn't usually one to cuddle. I liked my own space. But Chase was clingy and cuddly, and so help me god, I was used to it now.

I even liked it.

My dick liked it a whole lot.

It'd been far too long since I'd had any kind of action, and now my dick wouldn't quit.

The fact he was making all the sex jokes and innuendos didn't help, at all.

Then he basically offered to skip the movie night and stay in bed all night instead. Sex and blowjobs. He'd kinda been joking but he kinda wasn't, and normally I'd say yes just to get him to back down or shut up, but part of me was too scared.

Because what if he agreed?

What if he'd pushed me back onto the bed? Hell, the way he'd looked at me, looked at my dick—how he'd suggested I should make him suck my dick—I'd almost told him yes.

If I'd undone my fly, he would have.

No doubt in my mind, we'd be in bed right now doing everything we possibly could.

Fuck, I wanted to.

Which was crazy. And stupid.

He was my acting partner, nothing else.

It was in his nature to be playful and cocky, to push boundaries and imply sexual innuendos. That was Chase's leading personality trait.

But did he want me? Or was he acting?

Was he pushing boundaries and being a smartass? Would he have laughed and told me he was joking if I'd asked him to get on his knees?

I wasn't sure.

I was too scared to find out.

Because I'd be disappointed if he said no.

So yeah, lying on the beach with him between my legs

and his head on my chest wasn't ideal. I mean, it was amazing and it felt far too natural. But it wasn't doing my dick or my imagination any favors.

The movie helped. The horror of it, the fake blood, the huge fake shark, the fashion. It was awesome.

We laughed and chatted as the cameras filmed us, getting close-ups of me and Chase. Of me putting the straw to his mouth so he could take a sip of my drink. Of him threading our fingers on his chest.

Of him trying to get my hand to squeeze his pec.

I leaned down and whispered in his ear, "Leave your moobs alone."

He squeezed my knee which made me squirm, and of course that made him press against my dick.

Not helping. Not helping at all.

I knew the second he felt it because he froze.

Then he squirmed, deliberately rubbing against me.

"Stop it," I hissed at him.

He laughed. "Not a chance."

But he kept one leg bent at the knee and I was certain it was to hide his own erection.

"It's so big," Chase said. I dug him in the ribs and he laughed. "I was talking about the shark."

"Would you two be quiet," Didi whisper-shouted at us.

Chase laughed, jumped up to his feet, took my hand, and pulled me down to the water. Once we were far enough away from listening ears and camera microphones, he stopped, bent over with his hands on his knees. He was still laughing. "Holy shit."

I wasn't sure what this was about. "What are we doing?"

He took my hand again, threading our fingers like boyfriends would, and began walking down the beach. The lights of San Luco were twinkling on the water with the moonlight. It was a very pretty night. "We are getting away from the people," he said. "I thought you'd appreciate that."

"Well, yeah. I guess. The movie was fine though. Everyone was watching the screen and there was no need for small talk, which is the literal worst thing ever."

He chuckled. "And I need to walk off my hard-on. Which is one hundred percent your fault."

Uh . . .

I couldn't believe he'd just said that.

I sputtered. "Uh, I don't . . . I mean, how was it my fault? Christ, how can you just say that shit?"

"Because your huge dick was poking me in the back," he said.

Oh my god.

He was just going to say this out loud. To my face.

"And I haven't had sex in too long, apparently," he went on. "Because all this touchy-feely shit has my dick real interested, and I can't think about anything else."

I pulled my hand from his. "You're the one who's all touchy-feely, all the time."

He snatched up my hand again and pulled me to a stop. His face was even more beautiful under the moonlight, and my god, his eyes locked on mine. I was in so much trouble. "Because I like it," he said. "And I've never liked it before, not with anyone. I used to hate public displays of affection or whatever, but I like it with you."

Oh shit.

His voice was quiet. "Whenever I see you, I need to touch you. And sleeping next to you this afternoon put my dick on high alert, and I was gonna jerk off in the shower because I was trying to avoid this, but I didn't because I thought I could handle it. But then you had to put your huge dick against my back."

"Uh, you were the one who was lying on me," I tried to argue. "I'm innocent here."

He laughed. "Innocent. Yeah, right. You were hard this afternoon after our nap, and you were hard again just now. I'm not the only one with this problem here."

Good lord.

"I can't believe we're talking about this." I put my hand to my forehead, and he took that hand too. Now both our hands were joined between us.

"Why can't we talk about this?" he said gently. "We're both adults. We're supposed to be trusting each other for this acting project. I thought we did trust each other."

"I do trust you," I said. "It's just awkward and embarrassing."

"I've felt how big your dick is. You don't need to be embarrassed about anything."

I laughed and he smiled. For a long second, we just looked at each other, holding hands. My heart was knocking painfully against my ribs because this was far more intimate than I'd bargained for.

"I think we should fuck," he blurted out.

I stared at him.

So much for intimacy.

"Pardon?"

"I think we should take care of each other," he

amended. "If you know what I mean. We're not supposed to be seeing anyone else during this whole filming thing. At least not be seen with anyone else. So if we can't have sex with anyone else, then we should totally use each other. Like an acting perk."

I blinked. "Use each other. An acting perk."

"Well, yeah. What would you call it?"

"A terrible idea. That's what I'd call it."

"Is it, though?" he stepped in closer. "I know you're interested. I know your dick's interested, anyway. We both have needs and desires, and honestly, the sexual tension is killing me. If we just get it out of the way, then we don't have to worry about popping boners while filming."

Oh god.

"And this is method acting," he went on, like an executioner swinging the final blow. "It's what Dominic and Elijah would do. They would totally go back to Elijah's dorm room and Dominic would one hundred percent suck Elijah's dick."

Jesus.

My dick loved the sound of that.

"Does he want his dick sucked?" Chase whispered. He pulled me closer by my hands. "Because Dominic wants to suck him so bad."

"Fucking hell," I murmured.

At this rate, I wasn't even going to make it back to my room.

"Chase, I—"

He crashed his mouth to mine, pulling our hips together at the same time. His mouth, his erection; I didn't stand a chance.

It sounded as if the world had stopped. The sound of the ocean, the chatter, traffic, all of it disappeared, and all that existed was him and this kiss.

His full lips opened and his tongue against mine almost buckled my knees. This wasn't like the fake kisses we'd done a dozen times. This was a real kiss.

A great kiss.

And maybe this was Dominic kissing Elijah. Maybe it wasn't.

Because, my god, it felt good.

I raked my hand down his back, over his ass, and pulled him harder against me, and he groaned into my mouth. Then he broke the kiss, taking my hand and dragging me across the beach.

I had to remember how to walk, but he was on a mission. He never stopped until we reached my dorm, and even after I'd opened the foyer door, he snatched up my hand and led the way up the stairs.

"I thought you preferred the elevator," I said.

He spared me a glance over his shoulder as he took the stairs two at a time. "No time," he said. "Hurry the fuck up."

We made it to my floor and I was breathless. If it was from all the running up the stairs or from the way he'd kissed me earlier or maybe in anticipation about what we were about to do, I wasn't sure.

He stopped at my door and leaned against it, blocking me. "If you open this door, there will be dick sucking, just so you know. If you don't want that, don't open the door."

I held his gaze, pressed right up against him, inserted the key, and pushed the door open.

He smirked, fisting my shirt, and he pulled me into my room.

My blood was just about on fire. I was so hard and so turned on, I wasn't going to last a minute. God, even imagining the warm, wet heat of his mouth . . .

I kicked the door shut behind me and he was pawing at my shirt, trying to get it over my head. I pulled his off too, revealing his glorious chest and muscular arms. And then he was pulling at the button on my jeans, so I slid my hand under the waistband of his shorts and palmed his dick.

He froze and sucked back a breath, so I wrapped my fingers around him and he shuddered. "I'm too turned on," he bit out. "Too far gone."

So I went to my knees in front of him, pulled his pants down, and licked the underside of his shaft. He cried out and I was rewarded with a bead of precome. "Fuck. Gonna come so fast."

I licked the slit, tasting him, then took him into my mouth, sliding my lips down while tonguing the underside.

He fisted my hair. "Fuck, yes. Holy shit."

He was swollen, impossibly hard, and so close . . . so I sucked and took him in deeper and his body jerked, his cock pulsed in my mouth, and he cried out, a strangled sound as he came.

He twitched and moaned as I swallowed, groaning when I pulled off him. His cock was still hard, glistening wet, and he swayed on his feet.

"Holy fuck," he breathed.

I stood up and sat him down on the edge of my bed. His eyes were glazed over, he wore a lazy smile, and he was so fucking hot with his dick still hanging out.

But with me standing in front of him and him sitting down, he was the perfect height... So convenient. I opened my fly and took out my dick. I was so fucking hard, so ready to come.

His smile widened and he licked his lips, looking like he was about to taste his most favorite treat ever. "Fuck, yes," he whispered, pulling me closer.

No preamble, no warning. No licking, no tasting, he just sucked me right in, taking me in so far he gagged. But he didn't stop. He kept sucking, tonguing, moaning, his fingertips digging into my ass, and he set the pace.

He wasn't just sucking my dick. He was making me fuck his mouth.

This feeling, this euphoric feeling, I wanted it to last forever.

I wanted this sexual high, pleasure so divine, to never stop.

But then I looked down, and seeing Chase Soria, the hottest guy on campus with his lips around my dick and moaning like he was having a religious experience...

It was all too much.

"Gonna come," I warned. "Your pretty mouth is too good."

He looked up at me, heavy lidded and blissed out, his thick lips around my shaft, and he fucking smiled.

My orgasm ripped through me, and I came down his throat. He sucked it out of me, drinking down every drop.

The room spun, and I lost all sight and sound. The only thing that existed was him, his hands on my ass, and his oh-so talented mouth.

He pulled off me and caught me as I almost fell

forward. I was wiped out, and he laughed as he pulled me onto my bed with him. We were a tangle of limbs and laughter, trying to catch our breath.

Trying to not let reality crash the party.

I wondered how awkward it was going to get, how we still had weeks of filming left to do, and how this was a really bad, terrible idea.

Chase laughed. "That was the best thing ever."

I snorted, because of course he would think that. Of course optimistic Chase would think it was awesome, while pessimistic me was waiting for the dark cloud to roll in.

But I was too blissed out and boneless to care in that moment though.

"You think I have a pretty mouth," he added.

I gave him a shove, fighting to keep my eyes open. "Pretty and talented."

Did I just say that out loud?

Yep.

He laughed. "Well, that's the quickest I've ever come, just so you know. I normally have better endurance."

"Sure."

"It's true. You'll see. Next time, I'll last way longer."

"Next time?"

"There is going to be so many next times. Soooo many. Like, an infinite number of next times."

"Infinite. That's a lot."

He pulled back to look at my face. "Are you falling asleep?"

"You took my brain offline. Can't stay awake."

Chase laughed. "Well, no sleeping yet. We have an infinite number of next times to achieve, starting tonight."

I half laughed, half groaned, my eyes closing. "I thought an orgasm might shut you up for a bit, but apparently not."

"You shut me up with your dick earlier. That has to count."

I snorted. "True."

"Wanna do it again? I'm totally down. Your dick is delicious."

I groaned. God almighty. "Might need a few minutes."

The truth was, my dick was still out of my jeans and still half interested.

Chase rolled us over, putting me on my back so he could look down at me. "I don't. I'm ready to go again now." The best part of being a young college dude who hadn't been laid in far too long was the no-waiting time.

I looked down between us, and sure enough, his dick was semihard, hanging down toward mine. He lowered down until they touched, making mine twitch. He grinned at me, like the freaking devil, then pressed his dick to mine and rolled his hips.

Yeah. My waiting time wasn't too long either, apparently.

"You're sexy as fuck when you come," he murmured. "I wanna see it again." Then he dropped his weight on top of me, crushing his mouth to mine. He sank his tongue into my mouth, kissing me deep, invading my senses. My hands immediately went to his hair, pulling him closer.

I was lost to his kiss. The way his tongue tangled with mine, how he sucked and pulled my bottom lip between his. He had his eyes closed, kissing me like this meant something.

Like I meant something.

And he kept rolling his hips, rubbing against me, rutting, and soon he was moaning again.

That sound...

It did something to me.

It lit a fire in me like no one else ever had.

Resting on one elbow, he fumbled his hand between us, trying to get both our cocks in his hand. "Fuck," he hissed.

"Here, let me," I said, taking over. I wrapped my fingers around us both, and he thrust into my fist, sliding against me. He kissed down my neck, sucking and groaning, shuddering with each thrust.

"Fuck, this is so good," he breathed. Then he pushed up off me, his hands beside my shoulders so he could watch our dicks sliding through my fist. "Oh, holy fuck."

It was a glorious sight. So hot the way our cockheads peeked through my fist, leaking precome. Him, me, both of us together, making the slide wet. The slick sound was obscene.

I groaned. "So fucking hot."

Chase looked down at me, his eyes locked on mine then. Ablaze with desire and honesty, there was nowhere to hide.

His mouth fell open and he gasped, his eyes rolled, and he shuddered. "Gonna come again," he breathed, and his cock was so hard, so swollen, throbbing, pulsing against mine.

The pleasure was exquisite.

"Fuck, yes," I whispered. "Come. I wanna see you come."

He thrust hard, every muscle in his torso straining, his eyes closed, and his teeth clenched as his orgasm took hold.

He pulsed in my hand, against my cock, and it tripped me over the edge with him. Waves of bliss and fire ripped through me and I came, shooting come over my hand and onto my belly.

Tremors racked me, every nerve ending alight with pleasure.

I was too wiped, too blissed out to worry about reality or the consequences.

Chase collapsed on top of me, smearing our come between us, his breaths on my neck. "That was so fucking hot," he panted. "Two down, an infinite number of times to go."

I snorted, still too wiped out to speak, let alone argue.

Would I even argue?

Probably. There were a thousand reasons why this was a terrible idea, I just couldn't seem to think of any. Just not right now.

He rolled us onto our sides, and when I tried to pull away, he pulled me harder against him, throwing his leg over my hip as well. "Nope. You're staying right here. Need to cuddle."

"Has anyone ever told you you're needy?"

"Nope. Never needed to cuddle before, so shut up and enjoy it."

I snorted again. "How is it possible that you can make me come twice and I still find you annoying?"

He smiled, his eyes closed. "It's a special skill."

I gave up fighting it and sank into the boneless feeling. "Fucking hell."

"Yep, for sure. Next time you will."

"Next time I will what?"

"Fuck me."

I froze. "Oh, I will, will I?"

His smile became that smirk that both irritated and thrilled me. Then he pulled me in close, not even opening his eyes. "Yep. Definitely. It'll be amazing."

I was about to argue that. Not the amazing part, but the fact he assumed I would. I mean, did I want to? Would I fuck him if he asked?

Uh, hell fucking yes you would.

When I didn't argue, he chuckled and wiggled. "You thinking about it right now? What it's gonna be like to have your dick inside me?"

He gave him a shove. "Christ, shut up."

He squeezed me as he chuckled. "You totally are."

I sighed, hating how much I liked being with him like this. And hating how much I was now thinking about having my dick inside him.

My dick made its best attempt at agreeing but it gave up, and so did I.

I closed my eyes, relaxing into his arms. "You're so annoying."

2

THE NEXT MORNING, I was to meet Chase in the dining hall for breakfast with the crew. Cameras would be there; that was to be expected.

I didn't expect the crowd though.

And I didn't expect to be standing in the buffet line and

have Chase slip his arms around me from behind, his lips at my ear. "Morning."

I'd wondered how we'd fare this morning.

Would it be awkward? Would last night have ruined things between us? The comfortable ease strained now that we'd . . .

I should have known he'd have no concept of awkward. Much like he had no concept of personal space when it came to me.

"Are the cameras on us?" I whispered, not turning around.

"Don't know. Don't care," he replied, then kissed the spot under my ear that made me gasp. "Hmm," he chuckled. "Weak spot unlocked."

I sighed and tried to shake him off, but that just made him hold me tighter, his chin on my shoulder. "Can you grab a yogurt for me? And some fruit. Oh, and a juice. And maybe some toast."

I resisted groaning and did what he asked.

He was such a pain.

I took our tray over to the cast table in the corner, where all the cast were, where the cameras were focused. And I knew then that I had to leave Amos behind and become Elijah.

The Elijah who loved the fact that Dominic, aka Chase, was all handsy and clingy.

Was there a difference between my character and me?

I wasn't sure.

"Where did you two run off to last night?" Phoebe asked, smiling with her straw to her lips.

"Important boyfriend business," Chase said. I mean, Dominic.

Goddammit.

They all laughed, and Jess eyed me strangely. "Elijah, are you blushing?"

Shit.

"No. I'm a little sunburned," I replied, feeling my burning cheeks.

Chase leaned into me and laughed. "So, how did *Jaws* end?" he asked, and chatter around the table began.

After yesterday, we'd discussed some topics for small talk and banter and the plot points we needed to bring up in casual conversation, and it made the ad-libbing flow so much easier, and thankfully we had a seamless scene until it was time to go to class.

Today's filming would involve Max and Holly's story arc, and Jess and Phoebe, so Chase and I were off the hook.

I mean, we'd still have Daniel and Bridgette following us with their cameras, but mostly for small-scene stuff.

I slid the tray into the receptacle and Chase took my hand, smiling as he pulled me out the door. People were watching—some had their phones out and were filming us, which was stupid.

"You'd think they'd have something better to do," I murmured.

Chase laughed. "You didn't see? You really need to start checking the socials."

"See what?" God, did I even want to know?

"Uh, there's footage and photos of us last night online."

I stopped walking, feeling cold all over. "Of where?"

He snorted. "On the beach, silly. Where else would they

have footage from? Got cameras set up in your room I don't know about?"

I rolled my eyes. "You could have led with that." I put my hand to my heart. "Jeez."

He laughed and pulled me a little closer by our joined hands. "Kissing on the beach. It's dark and grainy, but it's us."

"Fuck."

"Not yet."

I groaned. "Really?"

"Oh, yes."

I ignored the innuendo, the hint, the look in his eyes. "Well, I guess it's good for the show or whatever."

Smiling, he bit into his bottom lip. "It was good for me too."

Oh my god, he was so annoying.

"I have to go to class," I said.

He stepped in close, his eyes on my mouth. "I'm going to kiss you, okay?"

I could see Daniel out of the corner of my eye, his camera on us. "Okay."

Chase slid his hand up to my neck, to my jaw, and pulled me in for a kiss. Slow, tender, lips open enough but no tongue. It was incredibly sweet and a little bit hot.

He broke the kiss, and with a groan he put his forehead on my shoulder, his hand on my ass. "Gonna be hard all day."

I shoved him and he took a few steps back, laughing as he turned to run off to his class. I stood there, gripping my backpack strap, annoyed. With a huff, I turned and walked to class.

Ignoring how people looked at me, ignoring the smiles and hellos from people who never knew I existed before now.

I wasn't interested in any of their fake attention.

Chase might love it, the way people fawned all over him, but I didn't have any time for it.

I took my seat in class and ignored it all.

"Doesn't it annoy you?" Mason asked me. I was two minutes into my shift at the Bean Necessities. I liked Mason. I'd worked with him a bit over the last two years, and maybe I'd even go so far as to call him a friend. "You don't seem the type to like the attention."

I smiled because yeah, he knew me that well at least. "Yep. Not a fan."

"Yet you're an actor," he said. "How are ya gonna handle making it to the big-time fame of Hollywood?"

"I'll be the recluse kind of actor."

"The kind that look homeless when they buy coffee in LA?"

"Yep. That's the plan."

He laughed. Then when the door opened and customers walked in, he sighed. "Well, don't look now but your fellow cast and crew are here."

I looked up, and sure enough, Max and Holly came in, their camera duo with them.

"I'll take their table," I said. Then I gestured toward

them. "Unless you want to be on camera for your fifteen minutes of fame."

He made a face. "No thanks. All yours."

I grabbed the notepad and went over to Max and Holly's table, and honestly, if they were going for an awkward first date, they were nailing it.

"Hey guys, what brings you in?" I asked.

They both lit up when they saw me, like I was their lifeline. "Oh hey, Elijah," Max said. "Just grabbing coffee."

"Great place to do that," I said, trying to save the scene.

"Where's Dominic?" Holly asked.

"He was gonna hit the gym and pool after class," I said. I didn't really have a clue but that sounded like a safe assumption.

"Explains where he gets his physique from," Holly said.

And I was hit with flashes of his naked torso above me, every muscle taut as he fucked my hand. The way he moaned, and his face when he came . . .

So then of course I blushed. "Ah, yeah. Something like that."

They both laughed.

I cleared my throat. "What can I get for you?"

I took their order and went back to the counter, distracting myself with work and keeping myself busy.

He was really beginning to mess with my head. He—Chase, Dominic. Both of them.

Mostly Chase.

I kept picturing him, seeing his stupidly handsome face in my mind, thinking about what we'd done. Trying to tell myself to regret it but not quite being able to . . .

"Your boyfriend's here," Mason murmured beside me. It was almost closing time, and I'd been so distracted . . .

I looked up, and sure enough, there was Chase, walking through the door with that smile that I hated.

Hate that you don't hate it . . .

And Daniel was right behind him.

Great.

"Hey," he said, coming up to the counter. "I was hoping I could grab a takeout order." He raised his hand to my height. "He's about this tall, dark hair, gorgeous, a little moody. Killer smile."

I couldn't help it.

I freaking smiled, and then I got mad at myself for falling for it.

"You'll need to wait," I replied. "He's busy for another—" I checked the time. "—twenty minutes."

"It's okay. I can wait."

I handed him the dirty-cup tub. "If you're gonna wait, you're gonna help."

He grumbled, but took the hint and went and cleared the last table of cups and plates, then he waited by the door for us to finish.

"Night, guys," Mason called out as we were leaving.

Then it was just me and Chase . . .

And Daniel with his camera.

I wanted to sigh and complain, but this was acting. Method acting, at that. Immersing myself into my character.

Chase picked a speck of lint off my shirt and gave me a soft smile that totally should not have made my stomach swoop. "Wanna come back to my place?" he asked, his voice low and inviting.

"Not really," I replied. When his eyes gave me a what-the-hell look, I followed it with, "Will your housemates be there?"

He grinned and took my hand, all but pulling me toward my dorm. "Oh, thank god. I was hoping you'd say that."

I laughed. "Don't you have friends to hang out with or something?"

"But what we do together and what you did to me last night is way more fun."

Oh my god.

Daniel got that on camera.

He's acting. This is for the show.

Right. Acting.

Yes, Amos. You should try it sometime. Be Elijah. What would Elijah say right now?

"Oh, do we still have your mom's birthday thing this weekend?" I squeezed his hand, hoping he'd roll with it. Discussing plans and family is what boyfriends of one year would do, right?

"Shoot. I forgot about that. I still haven't gotten her anything. We'll need to go shopping some time."

"Correction. You'll need to go shopping some time."

"But you have better taste than me."

"Well, that is true."

"I mean, you chose me so clearly you have exceptional taste."

"You're so full of yourself."

"Gonna be full of you later."

I tripped over my feet and he laughed as he kept me from stumbling. A group of guys crossed the road ahead of us. "Oh, isn't that your ex up there?" he whispered.

I tried to make out the figures. "I dunno. Why?"

Jeez. Was that Dominic asking or Chase?

We walked up the steps to the dorm entrance, and once inside, we caught a glimpse of Taylah and Georgia coming our way. "Woah," Chase said, pulling me toward the elevator. "Speaking of exes."

We dashed into the elevator, Daniel slipping in behind us. The elevator was small, and Chase leaned against the back wall, tugging me closer. "That was close."

Chase had a heated look in his eyes, his smirk that made weaker people crumble. And maybe I would have if Daniel wasn't right beside us, filming it all.

Were we doing this? Were we going to go that far for this show, on camera?

Clearly seeing the war in my gaze, Chase chuckled and pulled me in, our hips colliding, just as the elevator dinged and the doors opened.

"Saved by the bell," Chase said, then led me by the hand down the hall to my door.

Daniel was right behind us and I fumbled getting the key into the lock, and Chase laughed. "In a hurry?"

I growled at him, pushed open the door, shoved Chase up against the wall, and slammed the door shut, right in the camera's face.

It would be a great shot for the show. Kinda getting hot and heavy, desperate even, without actually doing anything.

But I still had Chase pressed up against the wall. His smirk was filthy, the erection in his shorts not helping at all.

"Camera's gone," he whispered, sliding his hand down over my ass and holding me right where I was. "You can let go of me now."

"You're the one holding me," I murmured. Then I took his hand and pinned it to the wall above his head.

His nostrils flared and his eyes darkened, and he hitched his leg up around my hip so I could press him against the wall even harder. "Fuck yes," he said. "I can't stop thinking about what we did. What you did to me. I want you to do it again. I want more. I want it to last for hours."

Fucking hell.

I crushed my lips to his, dipping my tongue into his mouth, deep and hard. He tried to pull his hand down, but I kept it pinned above his head and he groaned, rolling his hips, seeking friction.

Then he whined, and the sound set fire to my bones.

I let go of his hand so I could grab his ass, and I rubbed my hard-on against his as I devoured his mouth. His hands found my hair and he tried to climb me, tried to lift his other leg.

But he was bigger than me, stronger and heavier, and there was no way I could hold him.

So I backed up, pulling his shirt and pushing him onto my bed. I wasted no time following him onto the mattress, and as soon as I was between his legs, he lifted both knees to his chest.

Letting my hips fall right where he wanted me, like he was offering himself to me. If we were naked, I could push into him, just like this . . .

Just like he wanted.

Christ, he really was a bottom.

I wasn't sure why I'd doubted that, but then he began to rock and whine. He took my face in his hands and pulled me back, his eyes dark and his full lips red and swollen. "I wasn't kidding before. I want to be full of you. Tonight. Now. It's all I can think about since last night. Knowing how good you feel, I want you to fuck me. Please, say you'll fuck me."

I shivered as his words danced up my spine, electric fingers making it impossible to say no.

Not that I was ever going to say no.

"Are you sure?" I asked.

"Fuck, don't make me beg."

I smiled at that, kissing him, slower this time. Teasing and tasting his tongue and slipping my hand down to palm his dick. His back arched and he hissed. "Fuck. Please."

Oh god, that's hot.

I pulled back, resting on my haunches. His eyes shot open, angry . . . until he saw me smiling at him. "In a hurry?"

He snarled at me, which was funny as hell until I pulled his shorts down and his underwear, leaving him exposed to me. His thick cock lay toward his hip, his balls tight.

He sat up, six-pack bulging as he pulled his shirt over his head and tossed it. "Your turn."

I climbed off the bed and kicked off my Chucks, pulled my shirt off, then faced him as I popped the button on my fly. I watched as he enjoyed the show of me pulling my dick out and stepping out of my jeans. I grabbed the lube from the top drawer and found a condom—thank fuck—it'd been a while since I'd needed them. I tossed them on the bed, then took my place back between his legs.

He looked so fucking hot, lying there, waiting for me.

Chase Soria, of all people.

He bent one knee, his foot flat on the bed, and stroked his cock. "You like what you see," he murmured. "Don't try to deny it. I can see how you look at me."

I leaned over him, my hand on the mattress beside his head. "Don't flatter yourself," I said. I kneed his thighs apart and his nostrils flared, his eyes dark. But as soon as I cupped his balls and began to tug on them, the cockiness was gone and the desperate, close-to-begging Chase was back.

"Oh fuck. Don't make me come yet."

I smiled down at him before I kissed him, licking his tongue. I tweaked his nipple, making him jerk in surprise. "Ow."

I laughed, needing a moment of clarity. To calm down, to make this good for him. To make this about him.

I took the lube and slicked my finger, rubbing his hole. He instinctively lifted both legs. So fucking easy. I fucked him with just the fingertip, then to my knuckle, then more lube and a second finger.

"Oh fuck. Don't tease me, please. I just need to feel you."

God, if he kept talking like that, I was going to last one minute. I was thanking my stars that he'd made me come twice yesterday, otherwise this'd already be over.

I rolled the condom on, hissing as I smeared lube over myself. I was so ready for this . . .

With my hands on the backs of his thighs, I pushed his legs up to his chest, positioned myself at his entrance, and pressed in. Just the tip, in and out, until there was no resistance. And I watched it in his eyes when I pushed the head in. The pop of surprise when I breached him and slowly sank in.

Slow, inch by painful inch.

Chase's eyes rolled back as his eyelids closed, his mouth open. "Fu-uck," he said, his breath hitching.

So I took his cock in my hand and began to gently stroke him. He'd softened a little, but with a few deep breaths and a few strokes, he relaxed, and only then did I begin to move.

Stroking him in time with my thrusts. As slow as I could manage.

His hole was tight and hot, the warmth drawing me deeper inside him. I tried not to think about how good he felt.

I made myself not think about how good he felt.

How amazing he felt.

Like nothing I'd ever felt.

I dropped to one elbow beside his face and kissed him. Open mouths and lazy tongues, shuddering with restraint as I pulled out only to slide back in, deeper, further, hotter.

Better.

"I'm not gonna last," I bit out, rolling my hips. "You feel too good. Fuck."

He groaned, long and loud, and his hand went between us, stroking himself harder and faster. So I fucked him the same way.

Harder, faster.

I was so close, reaching the point of no return. I couldn't hold it back now. I was too far gone. Too lost to the ecstasy, and I drove up into him with a strangled cry as my orgasm ripped through me, and I came into the condom.

He gripped my ass and kept pulling me in, deeper, rocking his hips to take it. Every pulse, every spurt.

"Oh fuck, yes," he said, and I realized through my hazy brain that he was stroking himself. I tried to pull out but he stopped me. "Stay inside me. I'm so close."

So I took over his ministrations, drove my sensitive cock in harder, and his whole body clenched, his back arched, and he threw his head back as he came, shooting a stream of come onto his abs.

"Fuuuuuuuck," he groaned, collapsing and twitching, then laughing. "Fuck."

I pulled out of him then, and he shuddered at the loss. I discarded the condom and he grabbed me blindly, pulling me in for a cuddle.

Which I was beginning to like.

We lay in each other's arms, panting, our chests heaving.

I really wasn't sure what *that* was or why it felt so different with him. It wasn't just sex. It was mind-blowing and better than anything I'd ever experienced with anyone else.

My orgasm-addled brain tried to connect the dots but came up with nothing.

It was better because it just was. No reason necessary.

No. It was better because it was with Chase Soria and you've wanted him for years, and he's fucking gorgeous and you like him, and he took your dick like a champion. And you like him.

And you like him.

I frowned at the stupid voice in my head—that was clearly just on some euphoric orgasm high—and told it to shut up and mind its own damn business.

"I should get something to clean you up," I mumbled.

He tightened his arms around me. "No," he whined, his eyes still closed. "Sleep."

So I gave up fighting it and closed my eyes with a sigh, and all of a sudden, sleep sounded like a really good idea.

2

"Wake up." Someone shook my shoulder. "Waaaaaake up, sexy sleepyhead."

I cracked one eye open. It was Chase, of course, his face far too close to mine, his eyes bright and his smile wide, even in the dark.

"What is it?" I asked, confused.

"I'm hungry."

I'm hungry...

I repeated that over and over in my head a few times. Still couldn't get it to make much sense. "What?"

"I'm hungry."

"What are you telling me for?" I was annoyed now. "What time is it?"

"Dunno. Midnight, probably. Maybe one."

Jesus H. Christ.

"What the hell did you wake me up for? I was having the best sleep ever."

"Because I'm hungry. And you were having the best sleep ever because we had the best sex ever."

I remembered . . . how I sank inside him . . . his face when he came.

Fuck.

"I need to shower. I'm covered in crusty jizz."

That kinda woke me up. Because I hadn't taken care of him afterward at all. "Oh, let me get up," I said, trying to roll over and not roll off the bed. I stood up, helping him stand as well. "Are you . . . do you feel okay?"

"I feel great," he said, giving me that smile . . . that certain smile that kickstarted my heart. "Actually, I feel better than great." Then he froze and his eyes met mine. "No, actually, I feel hungry."

I shoved my towel at him and pushed him toward my shower. "Go. I'll find you something."

Something to wear. Something to eat. I wasn't sure.

I pulled on some underwear and went through my stash of snacks. I found him a bag of chips. Figuring he'd probably be going home, so he could eat them on the way.

He came back out, hung my towel up, then got back into my bed, stark naked.

"What are you doing?"

"Correction. What are *we* doing. We," he said, "are gonna watch one episode of *Rick and Morty* while I have a little snacky snack." He opened his hands for the bag of chips. "Gimme gimme."

I tossed them at him. "You're so annoying."

He patted the bed. "Come on." Then he noticed . . . "Why'd you get dressed."

"I hardly call putting on underwear getting dressed."

He shoved a chip in his mouth. "Start the show and get in here. Big spoon or little spoon?"

"The spoon that sleeps while the other spoon gets crumbs in my bed."

He laughed. "Little spoon you are."

I sat on the edge of my bed, annoyed at being woken up, annoyed at him eating in my bed, annoyed at him being so damned cute.

"You're so annoying."

"Shh, it's starting."

He demolished the chips, then half the bottle of water from my nightstand, and was sound asleep before the credits rolled.

In my bed, as the big spoon. His huge body wrapped around me, his beautiful face almost surreal in the moonlight with his head on my pillow.

So annoying.

"But that's my favorite shirt," I said, taking it out of his hand.

"But that's why I chose it."

It was bad enough he'd spent the entire night, slept in my bed, and woke me up this morning by sucking my dick. It was also bad enough that I'd made him straddle me so I could suck his.

But now he wanted to wear my favorite shirt. "It's not a replica. It's an actual vintage Grateful Dead shirt."

He snatched it back and pulled it over his head. "Even better."

"God, I hate you."

He laughed. "Ah, no you don't. Pretty sure you saying 'get up here and feed me your dick' is the opposite of hate. And then giving me a blow job like you're winning gold at the suck-a-pea-through-a-straw Olympics—"

"Shut up. I did not say get up here and feed me your dick."

He scoffed. "You did so! I mean, it was right after I made you come so hard you almost blacked out, so that probably explains why you don't remember."

I sighed, trying for any patience the universe could spare me.

"And anyway, do you want me to leave your room wearing the same clothes I wore yesterday?" He raised an eyebrow. "Now, I'll gladly do the walk of shame—"

I shoved his bag against his chest. "Christ, do you ever shut up?"

He laughed, pulled the door open, and held it for me. "Only when you shove your dick in my mouth."

I stood there, stunned.

"Morning," Daniel said brightly, clearly amused.

Chase stuck his head around the door, his eyes comically wide, and Daniel lifted his camera. "Wanna say that again so I can get it on the record."

I gave Chase a shove out of my room and pulled the door closed. "Sorry. He was being ... himself."

Chase put his arm around my waist and gave me a squeeze. "But baby, I do love it when you shove your—"

I shoved him toward the stairs. "Please fall down them. I'll tell people it was an accident."

Daniel stopped walking, I realized, to start filming. And Chase was quick to put his arm around my shoulder and whispered so Daniel couldn't hear. "Now, I know we've already eaten this morning, but what do you want for a second breakfast?"

"You are so crass," I said, but god help me, I couldn't help but smile. Waking up to a BJ and then returning it was an awesome way to start the day, despite the fact it was with the most annoying person on the planet.

We walked to the dining hall, Chase's arm around my shoulder, and he was smiling with a spring in his step.

"I think sex makes you more annoying," I mumbled.

He laughed as he held the door for me and spoke loud enough for everyone to hear. "Baby, you have no idea."

I went to the table where everyone sat, ignoring their smiles aimed at me. "Just out of curiosity," I asked, throwing my bag onto my chair. "Can we sell boyfriends on eBay?"

Max laughed and spoke around a mouthful of blueberry muffin. "Nope. Try Craigslist."

"Or Grindr," Jess added with a wink. "You'd get good money for him there."

"Hey," Chase said. "I heard that." He dumped his bag near mine and slid his hand along the small of my back. "Want me to grab you something?"

I was a little taken aback by his offer. I wasn't used to having someone ask or offer or even think of me.

"Sure. Coffee and a blueberry muffin would be great." Max's had looked good before he shoved it in his mouth. "Thanks."

I dumped our bags on the ground and sat down, ignoring the smiles aimed at us. And the crowd watching, who were, thankfully, mostly silent.

I did notice that some students were oblivious to our filming now and just carried on about their day, which was good. Discussion around the table turned to our finals and graduating, which were fabricated for the purpose of filming.

After all, what else did college students aim for?

We had our plot points to keep prodding along as secondary points of interest. Though our relationships were the main focus.

Each pairing was deliberately slated at different stages of their relationship, and each had their issues to work through, except Chase and me. Dominic and Elijah were the established couple. Stupidly happy and in love.

Emphasis on the stupid part.

Because being seniors in college and being in love was ridiculous enough. But finding your forever-love?

It was stupid.

Right?

Chase slid the tray onto the table and handed me my coffee. "Here, babe. Careful, it's hot."

I wasn't sure when or why this *babe* or *baby* business had started, and I had to remind myself that Elijah loved the terms of endearment.

"They only had apple muffins and chocolate muffins left, so I got you both," he said. "I'll have whichever one you don't want."

Oh.

Well, that was kinda sweet.

"Thanks."

I opted for the apple, for no other reason than I knew he loved chocolate muffins, and his smile and shoulder-nudge when I left him the chocolate muffin told me I'd made the right call.

"Do you work tonight?" he asked quietly.

I nodded. "Yeah. Four till close."

He made a face. "Tate and Jimmy asked me to go with them to the bar tonight." He pulled the bottom off his muffin. "But if you're working—"

"You should go with them," I said, pulling the bottom off my muffin too. "You haven't seen them much lately."

"Yeah, but you—"

"I'll be fine. In fact, a night by myself'd be nice."

He gasped and frowned. "What are you saying?"

"Nothing. Just a night by myself would be nice. I have to work, and when I get home, I need to hit the books."

"I could help you study."

I snorted. "Yeah. Our definitions of *help* are wide and varied. And maybe having my bed to myself tonight means I might actually get some sleep."

Someone cleared their throat, and Chase and I both turned to the table. I'd kinda forgotten where we were, being caught in one of our private conversations again, and everyone was staring at us, cameras rolling.

Shit.

Chase, completely unfazed, laughed. "He hogs the bed anyway."

I shot him a look. "Oh please. You . . ."

I trailed off because I realized saying anything incriminated me even further.

He popped some muffin in his mouth, smiling as he chewed. "You were saying? I what?"

"You need to shove more muffin into your mouth and stop talking."

Chase laughed again, his eyes alight. I swear, the more I insulted him, the more he liked it.

"I was just saying," Didi said, signaling with her eyes for us to play along. "There's a party on Saturday night."

"Oh," Chase said. "We can't. We have a dinner thing for my mom's birthday."

Which I'd forgotten all about. I really needed to start a calendar for all of Elijah and Dominic's fake appointments.

"Oh yes, we do, that's right," I said. "Did you get her a gift yet?"

"No, because you wouldn't come with me," he whined.

"I had to work."

"We'll have to go tomorrow," he declared.

I wasn't going shopping with him, in character as Elijah or as myself. Absolutely no way. Uh-uh. Hell no.

Chase grinned and went back to his muffin. "Cool. We can go after class."

Filming wrapped up and talk around the table turned to the party, which I still wasn't sure whether it was real or fabricated for the sake of filming. I didn't care either way because I wouldn't be going.

I couldn't help but notice that Max looked sullen and Holly looked frosty. Their chemistry wasn't great, and while I understood why—real-life relationship pressures—it kinda made it hard for all of us.

I hadn't paid much attention to any of the social media hype, but word was that Max and Holly's on-screen relationship was an issue between the shippers and the people who knew them in real life.

It had to suck especially that Holly's friends and Max's friends knew the reality. And because they were all friends with Max's girlfriend Jenna.

I was just very grateful that Chase didn't have a boyfriend or girlfriend that was upset with me.

We had the audience's full support.

Max and Holly didn't. Which, yes, sucked for them, but having viewers invested and getting the students of Franklin U to support *all of us* was paramount. And social media was an instant indicator.

If we sucked, if the show was lame, we'd get told.

In no uncertain terms.

And it wasn't really a fear of failure or embarrassing ourselves in front of our friends that filled me with dread.

Not being convincing enough. It was not being *good* enough. That's what I feared most.

Any story or script can be convincing with the right actor, and a failure to deliver it was a failure on the actor's part, right?

"Whatcha thinking about?" Chase murmured. "Or did the table make you mad?"

The table?

"Huh?"

"You're frowning at the table." Then he weaseled his way in and shoved his stupidly attractive face right in front of me, with that stupidly attractive grin. "Is that better?"

"Remarkably worse."

He snorted but made no attempt to move. "I know what it is," he said. "You're mad at yourself for telling me you don't want to see me tonight. That's it, isn't it?"

"One hundred percent incorrect. In fact, that is so

wrong, I think the CDC wants to examine it for stupidity fusion proteins. There might be hope of a vaccine."

Chase scowled at me. "Now, I did my very best to forget everything I was forced to learn in biology, but did you call me stupid?"

Yes.

I sighed. "No. Sorry."

He put his hand over my heart, looking me right in the eyes. "You sure you're okay?"

I nodded, and so help me god, he made me smile. He also made my heart feel too big and my blood run too warm. That was beginning to feel like emotions.

Or maybe it was encephalitis.

I palmed my forehead to feel for a fever. Nope. It must be emotions. "I'm fine. Just thinking."

He pulled me a little closer, so I was almost standing between his legs. "About?"

There was no way I was telling him I worried we weren't being convincing enough, because . . . because if we were any more convincing, we wouldn't be acting.

I wasn't even sure we were at this point.

And I didn't want to think about that . . .

"I was just thinking about how mad I am at myself for telling you I don't want to see you tonight."

He grinned. "I knew it!"

I chuckled, and with his hands on my hips, he pulled me snug against him. "What are you doing?" I murmured. We were still in the dining hall for god's sake. Daniel was talking to Deirdre, so the camera wasn't on us, but there were other eyes on us. And my dick liked being in between his legs with him looking at me with his perfect face and perfect, full pink lips. "This is a dangerous game."

He laughed. "It's why I'm playing it. So you'll want me to stay at your place tonight."

I sighed, resisting the urge to roll my eyes. "Do you not think we've seen enough of each other this week?"

He inhaled deeply, as if he was considering the question. "No." Then he murmured, "I'd like to see a whole lot more of you. Naked, preferably."

I groaned but stood my ground. Because he was so used to getting what he wanted, I couldn't let him win on principle. No matter how much I liked the idea of being naked with him. "No." I picked up my bag and tossed his into his lap. "I'm working. Go hang out with your friends. I'll see you tomorrow night."

He whined. "But babe." He caught up to me, slung his arm around my shoulder so he could whine some more.

I pushed him into the door and went to class.

2

For all the good standing my ground did me, I got back to my room after work, showered, and sat down with my books to study when there was a knock at my door.

I considered not answering it, considering the late hour, but with a long-suffering sigh and against my better judgment, I opened the door.

Chase stood there, leaning against the door frame, a bit tipsy, wearing the cutest pouty smile that I had zero defense against.

"I tried," he said.

"You tried what?"

"To not see you. To not come here. And I tried to walk home, but my feet took me here." He looked down at his feet as if *they* were the problem. Then he pointed down the hall. "And up the stairs. The stairs, Amos. I took the stairs. And now I'm here."

Okay, maybe a little more than tipsy.

"And how much have you had to drink?"

"Enough." He laughed. "Not a full sesh. More like a half-sesh. It's very important to contribute to the socio-economic prosperity of the local liquor establishment. Don't you think?"

Why was I smiling at him?

I had to make myself stop.

"Jimmy and Tate wanted me to stay for a full session but . . ." He shook his head. "I didn't want that. Because I kept thinking of you. And now I'm here."

I stared at him.

"I tried not to," he added. "Don't be mad at me. I don't like it when you're mad at me."

He kept thinking of me.

How could I possibly be mad?

"I'm not mad," I said quietly. "Infuriated and annoyed. I was about to study."

He grinned. "So can I come in? I promise I'll be quiet."

"You don't know how to be quiet."

"You can study and I'll watch *Rick and Morty* and eat some of your chips. I know you have a stash."

I was just impressed that he asked permission to enter

instead of trying to use that damn grin and maybe even manhandle me into my room. But nope. He asked.

I stood aside, and god help me, the smile he gave me. "I'll be good, I swear."

He wasn't good.

He wasn't quiet.

He didn't behave himself.

I didn't get much studying done, but the orgasms were amazing.

Chapter Thirteen
Chase

Jimmy and Tate could try to rattle me all they liked. I was done pretending and I was done trying to hide it. And they could tease me all night, I didn't care.

Hell, I probably deserved it.

For years I'd sprouted my anti-boyfriend rhetoric. For years I'd laughed at them and told them they were a special kind of stupid for wanting to get tied down to one person.

We were in college, for fuck's sake.

We were supposed to be sowing wild oats and playing the field and whatever godawful clichés my parents would use. We were young and it was our rite of passage to rack up a body count.

It was our duty to service anyone willing. And repeats were fine, as long as they understood that dating was not on the table.

No responsibilities, no obligation, no blame.

I'd been the preacher of this mantra for years.

And what was I now?

Whipped, according to Jimmy.

Who thought it was the funniest thing in the history of ever.

And I didn't even care.

All I could do was smile and agree because yes, I was.

And it was as pathetic and tragic as I'd always said it would be.

And it was also completely wonderful.

"He's a goner," Tate said, clinking his beer to mine. "RIP to the manwhore."

"Well," I amended, "I'm still a whore. It's just now with one person. And lemme tell you, he's fucking good at it."

Jimmy laughed. "I thought you were supposed to be acting."

"We are."

"So sex is part of the job?" Jimmy's eyes almost fell out of his head. "Hell, how do I sign up for that?"

I shook my head. "No, not like that. We are acting, but then in private, there are perks to having to be so handsy in public, right?"

"So it's not acting in private?" Tate tried to clarify. "So what are you, exactly? To each other."

"Boyfriends."

"In public," Jimmy nodded. "Yeah, we get that. But in private? I mean, what happens when the filming stops? What are you then?"

I . . . I didn't know.

I threw my bar coaster at him. "Don't ask me difficult questions, dickwad. It's your turn to hit the bar."

He'd laughed and slid off his stool and headed toward the bar. He got chatting with some guys there, and Tate gave me a nudge. "I think it's good," he said. "I'm happy for you."

"I'm happy for me too."

"Maybe just ask Amos what happens when the filming stops."

I sighed and drained my bottle. Asking Amos that was not a conversation I wanted to have. I just wanted to enjoy the now, to enjoy being with him, being boyfriends, without reality crushing it.

And I'd tried to enjoy my night with the guys, drinking and talking shit. But after that conversation about Amos, my mind kept going back to him.

About what we were.

Because we weren't just acting. Well, I wasn't. And we weren't just college kids. We were almost out of college, as grown-ass adults in the real world, and maybe—just fucking maybe—Amos was someone I could see myself being with.

In the real world.

I wouldn't mind annoying him every day as live-in boyfriends as we went off to LA to chase our dreams on the silver screen.

Like I wasn't getting way ahead of myself on that front.

Just like how I did honestly try to go home when I left the bar but somehow found myself knocking on Amos's door.

He was so fucking cute, the way he tried not to smile.

He was also really fucking hot, the way he fisted my hair as he came down my throat. And the way he returned the favor, of course. Then the way he let me snuggle in and sleep, all wrapped around him, and with a few beers under my belt, I slept like a log.

For some reason, I was awake before Amos, and by the time he got out of the shower, I was dressed and ready.

He stopped when he saw me. "That's my shirt. Again."

"Correct."

"When am I getting the other one back that you stole?"

"I didn't steal it. I borrowed it. And you can get both shirts back after you spend the night at my place."

"That's blackmail. And coercion. And bribery."

I grinned at him. "I know. But it works. Come on, I'm starving." I shoved his bag at him and went to the door. "Why are you so grumpy today?"

"Because you snored all night, that's why. And you hog the bed. And you're clingy. It's like sleeping with an octopus."

I laughed as I pulled the door open . . . and there was Daniel, camera rolling. "Thought I'd find you here," he said. "Who sleeps like an octopus?"

Amos brushed past me. "He does. With magnetic tentacles that strangle me all night."

I slung my arm around him as we began our way down the stairs. "And you love every minute."

Amos leveled a glare at me that told me in no uncertain terms that he did, in fact, not love every minute. "I'm sorry, babe. I'll make it up to you. What do you want for breakfast?"

"To be left alone."

"Well, sure. I can do that. If being alone includes me."

He sighed. "You're insufferable."

"Some people would call me cute or charming."

"They don't know you like I do."

"No, they do not. No one knows me like you do."

I wasn't sure why I said that, but once the words were out, I realized it was the truth.

Amos glanced my way and sighed, and as I held the door for him into the dining hall, he rolled his eyes. But he also kinda smiled, so I was taking it as a win.

He went to the table where the others were, and I went in search of coffee and those muffins he liked, and once I'd secured the goods, I slid into the seat beside him.

He was now watching something on his phone while everyone watched him. And then I realized what he was actually watching.

Me, being filmed at the bar last night.

Jimmy calling me "totally fucking whipped" as I, clearly drunk and all smiles, flipped him the bird before walking out. Jimmy roared laughing, then looked right at the camera and said, "That idiot is so in love and doesn't even know it."

To a view count of twenty thousand people and rising.

Amos hit Stop and turned his phone upside down on the table. His cheeks were pink, the tips of his ears too.

I was still trying to process what Jimmy had said . . .

I was going to kill him.

"Well, he's off my Christmas card list," I said, putting a cup of coffee in front of Amos. "Clearly he's full of shit. And he was drunk, and I hope he's so hung over he pukes for two days."

Amos's eyes met mine.

"What?" I said, putting his muffin in front of him. "He called me an idiot."

Like that was what we all took from what Jimmy had said.

Well, it's what I was taking from it while trying to pretend everyone at the table wasn't staring at me and that I wasn't embarrassed and dying inside.

"I got you blueberry," I mumbled. "I got chocolate if you want to swap."

"Okay, cut," Daniel said as he lowered his camera.

I groaned. "I'm sorry. And for what it's worth, you can show the police that video if they ask what reason I could possibly have had for killing Jimmy with my bare hands."

Deirdre came up to us, oblivious to the awkwardness. "Okay, guys, we'll meet in the rehearsal hall after lunch. One o'clock. Don't be late."

She gathered up the camera folks and they left, and there was silence at the table. "So," Jess said, looking right at me. "That was great for ratings."

I groaned and looked at everyone around the table. "If anyone else would like to embarrass themselves live on camera instead of me, that'd be great. I mean, I can't keep carrying the ratings like this. It's supposed to be a team effort. Someone else needs to pick up the slack. Come on, guys. Be fair."

They laughed but I couldn't ignore the way they looked between me and Amos. And the way he picked at his muffin and wouldn't look at me.

Goddammit.

So I shut my mouth for the next ten minutes and

managed to choke down half my breakfast, but really I just wanted to leave. I pushed my plate away and stood up. "Gotta go grab my stuff," I said to no one in particular and left.

I didn't look to see if Amos followed me, because I was pretty sure he wasn't following me, and I couldn't deal with turning around and finding out.

Or worse, to find Daniel following me and not Amos.

I couldn't deal with the cameras right now.

I all but jogged back to the house, ran up the steps, and through the front door, and found my least favorite best friend in the kitchen. He didn't look particularly healthy. "Oh good," I said. "Just the person I wanted to see."

Jimmy squinted at me. "Can we not yell? My head hurts."

"A head like yours should hurt."

"Now, I might be hungover and not thinking too clearly right now, but I'm picking up some negative vibes."

I inhaled deeply and tried counting on the exhale. I knew, rationally, it wasn't his fault. I had admitted to him that I had feelings for Amos, and just last night I was resigned to giving into those feelings. Maybe that was the beer doing the feeling for me, but still . . .

And Jimmy hadn't signed up to be filmed. I had. Not him, not Tate.

I growled and ran my hands through my hair. "Fucking hell."

"What's up?" Tate asked as he walked in. At least he was showered, and he was clearly faring better than Jimmy.

"Last night in the bar," I said, "someone was filming us, and Jimmy here decided to announce to the world that I'm in love with Amos. Twenty-something thousand people and climbing have watched it, and considering it's eight in the morning and not everyone is even out of bed yet, that's a pretty good view count."

Jimmy stood there with a stupid look on his face as if he was trying to remember . . . "Oh. Shit. I'm sorry. When did I say that?"

I sighed and shook my head. I wasn't mad at him. I was mad at me.

Tate had his phone out. "First thing that came up," he said, showing us the screen.

I didn't need to see it again.

Tate watched it through, then scrolled some comments. "People love it. Saying Jimmy's spitting facts. 'Drunk facts are honest facts.' That kinda stuff."

"It's not facts," I said, lying through my teeth.

"Well, it kinda is," Tate mumbled. "And if Amos has seen this, then now he knows, so is that a bad thing?"

I wasn't sure if Tate was stupid or incredibly smart.

Not that it mattered.

"It's bullshit and a very bad thing, because now Amos won't even look at me."

Tate stared at me, and when I looked at Jimmy, he was staring at me too. "Shit, man, I'm sorry."

I wanted to pull my hair out or punch something or scream. Or all three. I had a pent-up ball of rage inside me that I needed to let out, and there was only one way that I could do that.

"Fuck everything today. I'm hitting the pool."

Tate checked the time. "What about class?"

"I'm not going to class," I said, heading up to my room.

"And I'm not taking my phone. If anyone asks where I am, tell them you don't know."

Not that anyone would ask.

This. This shit feeling was why I'd stayed single all these years. Why no-dating, no-caring, had worked so well for me.

I grabbed my swim bag and jogged to the aquatic center, keeping my head down and not making eye contact with anyone.

I hit the pool, ignoring everyone else there, and started doing laps.

One after another, just following that black line for miles, up and back. Regulated breathing, unhurried strokes, measured and even, peaceful, mind-clearing.

I don't know how many laps I did. I had no idea of the time, but my legs and arms ached and I was out of breath, so I could safely guess it was way more than usual.

Good.

I felt marginally better.

Until I looked over at the bleachers, where I'd dumped my bag, and found Amos sitting there, watching me. Waiting.

Fuck.

No time like the present to have your heart broken.

I pulled my sorry ass out of the water, my arms barely having the strength to manage it. Still puffing, I walked over to him. He tossed me my towel.

"I told Jimmy and Tate not to tell anyone where I was," I said, patting my face.

"I never asked them," he replied. "When you weren't in class or at your house or in my room, there was only one other place you'd be."

"Sorry for being so predictable."

Was I really that predictable?

"Feel better?" he asked.

"Not really."

His eyes met mine, and you know what that fucker did? He smirked.

He fucking smirked.

"Get dressed," he said, standing up. "Deirdre wants to see us."

Deirdre?

"Well, I don't want to see her."

He threw my shirt at me. Well, it was technically his shirt, but today it was mine. "Put that on and put your emotional support tiddies away."

What the hell?

Was he just going to pretend this morning hadn't happened?

I wasn't sure if I was relieved or annoyed.

I put my wrinkled hand to my pec and squeezed. "If there was ever a day I needed these babies, it's today."

"Don't squeeze your moobs and say the word babies," he said. "Gross."

"They're not moobs."

"Okay."

I pulled my shirt on. "Stop calling them moobs. They're pectorals."

"Or tiddies."

"Correct."

I threw my now-wet towel at his stupid head, then proceeded to pull down my swimming trunks, right there for everyone to see. I was all out of fucks today.

"Jesus," he hissed at me, rushing in and holding the towel out to shield anyone from seeing. "Was being caught on camera once in the last twelve hours not enough for you?"

I pulled on my dry shorts. "Apparently not."

"Are you just gonna freeball it today?"

"All day."

He rolled his eyes. "I'm changing your name to Petulant Hollywood."

I made a point of readjusting my junk while holding his gaze. "Better than generic Hollywood."

His nostrils flared. "You are insufferable."

"So you keep saying, Mister James Dean, rebel without a clue."

His gaze turned to steel and he dropped my towel. "Have you been told to fuck off today?"

"Not yet."

"Might wanna brace yourself."

"Boys," the swim coach yelled at us.

We both turned to him, then back to each other and I realized then that we'd been inching closer.

"Get a room," someone from the swim team yelled.

I turned to the group of them, not knowing who said it. "Suck a dick."

"Mr. Soria," the coach chided me.

I was about to tell him to go suck a dick too but decided not being expelled was probably for the best. I snatched up my shit and trudged out, and before I could decide which way to go, Amos grabbed my arm and dragged me toward the rehearsal hall.

"I don't want to see Deirdre today," I said. "Or anyone, for that matter. Including you."

"Well, too fucking bad," Amos muttered.

He was stronger than he looked, and that annoyed me too.

"How are you this strong when you don't work out?"

"Because I have to carry all your bullshit," he said, pushing through the doors and dragging me to Deirdre's desk.

"Ah, here you are. I was wondering where—"

"I don't want to be here. I was busy swimming laps," I said, gesturing to my still-wet hair. "And now I'm tired and need a nap."

She stared at me.

I wasn't sorry. In fact, I'd meant every word.

Especially the part about the nap.

I palmed my forehead. "Sorry. Did you need me for something?"

"Yes," she began. She put her iPad down on the desk and I knew this was serious. "You both know you're the public favorite. That's no secret. The most likes, the most hashtags and reposts. And it's one hundred percent because of your on-screen chemistry. You've put in the effort to appear as an actual couple, going above and beyond, really."

She had no idea just how above and beyond we actually went.

"And Chase," she continued, "the scene with your friends in the bar last night was amazing. Having your friend drop the L-word was a stroke of genius."

I held my breath, squeaking on the exhale.

Oh boy.

There it was, right in front of our faces all over again.
So, so bad.

"So I was thinking for ratings, we could do a public breakup and reconciliation for the finale."

I stared at her.

God, that was worse.

Amos stared at her. "A third-act breakup scene? Really? That's so cliché."

I agreed. "Yeah. I'm not a fan."

"The viewers would eat that up," Deirdre added.

"Uh, no. They'd see it for what it is," Amos said. "Fabricated drama for the sake of ratings is poor form, and quite frankly, it's lazy."

"It's what all reality TV shows do. All the made-up and scripted fights and arguments." Deirdre smiled at both of us. "I think it could be good."

Amos shook his head. "Then have one of the other couples do it. Just for once, can we have a positive gay relationship on-screen—"

I put my hand up. "Bisexual. Not gay."

He gave me a nod. "Sorry, queer representation—"

"Thank you."

He sighed. "Can we not have a positive queer relationship on-screen without the contrite bullshit. Just happy people with solid communication skills in a healthy relationship. Just once. Make the heterosexuals dysfunctional for a change."

"Yes!" I crowed. "What he said."

Deirdre seemed to consider it. "Well, what can you two as a couple bring to the finale that fans will love?"

The look Amos gave her was the one where he couldn't believe he had to say shit out loud. I knew that look well.

"We give them a healthy relationship. Where we're happy, with solid communication skills." He looked at me. "Isn't that right, Chase? Where you don't run off and try drowning yourself in the pool."

I shot him a what-the-hell look. "I did not try to drown myself. I do laps. That's what I do." Oh, good lord. "Is that what the whole solid communication shit is about? Me?"

"I don't know if you could even act it out," he snarled. "I don't think you're that good of an actor."

I glowered at him. "What the fuck does that mean?"

"Uh, okay boys," Deirdre tried, her eyes wide. "That's not what I—"

"You know what?" I said to her. "I had it right in the beginning. Don't date, don't get involved, and sure as hell don't ever fall in love. Not even for an acting role, because this sucks!" I suddenly realized, I knew in my heart, that I'd crossed a line. And more importantly, that I was done. "You know what's worse for ratings than not having your most popular couple in some pitiful third-act breakup? Not having them in it at all. Because I quit."

I stormed out, slamming the door open on my way out, even more pissed off than I was before.

Honestly, fuck this. Fuck that and fuck him.

Fuck him in particular.

I heard Deirdre call out to me, but I kept walking. She could fail me for all I cared. I walked back to my house, trudged up to my room, threw myself onto my bed, and buried my face into my pillow.

Then I screamed into it.

I cocooned myself up in my covers and wallowed like a sad burrito until I fell asleep.

I WOKE up when someone sat on my bed. I peeked at who it was, hoping with all hope that it was Amos.

It wasn't.

It was Jimmy.

I groaned and covered my face with my comforter, rolling back over to the wall. "You're not him."

"Nope. I'm not. Wanna talk about it?"

"No."

"You okay?"

"I'll be fine. Just need to be dramatic first."

He snorted.

"This is your fault," I mumbled. "You told everyone I'm in love with him."

"Chase," he said.

"I said I don't want to talk about it."

"But—"

"But nothing. I'm going back to the old me. To the me that doesn't do repeats. That doesn't date. That doesn't feel things."

"Uh, Chase—"

"Feeling things is awful," I added. "Why would anyone do this willingly?"

Two very strong hands grabbed my burrito cocoon and sat me upright. "Dude," Jimmy said sternly.

I peeked out of my blankets to see Jimmy sitting there, a

worried look on his face.

And Amos standing behind him.

Chapter Fourteen
Amos

Chase's eyes went wide when he saw me. Then he threw himself back down on his bed and pulled his blankets over his head, making a pitiful sound. He mumbled through his covers, "Why didn't you tell me he was here?"

"I've been trying to tell you," Jimmy said. "He came to find me, said he needed me to let him into the house. The door was locked and you wouldn't answer your phone."

He huffed.

Jimmy stood up and gave me an apologetic shrug. "I'll leave you two to talk."

"I don't want to talk," Chase mumbled, still hiding in his blankets.

"Well, you're going to," I said. "Are you done being dramatic yet?"

"No." Then he shot up, pushed the blankets away, and glared at me. "You said I tried to drown myself and that I'm not a good actor."

Christ. He was such a child.

I sighed and sat down on his bed. "I'm sorry I said that. I was mad."

"You were mad? What reason do you possibly have to be mad at me? I'm the victim here."

I tried not to get mad again, but gawd, he didn't make it easy.

I used my best speaking-to-a-child voice. "Why are you the victim?"

"Because," he said, then he threw himself back down and pulled the blankets back up over his face. "Because I am. Because you said I wasn't a good actor."

"Is that all?"

"Yes."

It one hundred percent was not.

"And because of that fucked-up footage from last night," he added. "And you saw it and you heard what he said, and then you couldn't even look at me."

"Chase," I whispered.

"I'm sorry," he said, his voice catching.

I pulled the bed covers away from his face so I could see his eyes. His sad and teary eyes. "Don't be sorry. You didn't do anything wrong. It was Jimmy who said it."

He sighed, his whole face a mask of sadness. "This really sucks."

I wasn't sure what to say. If I'd make it worse or better, but it needed to be said.

"Separating feelings," I began. "It's confusing. Method acting is hard. Being our characters every minute of the day was a huge ask."

He was quiet for a long moment. "Feeling anything is terrible," he said. "I'm never feeling anything again."

"Is that right?"

"Yep."

I dug a finger into his ribs.

"Ow."

"You felt that."

"I hate you."

"Hate is also a feeling."

"Then I shall feel nothing but hate ever again."

"Okay, Anakin."

He tried not to smile. "I totally get the draw of the Dark Side now."

I sighed and fished his hand out of the bedding so I could hold it. "Did you really quit or were you just being dramatic?"

He pouted. "And you said I couldn't act."

"It was pretty convincing."

"I don't know if I can do it," he admitted quietly. "Maybe I'm *not* good enough of an actor."

"You are a good actor," I said. I had to lean down and catch his eye so he'd look at me. "You were made for Hollywood. Or Broadway."

He rolled his eyes, but he totally loved the compliment. I could tell by the twitch of his lips.

"The Chase Soria I know, who can belt out 'Empty Chairs at Empty Tables' and then take his shirt off and be hot as all hell, is the next Hugh Jackman for sure."

He scoffed and rolled his eyes. "Hot as hell, huh?"

"You know you are."

He frowned at me. "Why do your compliments always sound a little bitey? Like how can it be nice to hear but also sounds like it should hurt?"

"It's a skill. I like to keep you on your toes. But I think it's similar to how I can like you, but never has anyone ever annoyed me like you do. I think it's like that."

His lips twitched again. "You like me, huh?"

"I do. Against every fiber of common sense, yes. And as much as I try to talk myself out of it, and as much as I even hate myself for it, I do."

"See, like that. That should be a compliment but it kinda stings at the same time."

I chuckled and played with his fingers for a bit.

"There's a but coming, isn't there," he whispered. "You like me, but . . ."

I swallowed hard. "I do like you. But I don't know what it means outside of filming. I mean, you don't date. You don't want a relationship. You don't like feeling things."

"Because you don't feel the same."

My eyes shot to his. "Feel the same as what, Chase?"

My heart was thumping hard now, my belly full of butterflies.

"You haven't actually said how you feel," I whispered. "You just said it was terrible—"

"Because it is."

I snorted. "So is that your answer?"

"My answer to what?"

Sweet mother of all that is holy.

"To how you feel, Chase?"

He frowned at me. "Do I have to say it? Out loud?"

"That's generally how communication works."

"I don't know," he cried. "I've never done this before."

I gave him a sad smile, still playing with his hand. "Jimmy said you'd never liked anyone before. He said he'd never seen you play the boyfriend role before, and even though you were acting, you kinda weren't."

"Jimmy has to a lot to answer for," he said. "And he needs to start advertising for a new best friend."

"He brought me in here and let me in."

Chase scowled at me. "Don't take his side."

I sighed, not sure what exactly we'd accomplished, but at least he was talking to me.

"Don't quit the show," I said gently. "If you fail, you'll need to retake the class and it'll push your graduation back. Just see it through. We only have a few days left of filming. How about we just take a backseat for now? I think Max and Holly are filming their big scene today. We should probably be there right now, but..."

Here we were in his bedroom trying to have an adult conversation while he was still wrapped in his bedcovers.

"I'll finish filming," he said quietly. "But I don't think we should do anything more than that. As good as the BJs were, and the sex was amazing . . . I just don't think I can take that. I think that's where I got mixed up. You can compartmentalize it so much better than me, and I know it's because I've never let myself be all cuddly with anyone before and I now realize how amazing that actually is." He frowned. "No one ever told me that being a boyfriend is cuddling while watching *Rick and Morty* and then having awesome sex. I mean, what's not to like about that?"

I snorted. "It was kinda great."

"Was it? For you too?"

"Well, it wasn't . . . what did you call it? Terrible."

He pouted and sighed. "No, that part wasn't terrible.

The after part was. The feelings part. When you said you didn't feel the same."

"I never said I didn't." Fuck, now even I was confused. "No, you said it was terrible. I said it wasn't."

He narrowed his eyes at me. "When?"

"Just now."

"But not before."

"You didn't either."

I groaned and ran my hand through my hair. "I'm so glad there are no cameras here right now."

"Same."

"Look," I said, trying to clear this whole mess up. "I said I like you. I know Jimmy dropped the L-word and it caused you to freak out—"

"I didn't freak out. You freaked out."

"What did I do that could be constituted as a freak out? Run off and swim fifty laps and quit the drama production?"

He opened his mouth, then promptly shut it, then threw himself back down and pulled the covers over his head. "Feel free to leave at any time," he said, mumbling from somewhere in the middle of his blankets.

"I'm not leaving. Christ. You're such a child," I growled, frustrated and annoyed. "How is it possible for you to annoy me so fucking much and for me to still be here? How is that possible? I can't decide if it's because I like you so much or if it's because I hate myself more."

He threw the covers back. "You do like me?"

I groaned and stood up. "Be right back. Going to walk into traffic."

He reached up and grabbed my hand. "No, don't leave.

Stay here. I'm sorry. I'm a mess of . . . feelings. And it's awful."

I groaned again.

"Well, it's not all awful," he amended. "There are some good parts."

I stared at him and he pouted.

"I like you too," he mumbled. "And it's not the L-word like Jimmy said, because he's full of shit, and that's ridiculous. I absolutely do not L-word you. And I *don't* want to spend every night with you, and I do *not* want to touch you all the time. And I absolutely, *absolutely* did not envisage us moving to West Hollywood together and sharing a tiny condo and going to auditions and chasing the big Hollywood dream. That was just a post-coital brain fugue of stupid wishful thinking, and in no way an accurate representation of my feelings."

Uh . . . what?

I snorted out a laugh. "What?"

"Nothing. I said I *didn't* do that. Weren't you listening to anything I said?"

I sat back down, tired from the circles of this conversation. I took his face in my hands, and his beautiful blue eyes met mine. "You are insufferable. Has anyone ever told you that?"

"You do. A lot," he said, pouting because I was kind of squishing his cheeks.

"But you're really fucking cute. And you drive me so crazy I could scream."

"In a good way?"

"No."

He made a squishy sad face. "Oh."

"So let's clear the air, start again, do this filming, stupid-ass reality-method-acting thing, and then we can decide what we want to do."

He sighed. "Okay."

"But you can't stay in here and wallow."

"I'm not wallowing." He rolled his eyes at himself. "Well, maybe just a little bit. But I'm allowed. I'm not used to feeling the feelings."

"Look. We've established that we like each other. That's enough feelings for one day. Let's just get through this stupid production. No sleeping at my place until it's over and you know how you feel for real."

"Whose stupid rule is that?"

"It was yours."

"Well, I take it back."

I sighed. "Chase. For the love of fucking god. Stop being a child." I kissed his pouty lips, then let his face go.

"See? There it is again. Sweet, with a side of ouch."

"Just keeping it real."

"Could you be gentle with me? I'm fragile."

I sighed. "You know that game Kiss, Kill, or Fuck? Well, you're all three for me, and I don't even know how that's possible."

He finally smiled. A proper Chase Soria smile. "You wanna kiss and fuck me?"

"And kill."

"Those odds are still pretty good."

I stood up. "You know what? I have to get to class while I still have some sanity left. If you want to fail, go right ahead. But we are expected in the rehearsal hall by one o'clock. I will be there because I cannot afford to fail. If you want to stay here and wallow, then be my guest. But we can't get a tiny condo in West Hollywood and go to auditions together if you're still in college because you failed."

He unfolded himself from his covers, tried to stand up, almost fell over, and somehow managed to right himself before he hit the floor. "I said I never thought that. You need to listen more."

"I don't even know what I'm doing here," I mumbled, turning for the door.

He grabbed my hand, his eyes finally serious. "Thank you. For coming to clear the air and to calm me down. I'm glad we talked."

This sincerity, the adorable, too-sweet, stupidly hot side of him. The side of him that wasn't a freaking child, that wasn't the confident guy he portrayed himself to be. The side of him that showed his vulnerability, his need to be liked.

The side of him you want to hold onto forever.

It's just a shame it's attached to the incredibly frustrating side of him.

"I'm glad we talked too. And in two days, when all the filming is done and we're back to just being us—just Chase and Amos, and not Dominic or Elijah—we'll see how we feel."

He nodded. "Okay. Sounds good." Then he licked his lips and frowned. "You know what I said about the no-sex thing? Well, that didn't include kissing." He pointed to his lips. His full, inviting, sexy as fuck lips. "Maybe a kiss will make me feel better."

Why did I put up with his shit?

Why did I fall for the cute, playful bullshit, every single time?

Because I want to kiss him every chance I get.

Because, despite how hard I tried not to, I'd fallen for him too.

I put my finger to his chin and tilted his face upward, making him look me in the eye. And I slowly pressed my lips to his. Soft and warm, never moving to deepen the kiss, just sweet and chaste.

It made my blood run warm and my heart skip a beat.

"Feel better?" I asked.

He nodded. "Much."

I rested my forehead against his and closed my eyes. "Same. I'm glad we talked." Then I sighed and pulled back. "I'm not glad I followed you here, found your house locked, then had to track down your best friend to come let me in. I could have done without that. I also missed a class today. I could have done without that too. I also had to explain a few things to Deirdre. Could have done without that. But yes, I'm glad we talked."

He narrowed his brows. "What did you have to explain to her?"

"That things got . . . *complicated* between us."

"Ugh." Then he shrugged. "Did you tell her the sex was hot as fuck?"

"No. I didn't tell her that."

"You should have. Then maybe she'd understand."

"I think she got the gist of what I meant."

"What's that?"

I shrugged. "That the physical closeness, the staring into each other's eyes exercises and the kissing exercises we did might have made us closer than she'd intended. And that it's really no wonder that Max and Holly were struggling with it." I shrugged again. "And I told her method acting sucks ass."

He nodded. "You know, eating ass is one thing I've never done."

I closed my eyes and sighed. "Christ."

He laughed. "Wanna try it?"

I grabbed his hand and pulled him out of his room. "Not today."

"Tomorrow?"

"Probably not."

We passed Jimmy in the living room. I waved over my shoulder. "Thanks!"

Chase, still being dragged out by his hand, yelled, "You're to blame for all of this."

Jimmy laughed. "You're welcome!"

And we walked outside to find none other than Daniel waiting on the sidewalk. "Hey guys," he said, holding his camera up. "Ready to roll."

I shook my head at him. "Not now, Daniel. No filming. Just give us a break for half an hour, please."

I kept walking, kept dragging Chase, until he pulled his hand free, only to put his arm around my waist. "Slow down."

"It's almost one. Deirdre already thinks you quit. She's probably spent the last hour or so in emergency meetings making contingency plans."

"It'll be good practice for her," he said. "And anyway, we're not doing the godawful breakup thing she wanted us to do on camera, so what does she even need us for today anyway?"

"No, we almost did the godawful breakup thing for real."

"Lucky one of us was the grown up and tracked the other one down."

I stopped walking and stared at him. I was about to rip into him but he was doing that pouty thing. I sighed and shook my head. "Remind me again why I bothered?"

"Because you caught feelings for me. You already told me you did so you can't take it back. I have a strict no-return policy."

"Christ, you're insufferable."

He laughed and took my hand, now pulling me toward the rehearsal hall. "Come on, or we'll be late. And I'm hungry. Did I nap through lunch?"

Fuck my life.

WE WALKED into the rehearsal hall where everyone—cast, camera crews, and production—was gathered near the stage. They stopped and turned to face us, clearly seeing us holding hands.

"Oh, thank god," Jess said. "Please tell me we're still good to go."

"We were about to kill off Dominic's character and give Elijah the role of the grieving lover left behind," Deirdre said with the hint of a smile.

"Awesome," Chase said. "*Days of our Lives* meets kill your queers. Love that for me."

Didi greeted me with a gentle hand on my arm, looking between us. "Everything okay?"

"It is now," I replied. "Just had to go mow down a melodramatic bisexual and talk some sense into him."

"Melodramatic bisexual," Chase repeated flatly with a slow nod. "Better than generic Hollywood, I guess."

"Are we good to continue filming?" Deirdre asked gently.

I gave a nod, and Chase did too, but then Deirdre nodded to the corner of the hall. "Chase? A word?"

She took him for a quiet, private conversation, no doubt asking him if he was happy to keep filming, if he felt up to it, and if he was okay, basically.

"You all good?" Tucker asked me.

"Yeah. We just need to get this filming done."

"Tell me about it," Max mumbled. I don't know if he meant for Holly to hear, but she did.

I hated this for them too.

It didn't help that most of the viewer comments about Max and Holly's relationship weren't good. Some people were rooting for them. Some were saying they should split; they had no chemistry.

It wasn't their acting skills.

Well, maybe a little. But the outside pressure was buckling them.

"You know," I said, "I think method acting would be okay if it was a character not like ourselves. I know why they made our characters like our real selves for this, so we could continue with our daily lives at college. But man, it's murky waters."

"So you'd rather play a serial killer and get all dark and weird in real life to become a character?" Phoebe asked.

"I wouldn't kill someone, if that's what you mean. But I think some characters might need that kind of dedication. Like *The Godfather*. I can see why Brando chose method acting. It's still talked about over fifty years later."

"I'd rather leave my character at the door," Max said.

"Same," Didi agreed. "It's easier for me to slip in and out of character. As soon as the camera rolls, it's like bam! Character is switched on."

I nodded. "Agreed. I'm all for research and spending a few weeks doing what that character does, like Wall Street or small-town sheriff or whatever. But *becoming* that character?" I shook my head. "Living and breathing as that character twenty-four seven? Not for me."

Holly gave me a twisted smile as she nodded toward Chase. "But you and him became your characters, right?"

I looked over at Chase, just as he looked my way. He smiled, and it made me smile, and of course my cheeks burned. "We . . . we don't know yet," I said, embarrassed and kinda mad at myself for admitting anything. "See, his character Dominic is very levelheaded and funny, whereas Chase is more of a wallowing, melodramatic kinda guy who does nothing but annoy and frustrate the hell outta me, so we're still undecided."

"I heard that!" Chase yelled.

I rolled my eyes. "Good. Saves me from saying it again later."

They all laughed, and he and Deirdre walked back over to us. "Ready to watch the recap?" she asked. "Then we'll run through this afternoon's big scene."

There were some groans, mostly for Max and Holly's scene, because everyone knew it wasn't an easy one for them.

"Look, guys," Deirdre said. "Tomorrow's the last day. I know it's been rough, but I think we can all say we've learned about the process and about ourselves as actors and production crew. And I'm telling you, as hard as this has been, it's nothing compared to what you'll go through in the real thing. If you want to work in LA or Hollywood, or on Broadway, this project is a walk in the park. Okay?"

We all nodded and mumbled ascent.

Chase sat beside me, leaning his head on my shoulder, and his hand slipped into mine.

So much for no contact or intimacy.

"You know," I murmured so only he could hear. "It's kinda confusing. You say you don't want physical contact, but then you do this." I bumped my shoulder so he'd know what I was talking about.

He never lifted his head. "It's not confusing to me."

I sighed. "Of course it's not."

"I meant no sex," he whispered. "Cuddling doesn't count. Cuddles have been scientifically proven to reduce cortisol levels and increase endorphins."

"Shh," Phoebe hissed at us. "Do you two ever shut up?"

I pointed my thumb at Chase, blaming him, at the same time he pointed to me.

She rolled her eyes and went back to watching.

It was a scene with her and Jess, goofing off in one of their rooms, and then Didi and Tucker were having lunch together, talking about a concert they'd just bought tickets to. Their feet were interlocked under the table and it was kinda cute.

Then Max and Holly appeared. They were walking to class together, Holly's big doe eyes looking at Max like he hung the moon, and Max . . . Max's smile didn't quite sit right.

It was awkward.

Awkward for them to act out, awkward for us to watch.

And then there was me and Chase. Filmed today. Me sitting in the bleachers by the pool and Chase being surprised to see me. I didn't even know Daniel was filming us. He was quite far away, filming near the locker-room door by the looks of it, and thankfully we couldn't really hear our conversation.

But then Chase whipped off his swimming trunks and I held up the towel just in time, before the whole world saw his junk. Everybody cracked up laughing. "Almost an Only Fans," Chase said, totally proud.

I groaned. "God, now you all see what I have to put up with?"

Then, on-screen, the swim coach yelled at us for language and Daniel's filming cut away as me and Chase made our way out. It looked absolutely candid because it was. I had no idea we were being filmed.

Viewers were gonna love it.

Little would they know that was filmed just before Chase quit, before he had a meltdown and cocooned himself in his bed . . .

I gave Chase's hand a squeeze.

They wouldn't know the personal cost. Like all viewers

of any form of entertainment. It's a different story when the cameras stop rolling.

And I got it. It was an actor's job to present a persona on-screen. Personal lives were purely incidental. Sometimes personal lives were fodder for ratings and social media clicks.

It was a very good reminder to swear that if I ever did crack the big time in Hollywood, be it TV or movies, I'd keep my private life exactly that.

It got me thinking about what Chase had said about us moving to West Hollywood together, chasing auditions and dreams.

It sounded perfect.

If not impractical and way too premature.

But perfect.

Chase snapped his fingers in front of my face. "Earth to Amos."

I startled. "Sorry. I was . . . thinking."

Chase's face lit up. "Of me?"

"No," I lied.

It's not like I could admit to wondering what our place might look like, apart from tiny and dingy, or why I imagined a *Rick and Morty* poster on the living room wall . . .

I hadn't realized everyone was off doing their thing, getting ready for this afternoon's big scene. Holly came over, looking uncertain but hopeful.

"Hey," I said. "Ready for this today?"

She shook her head. "Not really. I have an idea. It's not scripted, not that much of what we've done is." She rolled her eyes. "But I need your help."

Chase put his arm around my waist. "We'll do it."

Chapter Fifteen
Chase

I didn't know what Holly was going to ask, and honestly it didn't matter.

Because for all the shit that Amos and I were going through—okay, so the shit I put him through—it paled in comparison to what poor Holly and Max were going through.

I had no idea what Amos and I were, or if everything we felt was all because of this stupid acting project. Maybe being fake boyfriends, having to act all lovey-dovey together, made us think we were more than acting.

Okay, so yes. Maybe it made *me* think we were more than friends.

Maybe it made me think I'd finally gone and fallen in actual stupid love with him. Maybe it was all real on my behalf and completely fake and just acting on his.

That was the bottom line that had made me lose my shit earlier.

Because hearing Jimmy say that L-word made me realize

it was possibly true. And seeing Amos's reaction made me realize he didn't feel the same.

But then he'd said that he does like me. That he had actual feelings for me.

And waiting until after the filming was done made sense. It certainly didn't make sense to fail the unit—I could see that now.

But if we remove the filming, the acting, the make-believe stuff, then all that should remain was the truth.

And then we'd find out how we really felt.

And that made sense.

Even though I already knew my answer. I knew how I felt.

And maybe, just maybe, Amos felt the same.

God, I hope he does.

He acted all irritated but I was pretty sure he secretly loved it when I annoyed him. When I pretended to be joking and acting like a big old whiny baby and giving him that pout that made him smile.

He could deny that he liked that pout all he wanted, but I knew he loved it.

He wasn't the emo, dark, and broody guy that pretended to hate everything and everyone. He wasn't a sullen Keanu Reeves or a misunderstood James Dean.

He was Amos Beddington. An actor with diverse range, an introvert who just needed peace and quiet, who avoided crowds but put up with them for me.

He was amazing.

And he was going to help me help Holly. If Deirdre wanted a big drama to see the show out, then that's what she'd get. Was what Holly wanted to do risky?

Sure.

Would it work?

Totally impromptu and secret, so the reactions would be real and honest.

It would either be awesome or a disaster.

Either way, ratings should be good.

MAX AND HOLLY'S scene was to take place in the courtyard for optimal audience viewing. It was also kinda risky given the likelihood of some douchey student ruining a scene, but for the most part, the student body had been very respectful of our filming. Helpful, even.

But given the fan wars between the Max and Holly shippers and the Max and Jenna shippers or even their real-life friends, anything was possible.

As people took their places and the scene began, Amos and I were on a side quest to save the scene, or possibly ruin it. Deirdre could get mad at us all she liked, but she wanted a big finale, and that's what she was going to get.

We found Jenna hiding in the dining hall, right where Holly said she'd be. She had her phone out, watching the livestream of the show.

Watching her boyfriend about to declare his undying love for someone else.

"Hey," I said, startling her.

She put her phone screen-side down on the table. "Oh, hey."

"We need you to come with us."

Her eyes widened. "Why?"

"To be honest, I'm not entirely sure. Holly didn't say, exactly. She just asked us to bring you to the set."

She shook her head. "Oh no. I'm not . . . I can't. I can't watch that."

Amos glanced to her phone, hinting that she already was.

"In person," she amended.

Clearly asking nicely wasn't going to work.

I took her by the arm and pulled her out of the chair. "Come on. We're running out of time."

"I don't think this is a good idea," she tried.

Amos grabbed her phone and her bag and followed them out the door.

"Do you trust Max?" I asked, dragging her along.

"Yes, of course."

"Because you know he's acting, right?"

"Well, yes . . ."

"And so is Holly. That girl has your back, I promise."

We came into the courtyard and hit a wall of people. The onlooking crowd was way bigger than we'd anticipated, people standing on chairs to see over heads, and amazingly, they were being quiet.

I could hear Max talking, his voice carrying. "You know how I feel," he said.

"I'm saying no," Holly replied.

There was a beat of silence.

Followed by Max's very confused, "Uh, what?"

"Excuse me," Chase said, pulling Jenna through the crowd with him.

When people realized it was us, they parted to let us

through. And when they realized we had Jenna, people in the audience clapped and a few hollered, "Yes!" and "About time."

We burst through to the center, where Max and Holly were in a stand off with each other. Jess and Phoebe were behind them, Tucker and Didi too. There were wild eyes between everyone, silently asking us *what the fuck?* Max looked confused as hell.

And poor Jenna. Looking like a deer in headlights...

Amos pulled me back by the arm, and Holly stepped forward. "I'm saying no, because it's not me you love." She took Jenna's arm and faced Max. "Because every time you're with me, you're thinking of her. I know you tried. I know you did. But you're in love with someone else."

People in the crowd cheered.

"I know you wish I was her," Holly said. "I can see it in your eyes. You need to make the choice for you, not our families, not our parents. Be with the woman you love."

Holly even looked a little sad. Well, her character did. I'd maybe not given her acting enough credit, because she was nailing this.

But Max only had eyes for Jenna . . . and Jenna burst into tears.

He quickly pulled her into his arms. He kissed the side of her head as the audience hollered and clapped. Even Tucker clapped and Didi was laughing. Jess and Phoebe both stood there with their hands to their mouths.

Holly patted Max's arm, then she looked over at me and Amos. "Thank you," she mouthed.

Then she stood in the middle, raised her arms. "And scene," she yelled, and gave a bow to a standing ovation.

We all clapped.

Not only because that scene was awesome, it was, but because it was over.

Tucker ran over and gave Max and Jenna a big hug, and Jenna was laugh-crying. Max took her face in his hands and gave her a soft kiss before tucking her into his side.

Jenna looked at Holly. "Thank you."

She grinned at her. "You're welcome."

Deirdre appeared, somewhat bewildered, yet trying to maintain the outward appearance that she knew what was going on. People were still standing there, watching, so she was putting on her best stage face.

"Okay, team," she said, trying to round us up. "Let's take this back into the classroom."

We all made our way back to the rehearsal hall. I slid my arm around Amos's waist and he hung his arm around my shoulder. The happy outcome felt good, and I was proud to be a part of it, even if Deirdre was about to rip into us.

We filed in, and Amos sat on a desk so I stood between his legs and pulled his hand around my waist, threading our fingers. And we had to wait for Max to come in. He'd left Jenna at the door with a kiss and jogged in.

Deirdre signaled at the door. "Invite Jenna in, please, Max."

Oh great.

We were all gonna cop it.

"It wasn't her idea," Holly volunteered. "It was my idea. She knew nothing about it."

"Oh, I know that," Deirdre said. "I could see by the look on her face."

Max brought Jenna in, holding her hand. She looked

like a rabbit caught in a snare, so I offered a huge smile. "It's okay," I told her. "Deirdre wants to bite us, but she's legally not allowed."

Deirdre shot me a look. "Mr. Soria. Your daily limit of that smile getting you what you want has been exceeded today. Try again tomorrow."

I laughed, and Amos chuckled into my shoulder. "She knows you well."

"It was all my idea," Holly said again. "We needed to do something. My character was too meek. She clearly knew Max's character wasn't in love with her, and the audience knew it as well. You've read the comments. You heard the applause when Jenna arrived." Holly raised her chin, not the least bit sorry. "My character needed to find some self-worth."

"It was awesome," Phoebe said.

Jess held up her phone. "People loved it. Already. The view count is huge."

"It was pretty cool," Tucker said. "Kinda like Ross's 'I take thee, Rachel' scene."

I snorted. "I dunno about that. I think Amos and I came in with incredible timing, like at the end of *Avengers: Infinity Wars*. We totally saved the whole scene."

Everyone rolled their eyes.

"Okay," Deirdre said. "Look, it wasn't planned. But I have to applaud the improvisation and the ability to stay in character. Rolling with a mishap and making it look natural takes skill."

Of course she'd turn it into a lesson.

"Yeah, maybe a little heads-up next time," Max said. "When you said no, I was like uh, what the hell?"

Holly laughed. "If you'd known what I was going to do, we wouldn't have gotten to see the real reaction. It was visceral, and we nailed it."

We all went in for a high five. "Hell yes, we did."

"Okay, so final scene tomorrow," Deirdre said. She looked around the rehearsal hall. "Who wants to help the set designers turn this into a graduation after party."

I took Amos's hand and pulled him toward the door. "Sorry. Would love to stay and chat, but we have plans."

"We do?" Amos mumbled.

"Yes, we do." I waved them all farewell as we went out the door. "See you all tomorrow! Great show today."

We fell into the corridor and Amos laughed. "So what are we doing?"

"Anything but set design," I replied. "Oooh, I know. You could do me."

"I thought you said—"

"That was past-me. Now-me wants it, and future-me agrees."

"Chase," he murmured.

"Just a little orgasm. It doesn't have to be a big orgasm. Just a little one."

He looked up to the sky and sighed. "Can I just point out the mixed signals you give? You say you want something, then you change your mind. You say you don't want something, then you change your mind. How am I supposed to know what you really want?"

"I really want you to do me. That's what I *really* want."

"But earlier you said—"

"Earlier-me was a dick to now-me. We've been through this."

He snorted out a laugh and dug his fingers into his eyeballs. "You need to make up your mind and stick to it. Now if we do something, you could regret it and tell me you'd said you didn't want to do anything until the filming was over."

"The filming is over."

"For today. Technically it ends tomorrow."

Now it was my turn to sigh. Because he had a point. I had said we shouldn't do anything in bed until the filming was all over because I needed to separate us from our characters.

"Fine," I conceded. "If you won't give me an orgasm, the very least you can do is give me tacos. I missed lunch and I'm starving."

I just happened to say this somewhat loudly, and as people were walking past us, they laughed, and Amos let out a long-suffering sigh. "No one appreciates my pain."

Chapter Sixteen
Amos

I kept Chase true to his word, as difficult as it was. Especially after we ate tacos in the shade at the pier and he offered me one last-ditch effort of an orgasm.

I really wanted to.

God, how I wanted to . . .

But what he'd said was right.

We needed to see who we were when Dominic and Elijah no longer existed and we were just Chase and Amos.

And to be fair, what I'd said was right too.

He needed to stop saying shit he didn't really mean. I got that he joked a lot and he was very new to relationships, but we needed to talk.

If we were gonna do the whole boyfriend thing, that was.

And I was pretty sure that's where we were headed.

Did I want that?

With the most infuriating guy I'd ever met?

The warmest, most wonderful guy, with the most heart-stopping smile and kindest eyes I'd ever seen. Who was funny and loving, and vulnerable. Who shared my passion and my dreams.

Yeah, I was pretty sure I did.

But we needed to talk first.

"So, about tomorrow," I hedged. We were sitting on the steps facing the ocean. The mid-afternoon sun was getting low, the breeze was cool, and people were, thankfully, leaving us alone.

And now was as good a time as any.

"Yeah?" he replied. "Will there be orgasms tomorrow?"

I snorted. "That depends."

"On what?"

"What we decide. When the filming's all done and we have no obligation to hang out together."

"Obligation?"

"You know what I mean. If we decide if we wanna be boyfriends in real life."

"I've already decided."

"But you were the one who said you wanted to wait."

He sighed. "Earlier-me has a lot to answer for."

I snorted, but this was exactly my point. "You need to work on your communication skills before I agree to anything."

He shot me a look. "I was just kidding."

I stood up and wiped the sand from my ass. "We should sleep on it."

"Amos," he said, holding his hand out. I thought he wanted me to help him up, but he didn't. He just wanted to hold my hand. "Real talk. God, this is hard. And awkward.

Why is my heart beating so fast?" He put his hand to his chest. "Is this normal or should we call 911?"

I snorted. "I'm glad you wanted to have a serious conversation."

He pulled on my hand. "I'm sorry. I joke when I'm nervous. It's easier for people to think I'm joking in case it all goes to shit. That way they're laughing with me and not at me."

Oh man.

There's that vulnerable side to him again.

"I wouldn't laugh at you."

"I already know my answer. I know what I want. And before you make your decision, I need you to know I'm serious. And I'm sorry about before. I freaked out and panicked because I thought you didn't like me the way I like you. And it felt like I'd put myself out there—though technically it was Jimmy who threw me under the bus—but the way you reacted, I thought you were horrified, and it was the first time in my life that I'd ever admitted to liking anyone—"

"The way I reacted? I didn't react. I was in shock."

"But it wasn't a good reaction.

"He said you were in love with me!"

He blinked fast a few times and his mouth opened a second before the words came out. "And I don't know if he's wrong."

Oh.

Oh, holy shit.

Chase looked up at me then, his eyes reflecting the sun and the water. "I don't know. I think maybe he was right."

"Chase," I whispered. Not sure what else to say.

"See?" He stood up, on the verge of tears. "Not a good reaction, Amos. Not a good reaction. If you could just pretend you're Elijah just one more fucking time, pretend that you even like me, that'd be great—"

He was about to turn, but I grabbed his arm. His eyes met mine, fear and hope looked back at me. "I was never Elijah," I said. "I was never pretending. Every kiss, every touch, every time. It was me. All me."

He nodded. "Me too."

I cupped his face and brought his lips to mine. Soft and warm, with every emotion I couldn't name. I pulled him against me, his arms holding me tight, and I buried my face in his neck.

"Chase, I was never acting. Not with you. Not once. I kept telling myself 'it's what Elijah would do,' but it wasn't. It was what I wanted."

"Same," he mumbled, nodding. "I tried. I tried to separate it." He pulled back and looked me in the eye. "In the beginning, it was just fun and exciting. Then it was too much fun and too exciting, and I thought, wait, is this what having a boyfriend is actually like? Because if it is, then I want that."

I laughed. "I want that too."

His smile was everything. "Just so you know, I will fuck something up at some point. And there's a one hundred percent chance of it being epically bad."

I held up my hand and counted off my fingers. "No cheating and no lying. It's not hard."

"Is that it? Are those the rules? Because those are easy."

I thought for a second. "No sulking, no miscommunication. We're going to talk like adults."

"Okay." He nodded. "I can do that."

"And no being a wallowing, melodramatic bisexual."

He made a face. "Okay, look. There are limits. The bisexual is a constant, and the wallowing, melodramatic part is almost guaranteed at some point. You'll just need to learn how to deal with it."

I laughed and with my fingers under his chin, I tilted his face and kissed him again.

"So? Boyfriends?" he asked. "You'd technically be my first ever, so if you want the title, it's up for grabs."

"I want the title."

He laughed and threw his arms around me. "Does this mean there'll be orgasms?"

I wrapped my arms around him tight, laughing. "I think it might, yeah."

2

WE WALKED into Chase's house holding hands and as we were about to take the stairs, Jimmy poked his head around the corner.

"Oh, hey," Chase said. "Can't chat. About to get a dicking."

Oh god.

Jimmy laughed. "So does this mean . . . ?" He looked between us.

"Yes," Chase replied. "To all the questions. Yes, we made up. Yes, we're officially dating. Yes, he's gonna dick me so hard, and yes, if you break the lock on my door to film us, I will kill you."

Jimmy grinned. "I'm glad. Glad you worked it out, I mean. We watched the livestream. It was pretty cool. Max can finally stop moping."

"Yeah, it was pretty cool," I said.

Jimmy flattened down his shirt. "I, uh, I was just about to leave, actually. So you'll have the house to yourselves. Tate and I are heading down to the bar with the girls. Georgia asked me," he said, blushing. "Hope that's okay."

"Hell yes it's okay. She's a great girl. And tell her I told you to tell her to give having a boyfriend a try. It's awesome. There's sex on demand, *Rick and Morty* marathons, and snacks. And cuddles. Literally no downside."

"Yes, there is," I added. "Having a boyfriend with the attention span of a squirrel on speed."

Chase met my eyes and grinned. "Right. Yes. Upstairs. That's what we were doing." He took off up the stairs and I followed him.

"I'll lock the front door," Jimmy yelled.

"Thanks," he yelled back. "Have a good night!" Then he mumbled, "I know I'm about to."

Chase pulled me into his room, shut the door, and locked it, then turned to me.

"So, boyfriends, huh?"

I took the hem of his shirt and pulled him closer. "Unless there's a waiver period."

"Nuh-uh." He shook his head as he slid his hand over my ass and pulled our hips flush. He was already half-hard. "No waiver. I'm all in."

"Good." I captured his lips with mine, taking my time to kiss him properly. Slow and deep, our tongues tangling until he moaned, melting into me.

His erection was hardening between us, as was mine, and I was desperate to get my jeans off. To be naked with him, to feel his skin against mine. To have that closeness, that intimacy.

I needed it.

I slid my hand along his jaw to hold his neck and he moaned, breaking the kiss. He pulled his shirt off, then ripped mine over my head, fumbling for the button on my jeans.

"Need you naked," he said.

I stilled his hand. "Slow down," I whispered. "I need it too—I need to be inside you, but I want to take my time. We have all night."

"Oh god, you're gonna kill me," he mumbled. "Is it possible to die from not being fucked fast enough?"

I chuckled. "Not likely. Get on the bed."

He toed out of his shoes, pulled his socks off, then whipped his shorts and briefs off and was on the bed in record time. I toed out of my Chucks, and by the time I had my jeans off, he had a condom beside him, and with one leg raised, he was smearing lube over his hole.

So fucking hot.

Okay, so maybe going slow wasn't gonna happen.

I kneeled on the bed, crawling between his legs, taking in his solid muscle and tanned skin. His cock lay across his hip, thick and hard, but I ignored it for now. "You're so fucking hot," I murmured, kissing his ribs and then tonguing his nipple.

He hissed, so I sucked on it, hard. His back arched and his cock twitched as he whimpered. "Fuck."

Laughing, I kissed him, crashing my mouth to his and

delving my tongue in deep. He ran his hands down my back, trying to pull me closer. "Need you," he said.

I smiled, trying to decide how long to play this out. But then his brows knitted together. "I will not beg you, Amos. I'll just get mad."

No teasing him then.

I laughed and sat back on my haunches. "Then I better not keep you waiting." I took the lube, smearing his hole first, then giving his shaft a few slow pulls.

"Oh fuck," he said, raising his hips, sensitive and desperate.

So I fingered his hole, slipping a fingertip inside him, then a second. He stroked his cock and groaned, widening his legs for me.

Fuck yes.

I pulled my fingers out and he whined, his head shooting up with a mad look on his face, until he saw that I was rolling on a condom. "Just as fucking well," he said.

"You're so demanding," I said, pressing my cock against his slick hole. "And desperate. And hot. You're so fucking sexy right now." I pushed into him, as slow as I could, watching his eyes, his face, for every emotion, every feeling he couldn't say.

His eyes went wide, his lips parted, his breath caught. His hand went to my hip to hold me, to stop me. I almost joked that he didn't seem to have much to say now, but I didn't. "You okay?" I asked.

He nodded quickly. "Just . . . slow." His brows furrowed and his nostrils flared.

I stilled, the head of my cock barely inside him, and the

restraint it took. The restraint . . . Oh god. "Chase," I whispered.

He nodded again. "Okay."

I let myself push in, still as slow as I could, but so good. So tight, so hot. All the way in. "Oh, holy fuck," I ground out. So much for taking all night. I wasn't going to last two minutes.

To distract myself, I concentrated on him, his comfort, his pleasure. I moved with him, for him. I made love to him. Drove my pleasure into him, and he rolled his hips faster, his rhythm increasing with his urgency.

He clawed at my back, moaning and gasping as I sucked on his neck. "God, Amos, more. I'm so close, I need more. Don't stop."

So I kissed him as I thrust harder, and he slipped his hand between us to stroke himself. Then he cried out, arching his back and groaning as his orgasm took hold. He shot come onto his belly, groaning and twitching, his ass milking and squeezing.

I came so hard, so completely, I almost blacked out. The room spun and went dark and silent. All that existed was him and bliss. I collapsed on him, spent and boneless, out of breath.

"Fucking hell," I mumbled. "Did I die?"

He chuckled underneath me, but I couldn't even lift my head. "Boyfriend sex is so much better," he murmured. "So was that the big or little orgasm? I need to know which one for round two later tonight."

"Round two? I'm still dead."

He laughed. "Just kidding. That was totally a big

orgasm. I'll take the smaller one as a BJ or a hand job in the shower. Later. When you're alive again."

I sighed, so ridiculously happy in that moment I would've agreed to anything. "Okay."

I pulled out of him and discarded the condom and he pulled me back in for a cuddle. "Little-spoon nap time."

Laughing, I tightened my arms around him and closed my eyes.

Chapter Seventeen
Chase

Amos and I walked into the dining hall for what would be our final breakfast filming day.

I wasn't sure how I felt about that.

"Where were you two last night?" Jess asked us. "Noticeably absent, I see."

Tucker pulled my shirt collar. "Noticeable hickey, I see."

I rubbed my neck and Amos cleared his throat, his cheeks pink. The fact he'd left a love bite on my neck was one of my proudest moments. "That's not even the best one," I said, beginning to lift my shirt. "Wanna see the crowning glory?"

Amos grabbed my hand. "No, they don't."

They all laughed, and I fell into my seat, then regretted the sting in my ass. No one noticed, thank god. Well, no one but Amos. "I'll get you breakfast," he said quietly, disappearing.

"So, what did everyone get up to last night?" I asked.

"Not as much fun as you two, clearly," Didi said with a smile.

"Speak for yourselves," Max said. Jenna gasped and whacked his arm, making everyone laugh.

"Uh, yeah," Phoebe said. "Speak for yourselves."

Then she lifted hers and Jess's hands. They were holding hands?

"Oh my god," I said. "For real?"

They both nodded, shy and giggly. "Last night." We all clapped and cheered. I was so happy for them.

"That is so amazing!" Didi said, looking at them fondly. And when she realized people were all looking at her, then at Tucker, she scoffed. "Uh, no."

Tucker snorted. "Yeah, no."

Then Holly put her hands up. "Don't look at me. Read my shirt."

She stood up and pulled the front of her shirt flat so we could read it. In bright purple and orange groovy font, it read *My own self-worth is my HEA*. "I made it last night. One plain T-shirt and two Sharpies. That was how I spent my night."

Everyone smiled at her, especially Jenna and Max. "It's perfect," Jenna said softly.

Holly smiled with a sigh. "You know, for as not-fun as this whole project was, I'm gonna miss this." She looked at each of us. "Hanging out, doing breakfast, or meeting for coffee, all of us together."

"I was thinking that too," I admitted. "And yeah, while it had it's not-fun moments, I'm still glad we got to do it."

"Same," Tucker agreed.

"Same," Jess said, holding up her and Phoebe's hands.

We laughed again.

"We can still do this," Didi said. "Like *The Breakfast Club*, but for real."

Amos slid a tray onto the table. "I love that movie," he said. "What are we talking about?"

"Being *The Breakfast Club* instead of a reality TV version of *90210*," I said, snagging a piece of his toast. "Thanks."

"But no cameras," Max said.

"Definitely no cameras," Phoebe said.

"You know," I said, an idea forming in my head. "We should totally set up a projector and show movies, like once a month or something. Our favorite films, take it in turn to choose, and make a night of it." The more I thought of it, the more I liked it. "We could show them on the lawn at Liberty Court, open invitation. Bring a blanket and a picnic kinda thing. Whaddya think?"

"I like it," Jess said.

"Sounds awesome," Max agreed, and everyone nodded.

I grinned, excited. It was gonna be so much fun. I even caught Amos smiling at me. I bit into my toast and wiggled, quickly regretting the sting in my ass again.

Amos caught on, smirking sipped his coffee. "So has anyone seen the rehearsal hall? Looks just like a graduation party. It looks pretty cool."

"They did a good job," I added. "We snuck a look on the way here this morning."

"I can't wait for this to be over," Tucker said with a groan. Then he winced at Didi. "No offense."

She laughed. "None taken." Then she looked at me and Amos. "Hurry up and eat so we can get this over with."

2

We spent the morning rehearsing. This would be filmed and livestreamed, and with the crowd watching live at the outdoor theater and this being the final scene, there was extra pressure to get it right.

As we got dressed for the final scene, we also took turns having candid interviews. Together with our on-screen partner, and then just by ourselves.

Deirdre planned on releasing a whole bunch of interviews and bloopers after the livestream ended. And we'd get to watch it on the big theater screen on the beach with the whole campus.

No pressure at all.

And most of the student body were coming if the hype around school was anything to go by.

The final scene itself was the graduation after-party. The rehearsal hall had streamers, balloons, disco lights, and terrible music. There was a long table of drinks and snacks, and they'd kinda made it an actual party for the end of filming.

It was perfect.

The editing team, the production, and the sound guys all got to play extras, and it was fun!

And I got to dress in my suit pants, button down shirt and tie, and I could admit that I looked good. Amos wore suit pants and a vest, and fuck me, when he came out of the fitting room, he smiled at me, and I couldn't even speak.

He looked so damn good.

Holly nudged me in the ribs. "Close your mouth."

"New rule to the boyfriend clause," I said. "You need to wear this outfit every day."

Amos laughed. "You wish."

"Yes, that's why I said it."

He took my hand and lifted it, getting a proper look at me. "You look great. Those pants . . ."

"Tailored just for me."

He raised an eyebrow, appreciating the view. "I can tell."

Deirdre stuck her head in. "Okay, curtain up in five."

Curtain up. I snorted. This wasn't theater, but we knew what she meant.

We made our way out to find Holly fixing Jenna's hair. I was glad they were friends at the end of all this. Jenna wore a pretty dress that matched Max's tie.

"Oh man," I said, "we should have totally worn something that matched. Why didn't we think of that?"

"Because we're new to this, remember?" Amos replied.

"Well, for our real graduation, we're totally matching."

He sighed, just as Holly came over. She wore brown suit pants, her shirt with *My own self-worth is my HEA* on it, and orange suspenders. She looked amazing. "Well, don't you two make a fine couple," she said, giving us a bump with her hip. Then she looked around the hall. "This looks fun, don't you think?"

"It does," I agreed. "And Jess and Phoebe? That was unexpected."

Holly gave me a side-eye. "Are you kidding? It was the most obvious thing ever. Were you even watching them?"

I made a face. "Well, no," I said. "To be fair, I've been distracted . . ." I gestured to Amos.

Holly nodded. "Fair."

"Okay," Deirdre yelled, getting our attention. "Places, everyone."

And so filming began.

All I cared about was getting to slow dance with Amos. Sure, we had some lines and dialogue with the others and between ourselves. We laughed and we danced, and in a way, we said goodbye to these characters for the last time.

But for me, it was all about Amos and me slow dancing.

And when Deirdre yelled, "Cut! And that's a wrap!"

Everyone cheered. Everyone. All the cast and crew. But Amos just pressed his forehead to mine. "Goodbye, Dominic and Elijah."

"And hello, Chase and Amos," I replied, kissing him softly.

He laughed as we were pulled apart and dragged into the celebrations, but there was no time to waste.

"Okay," Deirdre said, cutting the music. "Let's go down to the outdoor theater. Can you hear the crowd?"

"There's a lot of people down there," Alex said.

Relief became nerves again. Live audiences were always a rollercoaster. "Let's go."

We made our way down toward the beach, toward the outdoor theater. Toward the few hundred people.

"Oh my god," Amos mumbled.

I grabbed his hand and dragged him along. "Come on. It'll be fun."

When people saw us coming, they started to clap and

cheer, which made everyone look . . . and then there was more clapping and cheering.

We stood in a curtain-call line, raised our joined hands, and took a bow.

It was a rush.

And for all the crap and stress over the last few weeks, this moment made it worth it.

Deirdre went to the front and asked for quiet.

She thanked us, the cast, but also everyone who worked in production, the camera crews, the sound and editing team. Then she thanked the students for being cooperative and enthusiastic, and the faculty and staff for forgiving any minor inconveniences.

The views for the series overall were huge.

It was hailed as a *Blair Witch*'s filming approach to a *90210*-esque reality series. The amateur nature of it all was its charm, it's what made it a hit.

"Now what you've all been waiting for," Deirdre said. "Some interviews, and the all-important blooper reel."

Oh great.

We stood at the side, watching with everyone else. The interviews were thankfully snippets and short, interspersed with clips of behind-the-scenes stuff. Given there was eight of us, it was a lot to get through.

There was footage of Amos and me on day one or two of preproduction, right back in the beginning. We were sitting on the floor, Amos had his back to the wall, and I was propped up between his legs, my back to his chest, and we were reading the script outline.

Then it cut to my interview. "Your character and Amos's character needed to get comfortable with each other right from the beginning. How did you manage that?"

I grinned on the screen. "By annoying him a lot."

The audience laughed and Amos chuckled beside me. He slung his arm around my shoulder. "So true."

"Method acting is an intense insight into the character you're portraying," the interviewer said. "Amos, how did you prepare for becoming a character twenty-four seven? And a boyfriend at that."

On-screen, Amos smirked, his cheeks pink. "Easy. We were never acting."

The audience cheered, and I leaned into his side, holding his hand at my shoulder. My cheeks were starting to hurt from grinning.

Then the video cut to snippets of us over the last two weeks. Walking, holding hands, laughing, sitting with his arms around me, with my arm around him. All the times I had no clue the cameras were even on us. In the dining hall, in the corridors, walking to his place, leaving his work, leaving the bar.

Then it cut to him frowning at me, scowling at me, and me grinning at him every time.

It was funny as hell.

Then it showed me whipping my swimming trunks off and him barely covering me with a towel just in time. The footage of us in my room, lying on my bed, courtesy of Jimmy. And footage of Amos running down to my house...

That must have been when I'd had my melodramatic meltdown.

I looked up at him. "You ran?"

He replied with a sigh. "Of course I did."

"Aww. You're so sweet."

"Don't push your luck."

The footage showed snippets of the others, all funny and dramatic and awesome.

Then it cut to the final scene, that'd just aired tonight. To Amos and me slow dancing, kissing. And the audience cheered. And then when Jess and Phoebe were dancing, foreheads pressed together and holding hands, they cheered again.

They cheered for Max and Jenna, and then for Didi and Tucker.

But they cheered loudest for Holly, as she danced by herself, holding a red solo cup in the air.

It was so awesome.

Then Holly's interview showed on-screen. She was wearing the shirt she had on now. "Not everyone's happy ever after has to end with being in love."

It cut to footage of Max and Jenna, and then to footage of Amos and me.

And then it showed us all together, the eight of us, laughing at our usual breakfast meetings, with Holly's voiceover. "Sometimes it's learning about yourself. It's about loving yourself and knowing your own self-worth and finding people to call friends. Sometimes that's the best happy ever after."

And that was how it ended.

Perfectly.

Had I found my happy ever after? With Amos? With knowing more about myself, about how I loved and needed to be loved? I was pretty sure I had.

Sure, we were young and we had our whole lives ahead of us, but I knew one thing for certain.

I wanted to start a life with Amos. He was the calm to my chaos, and I wanted that safe harbor forever.

Now that the filming was done, we could concentrate on just us, on graduating, and on maybe moving to LA together like I'd dreamed about.

Big dreams, big goals.

Big love.

Sounded about right.

Epilogue
Amos

It was easy to see where Chase got his need for physical touch. His whole family were huggers. His mom was the hugging, emotional type that was kinda horrifying, kinda nice.

"Ohh," she cried, sliding a box onto the kitchen counter. "Look at this place!" She took it all in as if it were the Taj Mahal. "It's so cute! You two will be so happy here, I just know it."

She called it cute.

My mother had taken one look at our place and cringed.

It was a one-bedroom apartment roughly the size of a shoebox, with marked walls and scuffed flooring. But the location was great and there *was* a balcony. The hot water seemed a little sketchy, but it was cheap enough.

Cheap enough for two budding actors here to chase the dream.

Mrs. Soria was lovely though. As pretty as her son, and she'd welcomed me with open arms. Literally. She'd hugged me, and I'd almost died. Chase had to pull me free, but being squished with welcoming hugs was so much better than facing disapproval, so I'd take the hugs and the happy tears, even if it made me die inside.

Chase had the exact same excited look on his face that his mother wore. "This is gonna be so cool," he said. "TV on that wall, sofa here. Bed in the sex-dungeon, obviously."

"Oh my god," I hissed at him, eyeballing the back of his mom's head. "Chase."

She didn't care. She just waved her hand and kept unpacking the box of kitchen stuff. "Oh, I'm used to him, dear." Then she gave Chase the look. "You just make sure you're on your best behavior when Amos's family gets here."

He rolled his eyes. "Puh-lease. They love me."

It was true. They did. They were perplexed, to say the very least, when they'd first met him. He was a blond-haired, blue-eyed ball of energy and I was . . . well, I was me: the tall, dark, and quiet type. But he won them over with his charm and that damn smile. And they could see that together, we just worked.

My dad and my brother came in, awkwardly carrying the bed. "Glad we could do this for you while you stand around," my brother griped.

"More boxes in the van," Dad added.

I laughed. "Yeah, okay, okay."

I pulled Chase out with me, running down the stairs to grab more stuff out of the van. "Here," I said, loading Chase up with his duffle bag over his shoulder and two boxes in his arms. I took two boxes myself and slid the van door shut with my foot. "You need to get your clothes unpacked and ironed for tomorrow."

"I know," he said. "God, I hope it doesn't suck."

He had a shoot with his agent tomorrow. Photos and whatnot. He'd scouted a few of the top agencies and his first pick had wanted him. It was kind of a huge deal, hence the big move.

"You'll be fine."

"Yeah, I know *I* will be," he said. "I meant I hope *they* don't suck."

I snorted. His confidence and attitude hadn't waned at all.

"And your first shift at the café," he reminded me. "Day after tomorrow. I'm not ironing your clothes. Just so you know."

I held the door open for him. "I wouldn't dare ask."

I followed him up the stairs. "Hm, the view here is nice."

"Stop looking at my ass."

"It's a beautiful ass."

"There'll be no ass tonight," he said. "We have dinner with our families."

Ugh. A joined family dinner to celebrate the big move and to see us off before our folks went home. It was nice and all, and I probably shouldn't whine because they were helping us move . . .

But our future was starting *today*, and I wanted to enjoy that with Chase.

"We'll have every night after this one for you to enjoy my ass," Chase said, just as my brother came down the stairs.

"Gross."

"Shut up," I replied.

He made a face at me. "Dad! Amos told me to shut up!"

I rolled my eyes and Chase laughed. He liked my brothers. He didn't have brothers so he enjoyed our childish bickering.

Dad took the top box off my pile. "Couch is next, and you're helping."

I bit back the groan I so badly wanted to let out. "Sure thing. Chase, go help them carry the couch." He laughed and gave me a playful shove as he followed my dad down the stairs.

We had the place set up in no time. Granted, we didn't have much stuff. A new bed, a secondhand couch, and Chase's TV from home. Our moms had pooled together some kitchen utensils and stuff, but the plates, silverware, cups, and glasses were all new.

Our families had gone back to their hotels for a few hours before we were heading out to dinner, and Chase fell back onto the bed, arms spread wide.

"Baby, this is gonna be awesome. Can you believe we're doing this?"

"I just have one more thing," I said from the living room. "Something I pictured when you first talked about moving here and us living together. Just gimme one sec."

He appeared in the doorway, looking around. "What is it? Is it a sex bench?"

I scoffed. "Of course not. That's what the couch is for."

He laughed and gave the armrest of the couch a good jostle. "It's sturdy too."

Then he saw what I was doing, what I was hanging on the wall.

"Oh my god," he said, grinning. "This is what you imagined?"

I stood back and took in the *Rick and Morty* poster. "Yep." It was a poster of the *Rick and Morty* toilet episode, which was stupid and childish. "It's the episode where the fucked-up moral of the story is not to let your dreams turn to shit, basically."

He laughed, sliding his arm around my waist. "It's perfect. It's an actual piece of art."

I kissed the side of his head and pulled him in for a hug. "Now this place is ours."

"Not yet," he said, shoving me toward the bedroom. "We need to christen the bed. And the shower, and the couch, and the kitchen counter. *Then* this place will be ours."

I chuckled and went willingly, pulling my shirt over my head. "Which do we christen first?"

"The bed."

"But we just made it, and we're all sweaty and gross."

"Then the shower it is," he said. "Not that it matters. We're going to christen them all. We have the rest of forever to do it everywhere." He pulled his shirt off and tossed it toward the hamper but missed.

"Pick that up. You're not leaving your shit on the floor."

He took my hand and placed it over his pec. "Feel your emotional support tiddies, take a deep breath in and go to your happy place."

I walked him into the bathroom, pushing him against

the small counter, kissing down his neck. "You are insufferable."

He laughed. "You're gonna love living with me. So much suffering."

I smiled as I captured his lips with mine. Because yes, he still annoyed me. How it was possible to love someone with my whole heart and be equally annoyed by them, I'd never know. But he made me so happy I couldn't even put it into words. "Let the suffering begin."

He pulled my shirt over my head, kissing my collarbone and grinding his erection against mine. "However will you cope?" he asked breathily.

I slid my hands under the waistband of his shorts and pushed them down over his ass. "I'm sure I'll find a way."

"Forever? Will you put up with me forever?"

I spun him around so he faced the mirror and I met his eyes in the reflection. "You're my one person, Chase."

The smile he gave me was warm and just for me. "I love you, Amos."

"I love you too. I don't tell you often enough," I whispered, kissing behind his ear.

"Yes, you do. Every time you call me insufferable. The very first time you called me that, I think it was day one of the method-acting thing. You said, 'you're insufferable,' but what I heard was, 'I love you and you're my one person, my forever person, Chase Soria, and the more you annoy me, the more I will love you.' That's what I heard because it's basically the same thing."

I chuckled at his ridiculousness. "Well," I said, meeting his eyes in the reflection. "I guess that means I'll put up with you forever."

He grinned. "Good. Forever starts in the shower."

He started the water, talking non-stop about dinner with our parents, our work, and the local studios that were well-known in scouting circles.

Sex seemed to be forgotten as we showered because his mind was now running on a different tangent.

And that was completely okay with me.

Would I put up with his short attention span, his sometimes frustrating and infuriating childishness, and his flair for the dramatic?

Yes, I would.

Forever?

Absolutely.

THE END

Thank you for reading Method Acting!

If you're curious about the stats professor (Jonah) who outed himself when he confused Benny with Emmet, be sure to grab their story, Twincerely Yours.

Want more from me?
Be sure to check my steamy EWB, or my sweeter Bloom! If you want to keep up on all my releases and fun stuff, join my Facebook Readers' Group!

Thank you for reading!

Meet all of the couples from FU2!

Perry and Theo:
The Hookup Mix-up

Harrison and Benny:
A Stealthy Situation

Blaise and Jordan:
Batting Style

Jay and Ryan:
Level Up

Silas and Everly:
Full Service

Dex and Austin:
Tongue-Tied

Chase and Amos:
Method Acting

Emmett and Jonah:
Twincerely Yours

About the Author

N.R. Walker is an Australian author, who loves her genre of gay romance. She loves writing and spends far too much time doing it, but wouldn't have it any other way.

She is many things: a mother, a wife, a sister, a writer. She has pretty, pretty boys who live in her head, who don't let her sleep at night unless she gives them life with words.

She likes it when they do dirty, dirty things... but likes it even more when they fall in love. She used to think having people in her head talking to her was weird, until one day she happened across other writers who told her it was normal.

She's been writing ever since...

nrwalker.net

Also by N.R. Walker

Blind Faith
Through These Eyes (Blind Faith #2)
Blindside: Mark's Story (Blind Faith #3)
Ten in the Bin
Gay Sex Club Stories 1
Gay Sex Club Stories 2
Point of No Return – Turning Point #1
Breaking Point – Turning Point #2
Starting Point – Turning Point #3
Element of Retrofit – Thomas Elkin Series #1
Clarity of Lines – Thomas Elkin Series #2
Sense of Place – Thomas Elkin Series #3
Taxes and TARDIS
Three's Company
Red Dirt Heart
Red Dirt Heart 2
Red Dirt Heart 3
Red Dirt Heart 4
Red Dirt Christmas
Cronin's Key
Cronin's Key II
Cronin's Key III

Cronin's Key IV - Kennard's Story

Exchange of Hearts

The Spencer Cohen Series, Book One

The Spencer Cohen Series, Book Two

The Spencer Cohen Series, Book Three

The Spencer Cohen Series, Yanni's Story

Blood & Milk

The Weight Of It All

A Very Henry Christmas (The Weight of It All 1.5)

Perfect Catch

Switched

Imago

Imagines

Imagoes

Red Dirt Heart Imago

On Davis Row

Finders Keepers

Evolved

Galaxies and Oceans

Private Charter

Nova Praetorian

A Soldier's Wish

Upside Down

The Hate You Drink

Sir

Tallowwood

Reindeer Games

The Dichotomy of Angels

Throwing Hearts

Pieces of You - Missing Pieces #1

Pieces of Me - Missing Pieces #2

Pieces of Us - Missing Pieces #3

Lacuna

Tic-Tac-Mistletoe

Bossy

Code Red

Dearest Milton James

Dearest Malachi Keogh

Christmas Wish List

Code Blue

Davo

The Kite

Learning Curve

Merry Christmas Cupid

To the Moon and Back

Second Chance at First Love

Outrun the Rain

Into the Tempest

Touch the Lightning

EWB - Enemies With Benefits

Holiday Heart Strings

Bloom

The Men From Echo Creek

Titles in Audio:

Cronin's Key

Cronin's Key II

Cronin's Key III

Red Dirt Heart

Red Dirt Heart 2

Red Dirt Heart 3

Red Dirt Heart 4

The Weight Of It All

Switched

Point of No Return

Breaking Point

Starting Point

Spencer Cohen Book One

Spencer Cohen Book Two

Spencer Cohen Book Three

Yanni's Story

On Davis Row

Evolved

Elements of Retrofit

Clarity of Lines

Sense of Place

Blind Faith

Through These Eyes
Blindside
Finders Keepers
Galaxies and Oceans
Nova Praetorian
Upside Down
Sir
Tallowwood
Imago
Throwing Hearts
Sixty Five Hours
Taxes and TARDIS
The Dichotomy of Angels
The Hate You Drink
Pieces of You
Pieces of Me
Pieces of Us
Tic-Tac-Mistletoe
Lacuna
Bossy
Code Red
Learning to Feel
Dearest Milton James
Dearest Malachi Keogh
Three's Company
Christmas Wish List

Code Blue

Davo

The Kite

Learning Curve

Merry Christmas Cupid

To the Moon and Back

Second Chance at First Love

Outrun the Rain

Into the Tempest

Touch the Lightning

EWB

Holiday Heart Strings

Bloom

The Men from Echo Creek

Series Collections:

Red Dirt Heart Series

Turning Point Series

Thomas Elkin Series

Spencer Cohen Series

Imago Series

Blind Faith Series

Missing Pieces Series

The Storm Boys Series

Free Reads:

Sixty Five Hours
Learning to Feel
His Grandfather's Watch (And The Story of Billy and Hale)
The Twelfth of Never (Blind Faith 3.5)
Twelve Days of Christmas (Sixty Five Hours Christmas)
Best of Both Worlds

Translated Titles:

Italian

Fiducia Cieca (Blind Faith)
Attraverso Questi Occhi (Through These Eyes)
Preso alla Sprovvista (Blindside)
Il giorno del Mai (Blind Faith 3.5)
Cuore di Terra Rossa Serie (Red Dirt Heart Series)
Natale di terra rossa (Red dirt Christmas)
Intervento di Retrofit (Elements of Retrofit)
A Chiare Linee (Clarity of Lines)
Senso D'appartenenza (Sense of Place)
Spencer Cohen Serie (including Yanni's Story)
Punto di non Ritorno (Point of No Return)
Punto di Rottura (Breaking Point)
Punto di Partenza (Starting Point)
Imago (Imago)

Imagines
Il desiderio di un soldato (A Soldier's Wish)
Scambiato (Switched)
Tallowwood
The Hate You Drink
Ho trovato te (Finders Keepers)
Cuori d'argilla (Throwing Hearts)
Galassie e Oceani (Galaxies and Oceans)
Il peso di tut (The Weight of it All)
Pieces of You - Missing Pieces 1

French

Confiance Aveugle (Blind Faith)
A travers ces yeux: Confiance Aveugle 2 (Through These Eyes)
Aveugle: Confiance Aveugle 3 (Blindside)
À Jamais (Blind Faith 3.5)
Cronin's Key Series
Au Coeur de Sutton Station (Red Dirt Heart)
Partir ou rester (Red Dirt Heart 2)
Faire Face (Red Dirt Heart 3)
Trouver sa Place (Red Dirt Heart 4)
Le Poids de Sentiments (The Weight of It All)
Un Noël à la sauce Henry (A Very Henry Christmas)
Une vie à Refaire (Switched)
Evolution (Evolved)

Galaxies & Océans
Qui Trouve, Garde (Finders Keepers)
Sens Dessus Dessous (Upside Down)
La Haine au Fond du Verre (The hate You Drink)
Tallowwood
Spencer Cohen Series
Thomas Elkin One
Thomas Elkin Two
Lacuna

GERMAN

Flammende Erde (Red Dirt Heart)
Lodernde Erde (Red Dirt Heart 2)
Sengende Erde (Red Dirt Heart 3)
Ungezähmte Erde (Red Dirt Heart 4)
Vier Pfoten und ein bisschen Zufall (Finders Keepers)
Ein Kleines bisschen Versuchung (The Weight of It All)
Ein Kleines Bisschen Fur Immer (A Very Henry Christmas)
Weil Leibe uns immer Bliebt (Switched)
Drei Herzen eine Leibe (Three's Company)
Über uns die Sterne, zwischen uns die Liebe (Galaxies and Oceans)
Unnahbares Herz (Blind Faith 1)
Sehendes Herz (Blind Faith 2)
Hoffnungsvolles Herz (Blind Faith 3)
Verträumtes Herz (Blind Faith 3.5)

Thomas Elkin: Verlangen in neuem Design
Thomas Elkin: Leidenschaft in klaren
Thomas Elkin: Vertrauen in bester Lage
Traummann töpfern leicht gemacht (Throwing Hearts)
Sir
So Unendlich Viel Liebe (To the Moon and Back)

Thai

Sixty Five Hours (Thai translation)
Finders Keepers (Thai translation)

Spanish

Sesenta y Cinco Horas (Sixty Five Hours)
Los Doce Días de Navidad
Código Rojo (Code Red)
Código Azul (Code Blue)
Queridísimo Milton James
Queridísimo Malachi Keogh
El Peso de Todo (The Weight of it All)
Tres Muérdagos en Raya: Serie Navidad en Hartbridge
Lista De Deseos Navideños: Serie Navidad en Hartbridge
Feliz Navidad Cupido: Serie Navidad en Hartbridge
Spencer Cohen Libro Uno
Spencer Cohen Libro Dos
Spencer Cohen Libro Tres

Davo
Hasta la Luna y de Vuelta
Venciendo A La Lluvia
En la Tempestad
El Toque del Rayo
Corazón De Tierra Roja
Corazón De Tierra Roja 2
Corazón De Tierra Roja 3
Corazón De Tierra Roja 4
ECB (Enemigos con Beneficios)

CHINESE

Blind Faith

JAPANESE

Bossy

PORTUGUESE

Sessenta e Cinco Horas

Printed in Great Britain
by Amazon